SCORCH

A DARK BRATVA ARRANGED MARRIAGE ROMANCE

WICKED VOWS
BOOK 4

JANE HENRY

Scorch: A Dark Bratva Arranged Marriage Romance

Cover photography by Michelle Lancaster (www.michellelancaster.com)

Cover art by Popkitty

ISBN: 978-1-961866-11-9

Cover art for Alternate Cover Print Edition by *Haya in Designs*

ISBN: 978-1-961866-14-0 (Alternate Cover Print Edition)

Playlist

Scan QR Code to listen to the playlist for 'Scorch: A Dark Bratva Arranged Marriage Romance" on Spotify©

SYNOPSIS

In the dark underworld of the Russian Bratva, I've finally claimed the object of my obsession: Lydia Ivanova.

Beautiful and passionate, she's fire and ice, and I want her. I need her.

Lydia is my prize. My spoils of war.

Only she doesn't know that yet.

Forced into marriage with me to protect her from those that would destroy us, I vow to keep her secure at all costs... even when she fights me tooth and nail.

Can I protect Lydia without consuming her, or will our love story end in ashes? The stakes have never been higher, and for Lydia... I will burn the world.

PROLOGUE

Ten years earlier

THEY WOULD PAY and pay dearly. Every last fucking one of them.

The purr of luxury cars and the rhythmic click of heels and polished shoes mingled with the swish of neatly pressed uniforms while Viktor maintained his distance.

Head down, dressed in nondescript, inexpensive clothing with his hands buried in his pockets, he looked like a nobody. Just like he'd planned. No one at Liberty Ridge Academy would give him a passing glance.

He looked at his watch. Though he'd come early before his session with his mentor, Kolya, time was ticking. Kolya detested tardiness, and it mattered to him to show up on time.

Where was she?

Sometimes, she'd be cloaked in a scarf and a knee-length sweater, concealing her figure as though shielding herself from the relentless, judgmental gaze of her peers. But today, she was conspicuously absent from the usual flurry of student arrivals.

His pace slowed, and he moved away from the throng, even though most students steered clear of him. He was a giant among them, a few years older and twice the size of the biggest varsity football player.

Fortunately, the lack of surveillance at the school was laughable. Anyone paying attention would have noticed the imposing young man who was always there. Always watching.

"Here she comes," one of the boys announced in a snide whisper about ten feet ahead of Viktor. "The fat girl with big tits."

Viktor clenched his fist in a surge of protective fury and made a pact: he'd deal with that fucker first.

He had only been training with Kolya for three months, but he had already begun to develop hard muscle under Kolya's tutelage. It would come in handy when he cornered that asshole in the dark alley between school and home.

Viktor's eyes narrowed as the familiar Lincoln purred to a stop at the curb. He held his breath. She was here, brought by her father. Viktor refocused his attention, his gaze icy and menacing as he contemplated knocking the boy's teeth out. He cracked his knuckles, tension rolling off him in waves.

One of the boys shot him a wary glance before nudging his friend as the car door swung open.

"Sit up straight," her father commanded from the backseat. "You represent the Ivanov family with *dignity*."

Viktor's breathing became labored. Time stood still for a moment when he saw her.

His angel.

Lydia Ivanova. The most beautiful girl he'd ever seen. The girl who lived in his dreams. The object of his utter obsession. He stroked the gold earring in his pocket and pricked his finger with the post to keep him focused.

Each tiny pain was a tether, keeping his thoughts sharp and his desire in check.

Viktor's mind was a constant whirlwind of thoughts about her: her scent, the way her eyes, a striking emerald flecked with hazel, flickered with a mix of defiance and vulnerability. He knew her every expression, every quirk. He had watched her for months, always from the shadows, always unseen.

He knew it was wrong, the way he tracked her movements, the way he collected items she had touched—like this earring, lost one summer night and now a permanent fixture in his pocket.

He was her shadow, her silent sentry, driven by a need he didn't understand, a desire so deep, it bordered on madness.

"Back off, motherfucker," he said softly under his breath when Sterling Eldridge took a step toward her. "Back the fuck *off*."

Lydia was fire in more ways than one. He'd watched the way her eyes lit up when she set things ablaze, the joy and freedom she found in the flames. It was a part of her he loved, the dark side she showed no one.

His fingers tightened around the earring, the sharp sting grounding him.

She stood facing her classmates, a defiant spark igniting her emerald gaze as she swung one long leg out, then the other, her plaid uniform skirt grazing the top of her knees. Her glasses perched precariously on the edge of her nose. When she tossed her head, thick waves bobbing defiantly in the breeze, her chin lifted in silent challenge.

Fat girl with big tits.

Viktor's blood boiled at the thought. She was *amazing.*

Despite her father's harsh, dismissive tone—always scolding, always belittling—she stood proud and tall. He fucking loved that about her.

But today, from his vantage point under the shelter of a thick maple, he saw the sheen of tears in her eyes. A public scolding only added to the torment inflicted by her cruel classmates.

Fucking losers.

"Awww," one of them said under his breath to the other. "Is she gonna cry?"

Viktor's hand curled into a fist.

He would be victim number two.

He noted the golden Lincoln still purring at the curb and narrowed his eyes before he zeroed back in on the boy with the big mouth and imagined what he'd look like missing his two front teeth. Viktor cracked his knuckles and rolled his neck. It would feel so fucking good when his fist connected with flesh and bone.

As Lydia walked toward the school, one of her books fell from the large pile. She bent to pick it up.

"Lydia," her father muttered. "Don't be so damn clumsy."

Always scolding, always dismissive and harsh. Viktor didn't know how anyone could withstand the constant berating. Did it make her feel small and unworthy? From what he'd seen, her father was relentless.

In his eyes, Lydia was neither overweight nor clumsy—she'd developed earlier than her other classmates, all curves and voluptuous temptation, and she simply hadn't grown into her own body yet.

And who the hell were they, anyway? Who decided what her body should look like, and who decided it didn't meet some set of random fucking expectations?

She was *perfect*.

Viktor stood taller and glanced at the time. He had seven and a half more minutes before he'd have to jog to get there on time.

Lydia's father frowned and sat up straighter. "I'll be here to pick you up today. We have something urgent to discuss," her father said, glancing at his watch.

"Yes, Father," she said in a clear, graceful voice. "See you then."

As the car left, she stepped forward and wobbled. A few of the boys made derisive comments. The leader winked at a tall, slender blonde girl exiting a silver Mercedes behind Lydia. They shared a look when the girl pressed her finger on her nose and wrinkled it at the girl as if mimicking a pig. Snickers erupted all around them.

Fucking spoiled, pretentious brats. Viktor delighted in imagining how he would punish them all.

"Lydia! You okay?" A thin girl, a full head shorter than Lydia, sidled up beside her. Maybe he'd spare that one.

"I'm good, thanks," she said in that beautiful voice that haunted his dreams.

The first bell rang. It was time to go. If he showed up late, he'd be in deep shit. Kolya didn't warn twice.

The blonde walked in front of the boys, standing tall and flaunting her breasts. She'd left a few of the buttons on her uniform shirt undone, her meager breasts pushed up on display. Pretending to sneeze, she made a big production of scattering tissues in Lydia's direction. Laughter erupted all around them. Lydia's pretty cheeks pinked.

Viktor's growl rumbled deep in his chest. This particular girl had been hinting at Lydia stuffing her bra for weeks now. Jealousy was an evil little bitch.

"Morning, Lydia," the girl said with fake camaraderie. "Need help?"

"No." Lydia held herself erect, not trusting the girl. She held her head high and turned away. The boys watched on and snickered.

"Fine," the girl said, shaking her head. "Not sure why you have to bring so many books home anyway. Show-off," she muttered under her breath. She flicked her hair over her shoulder and turned to walk away as one of the boys, the tallest and obvious leader of the group, discreetly stuck his foot out.

Viktor risked coming out of the shadows. If he could—*fuck*.

Lydia stumbled but quickly righted herself. Her cheeks flushed, and she turned on the boy.

"You fucking asshole! You did that on purpose!"

Pride surged in his chest.

Atta girl.

"Lydia!" A sharp voice came from several paces ahead where a tall woman with her hair in a merciless bun at the nape of her neck marched over to them. Snickers erupted all around them as she approached. "Come here at once."

Viktor's gaze hardened. Lydia might have stood up to him today, but it left her more vulnerable than ever to the cruelty of her classmates. His protective instinct, already fiercely attuned to her, flared. He could not stand by while she was mocked and isolated.

Stepping forward, his presence immediately silenced the group. His voice, when he spoke, was low but carried an unmistakable threat. "You find something funny? Maybe you'd like to share the joke with me."

The snickers died in their throats. Lydia, her gaze flicking briefly from the teacher heading her way then to Viktor, seemed to straighten even more, her eyes meeting his with a silent *thank you* that said she knew, at least for today, she wasn't alone against them.

No words passed between them, only a quiet understanding before her teacher reached her.

"This is the last straw, Miss Ivanova," the woman said severely. "But soon you'll be no bother to me. Perhaps your father will tell you of his recent decision and how it impacts your attendance here."

Lydia stared and paled. "They were—"

"I don't care what they were doing," the teacher dismissed.

Viktor kept careful note of all of them. The tall, pompous football player. The stuck-up blonde. The critical teacher.

They would all pay, and he would take his sweet time making it hurt.

"What are you talking about?" Lydia marched after the teacher. Her bag was slightly open, and a few papers and a slim, well-worn paperback book fell to the ground. Viktor bent and picked them up, but when he went to give them to her, she was gone.

Her classmates scattered like scared little ants.

He tucked the book under his arm and headed to meet Kolya and face the consequences of being late.

He came the next day.

And the next.

And the next.

But she never returned.

CHAPTER ONE

Present *day*

Viktor

"NAME A PRICE," Mikhail says. "I owe you, Viktor. It's time."

My oldest brother and *pakhan* Mikhail looks at me over the fuzzy head of his sleeping son and says, "I am indebted to you for everything."

I shake my head slightly, dismissing the weight of his gratitude. "You don't owe me. I did what I had to do. I did what you needed me to do. It was crucial that I take care of what's yours because we're family, and you know that." I pop the top of a beer and drink half of it in a few gulps.

I look out into the dark blue-black haze of a late September evening, the lights of the city twinkling in the distance from our vantage point in The Cove. We've had a tumultuous few months with a brief pause for our brother Nikko's wedding, but now it's time for us to continue to make our moves. We've made great strides here, and it's time we kick things up.

Since our father's death, we've been doing everything in our power to strengthen our ties and put down roots as the most powerful family in The Cove, nestled between Coney Island and Manhattan.

Every day that passes counts. Every strategic move a power play.

Mikhail's voice grows softer, more earnest. "You saved my wife's life, Viktor." Mikhail loves his wife Aria with all his heart, and on more than one occasion, she's been in grave danger. I'm not the only one who's protected her. We all have. It's what we do.

I shift in my seat, feeling the unease settle over me. "Family does for family. You'd have done the same for me," I respond, my eyes briefly meeting his before settling on the infant. "Just make sure you keep them safe. That's all I ask."

The room falls silent, the magnitude of my request left lingering. Mikhail nods, his expression solemn. "I will. And anything you need, Viktor, it's yours. You name it."

The other brothers present—Lev, our younger brother and Aleksandr, second in command to Mikhail—listen intently to our conversation. I can sense Lev getting restless beside me, tapping his foot as if he's holding himself back from interrupting.

"You guys don't get it." Lev speaks up from the back of the office, his voice cutting through the previous chatter. I'm honestly proud of him for speaking up. For years, he was the quietest, under the thumb of our father and overshadowed by the rest of us older brothers. Our youngest brother often keeps to himself but misses nothing. He and I have grown closer over the past few months while my brother Nikko was stationed in Moscow.

"Leave it, Lev." I shake my head. *Jesus.*

"What are you talking about?" Aleks asks, his curiosity piqued. Head of cybersecurity, he prides himself on noting everything, but he's been deep in the weeds researching a new development on the West Coast and hasn't looked up from his laptop.

Lev continues, his voice firm and clear. "He doesn't want money. He doesn't want *things.* Viktor doesn't want any of that. He already has his own house; he has everything he needs... well, almost everything that he needs."

The room falls into a brief silence as everyone processes Lev's insight, waiting for him to reveal what it is that I still need. I look away, my jaw tensing. He's read my fucking mind. When Mikhail offered me the proverbial genie's lamp, I immediately knew what I would wish for when I rubbed the golden sides.

I'd only need one wish.

"Fuck," I mutter under my breath. My brothers hide nothing from each other. I won't hide this.

"Lydia Ivanova," Mikhail says quietly, almost reverently.

Silence reigns for long moments before Aleksandr speaks up. "Is she available? Has anything changed?"

Lev shakes his head. "No."

Mikhail growls. "Since when does that fucking matter? You know our mantra."

Aleks's lips twist into a grim smile, his gaze hardening. "No one and nothing stands in our way."

I stand up abruptly, my voice low and resolute. "I don't need anything. I don't need any*one*. It's too risky."

Blowback from the *Ledyanoye Bratstvo*, the group to which Lydia Ivanova's been promised, is more powerful than we are and known for their ruthlessness. The retribution if we intervened would be swift and severe.

But before I can continue, Lev interrupts. He's smaller in stature than I am but a force to be reckoned with. His eyes gleam with intensity, his arms crossed on his chest.

"You've taken your eyes off the prize, brother. You haven't seen what the others have." He leans forward. "Do you have any idea what Timur Yudin plans on doing with her when they're married? What he plans to do to the Ivanovs?"

I draw in a sharp breath, willing my racing pulse to slow the way my mentor Kolya taught me to do when I was just a boy who didn't know his own strength.

It doesn't help.

"I get it," Lev presses on, his fierce gaze burning into mine. He isn't the young kid I once knew any more, but strong and powerful in more ways than one. "It would fucking kill you to see a woman like her treated like property. And if you killed Yudin like you wanted to, the blowback to the rest of us would be brutal."

I dig my fingernails into the palms of my hands. He goes on.

"Yudin plans on sharing her with his men. He's a filthy, sick son of a bitch. He's already filmed her and shared it. He's got one in his crew who jerks off every fucking night to pictures of her on his phone."

"Where?" I growl. "Who?"

"Sit down, Viktor."

I shake my head, and Aleks puts his hand on Mikhail's arm. "Let him. He'll turn into the fucking Hulk right here in front of you if you don't."

I pace, trying to let the rage bleed off me.

"He plans on decimating the Ivanovs. He's an insidious fucking snake and has already made strategic moves by infiltrating their ranks and spreading misinformation to sow distrust within their leadership. By marrying into the Ivanov family, he gains access to their secrets and vulnerabilities. And unlike us," he says, pausing for emphasis, "he doesn't plan on strengthening by collaboration. He plans on decimating for his personal gain. Over time, he'll destroy them. Sabotage business deals, assassinate the Ivanov power players." He shakes his head and lowers his voice.

"You've watched Mikhail, Aleks, and now Nikko get married." Mikhail married Aria, hacker extraordinaire. Aleks then married Harper Bianchi in an arranged marriage. Nikko married Vera – Lydia's younger sister. One by one, couple by couple, we've solidified our family.

"We've grown in strength here in The Cove, and we all know joining forces with the Ivanovs is complicated." He shakes his head and looks at Mikhail. "Lydia Ivanova's marriage to that self-centered prick would fragment our control as well. She'd be used and discarded." He looks to me next. "We *have* to intervene and fucking end this before their marriage."

Aleks and Mikhail share another look, an unspoken understanding passing between them as they consider Lev's words and the implications they carry.

I don't even want to think of actually... *having her*. If I let myself hope... if it doesn't happen... My mouth goes dry.

I pace in the office and shake my head. "*Fuck.*"

"Her marriage to him will bring severe consequences," Lev counters. "If we secure the hand of both Ivanov women, you know what that means for us."

I do. It means creating a foundation that decades of influence and legacy couldn't rival. It means allowing brutal devastation to our friends and family if we fail.

But it's complicated. So fucking complicated.

Mikhail holds my gaze. "Tell me what you know about Yudin."

I look away, my jaw tense. "I've stayed away."

I had to.

Watching her go anywhere near him sends my blood to boiling, and my gaze grows hazy. I have to focus on protecting my family and can't risk going nuclear on a man who means nothing to me. I can't expend energy on a situation that's out of my control.

I've watched. I've watched so carefully but from a distance. "He hasn't hurt her, and that's all that matters."

Timur Yudin buys her nice things, makes sure she has a guard on her, albeit a weaker one than I would have, and has never once raised a hand to her. I would know. If he did, I'd rip his dick off and shove it down his throat so he choked on it while I slit his throat.

"Yet," Aleks says, shaking his head. "Aria's got a file on him. We researched heavily after Nikko's marriage to Vera."

My skin prickles, and I swivel my gaze to Aleks.

Aria, Mikhail's wife, is our head of cybersecurity and excellent at what she does. When our brother Nikko married Lydia's sister Vera Ivanova, it became necessary to zone in on whoever might pose a threat to us.

I look away, not wanting to listen to the details.

What good will it do? I'll only want to fucking torture every cell in his body before I murder him with my own bare hands. I hate him for being near her. I despise him for not being worthy of her. If I find out one goddamn detail about him—

"He's a master at orchestrating these deadly catastrophes," Aleks says, his voice icy. "He makes sure people in his stable have fatal accidents, then he swoops in and collects hidden insurance policies."

I shake my head. Fucking douchebag move, but it's not out of the ordinary to—

Aleks goes on relentlessly. "He stages human trafficking. He sells women and children as if they're cattle. He's a top trader in the black market."

I clench my jaw and stare straight ahead. The fucking asshole. I'm no saint, but anyone involved in human trafficking deserves to be dealt with severely. He'll live to regret every vile action he's taken. No one harms the innocent on my watch.

And I want her. I want her so fucking bad it consumes my every thought. If I can't have her... if she ends up with that self-serving, sadistic prick...

Lev speaks up. "There's more. Don't shut this down, Viktor, and fucking listen." My gaze snaps to his. "Three months ago, his lawyer got him acquitted on accusations of ownership of child pornography, but he's guilty as fuck. He's just untouchable. Too much money and too much power."

"*Fuck,*" I growl.

Aleksandr delivers the final blow. "Aria uncovered accusations that were deeply buried. He brutally assaulted his last girlfriend. She faked her death to escape, but he found her. When he did, he broke her jaw before she threw herself into oncoming traffic."

Bile rises in my throat with the effort of restraining myself.

"It's not a question of *if* he will hurt her, Viktor, but *when*."

"You've been tailing him?" I growl. "Where is he?"

Aleks frowns, making a few clicks on his keyboard. "Two hours north of here. Near the Mid-Hudson Bridge." He reaches for his phone without breaking eye contact with Mikhail, signaling the gravity of the decision. He dials quickly, and the room falls silent, waiting for the call to connect.

"Nikko," Aleksandr begins when the call is picked up, "we need to discuss the Ivanov situation."

Nikko, always quick on the uptake, responds, "I've been waiting for this call. Go."

Mikhail takes over, his voice firm. "It's about Lydia. We need to secure her for Viktor." He fills him in.

From what I've seen and heard, Lydia and Vera are not close, but that was likely their parents' fault. They are still sisters.

Nikko pauses, the gears turning as he considers the implications, especially given his ties with Lydia's sister. "Alright, I see the angle. I'll set things in motion. But remember, this isn't just about owing us; it's about aligning our families for the long term." He needs the Ivanovs' buy-in. After the death of their *pakhan,* new leadership has taken position, and Nikko is the only one who has a working relationship with the Ivanov Bratva. He'll know how to play this.

They go on to discuss the details and how they'll make it happen while my mind races with possibilities. There's a faint buzzing in the back of my mind, a combination of disbelief in what we're about to do and the need to find Timur Yudin and destroy him.

As the call ends, the atmosphere in the room shifts from tension to a more calculated focus. Mikhail looks around, ensuring everyone is on the same page. "Nikko will handle the arrangements. We need to be strategic and careful. This isn't just about acquiring what Viktor wants but about positioning ourselves favorably within the community and ensuring long-term alliances."

"And dealing with the fucking blowback from Yudin," I mutter.

Aleksandr nods in agreement, his mind already racing through potential scenarios. "We have to consider every move as part of a larger game. Lydia is the key piece. Not only does Viktor get what he desires, but her connection through marriage ties us to a powerful family, strengthening our influence."

Lev, usually the quietest, seems fueled with his need to see this happen and adds, "And we need to keep this clean. No loose ends that can come back to haunt us."

Easier said than done.

I've been silently listening but finally have to speak up, my voice low and contemplative. "Make sure Lydia is treated with respect in this process."

I'll take good care of her. Such good care of her.

My brothers nod, understanding the delicate balance of fear and favor they need to maintain. This isn't just another acquisition; this is personal, and it has to be handled with precision.

Mikhail's expression darkens as he leans forward, the lightness of our earlier considerations gone. "While we aim to manage this smoothly, understand that Lydia will likely not come willingly. We'll need to compel her."

Of course she wouldn't. She might see us, or me in particular, as a threat. She's fiercely independent and resists being controlled or used in any of her family's political moves or machinations. Being forced to marry me after her engagement to Yudin will likely piss her off. Who knows what she thinks about me? Given what I know about her, she doesn't easily trust and almost never lets her guard down.

This won't be easy.

Mikhail smiles. "You know... we can align this necessity with an old Russian prophecy known to both our families, which we can use to our advantage."

Aleksandr, intrigued, raises an eyebrow. "A prophecy? Explain."

Mikhail nods, a grim smile touching his lips. "Yes, the prophecy known to families that hail from Moscow speaks of a 'Scourge'—a great turmoil that one family will endure, only to be saved by an alliance through marriage. It's vague enough to instill fear and acceptance. It's believed that rejecting the prophesied union will bring disaster, and embracing it will restore balance and prosperity."

I shake my head. "That's ridiculous. We're all too pragmatic to believe in old prophecies. No. If I'm going to have Lydia —" I pause and get my shit together before I continue. "I want it out in the open. I want to solidify our alliance with the Ivanov family like Nikko did and for the same reason." I shake my head. "She can't go to that monster."

I'll do way more than fuck him over.

I dislike manipulation and typically prefer brute force, but this situation requires a delicate touch. "I want the Ivanovs to believe that aligning with us is not only inevitable but beneficial."

I shake my head, still disbelieving that this could work, that Lydia... could be mine.

"And if it doesn't work?" I try to keep my tone light, pretending that what hangs in the balance could make or literally fucking break me. I fail. My voice cracks.

"It will work," Mikhail says. "I promise you."

When I finally leave Mikhail's office, I'm weary but energized.

Lydia Ivanova.

I drive to my home on the Manhattan border. I walk up the brick steps on autopilot, barely noticing where I'm going or what I'm doing.

Nikita, my large, muscular Tibetan Mastiff, meets me at the door, and I scratch her ears. "Give me five," I tell her. I need a minute before we go for a walk. I take the stairs to my bedroom two at a time and walk straight to the closet hidden deep in the back of the room.

I slip the key into the lock, and the door creaks open on its hinges. I give myself a moment to lean against the worn wood and take in a deep breath before letting my gaze roam over every damn piece I've collected.

A nearly empty bottle of *Opulence* I lifted from her locker at the gym a year ago. A lipstick-stained napkin I confiscated at a coffee shop where she met her mother a few months ago. A torn page from a notebook she carries with the simplest of shopping lists on it. A disposable, empty coffee cup with her name scribbled on the side in permanent marker. A ticket stub from a concert she snuck into when she was still a teen here in America. Her photograph from her senior year in high school and a more recent one I found online and had made into a print. Her copy of *Wuthering Heights* she left behind all those years ago that I've read so many times the pages are falling apart.

Lydia's shrine.

I lift the bottle. The heady, intense fragrance is her signature scent. I lift it and give myself the luxury of a deep, cleansing breath of it. Just smelling it conjures up the mental image I have of her.

I let myself linger through the shrine. I finger the napkin and press it to my lips. I read her shopping list and recite it from memory.

> Chocolate
> Coffee
> Oranges
> Something for dinner

I run my thumb along the edge of the coffee cup, where I imagine her lips graced. I place them all back down with reverence and stare at the picture of her as a teen and compare it with the way she looks now.

She's only grown more beautiful, more exquisite, more sensual with time. Curvy and lush, she's imposing yet graceful. Her long, dark hair cascades over her shoulders in waves, her eyes expressive and intense. She favors flowing tops and dresses that accentuate her curves.

Lydia.

With a sigh, I place everything back with precision, shut the door, and lock it behind me. I stifle a yelp when I almost trample Nikita beneath my feet.

"Jesus," I mutter, my heart hammering in my chest. "You should give me some notice you're there. *God.*"

I look at the locked door with a frown then turn around and face the bedroom. It's hard to even believe, but if this works... if Mikhail actually pulls it off and Lydia becomes mine... I might need a bit of a feminine touch to this room.

And fucking safety measures put in place.

I snap on Nikita's leash and head out to take her for a walk.

My phone rings with a call from my brother Nikko as I head out the entrance of my home, a few miles from the Romanov family headquarters.

"Yeah?"

"We spoke with Zofia." Zofia Ivanova, my sister-in-law Vera and Lydia's mother, is the Ivanov family matriarch in the wake of her husband's death. She and my brother Nikko are the ones who make all major decisions.

"And?" My heart smashes against my rib cage, my mouth instantly dry.

"Her mother's amenable to the idea, but I need more time. I'm working on it. Let's assume this is a go and work accordingly."

I swallow hard.

"Alright. Thanks."

"But you know we need to destroy Yudin, Viktor. You know

what he'll do in retaliation. We can't leave a single shred of him behind."

I nod. "Consider it done."

CHAPTER TWO

Lydia

I FIDDLE with my engagement ring, spinning it around on my finger, and stare. Diamonds inlaid in yellow gold, they sparkle under the overhead lights. I know they must've cost a fortune. Timur Yudin, a man of high taste and a high-ranking captain of the *Ledyanoye Bratstvo*, doesn't do cheap things.

My belly churns with nerves as I wait for him. The guard he's stationed by me stands, scrolling through his phone as I sit at a quiet table by myself. Timur said he'd be here any minute and instructed me to go and wait for him. He seemed a bit guarded, but that's not unlike him after a busy day of work.

I pick up my phone and pretend to make a call, then surreptitiously put my phone camera on so I can look myself over to make sure I'm flawless. Timur doesn't like anything less than perfection.

I'm wearing a soft green dress that highlights my curves and emphasizes the green in my eyes. My makeup's flawless, not a hair out of place.

I finish checking myself over and, when satisfied, put my phone back down. When he arrives, he won't like it if I'm on my phone. I'm expected to pay attention to him.

The flicker of the candle on the table pulls my focus. I'm drawn to the orange flame behind frosted glass. I reach out and run the tip of my polished fingernail around the base of the candle. I pause and note a drip of wax.

My heart races.

It's not one of those fake electric candles, but real fire. If I took the edge of this tablecloth and touched the flame, I know exactly what would happen. First, it would smoke—

I close my eyes and draw my hand back as if the glass itself scalded me. I hate that my mind goes there when I'm stressed or under pressure.

No.

I worked too hard and too long to go back there now. I can't.

I won't.

I can still hear my mother's tearful plea while my father slammed my suitcases into the back of the car that took me to boarding school. *"Why, Lydia? Why did you do it?"*

I heard the questions she didn't ask as clearly as I heard the ones she did.

Where did I go wrong?

I take another sip of wine, aware that I've likely only traded one vice for another, but I don't fucking care.

I take a few minutes to look around the upscale restaurant. It's difficult to get into *Le Jardin de Lumière*, but I'm excited because the name reminds me of *Beauty and the Beast*, my childhood favorite. Who am I kidding? It's my favorite even now in adulthood. They're booking six months out here, but Timur likes expensive, hard-to-get things, so it makes sense he would want to come here. I'd expect no less from him.

Quiet instrumental music plays in the background. The tables are set with fine china and crystal wine glasses, the utter picture of sophistication. The basket of fragrant, warm bread is accompanied by slabs of homemade butter topped with crystalized truffle salt. *Delicious.*

My phone buzzes with a text. My heart leaps, thinking it might be Timur, but when I look at the screen, I sigh.

Vera: Lydia, can you talk now?

Vera gets so caught up in her studies she doesn't talk to me for weeks at a time, and now that she has a break, she wants to chat? I shoot her a quick response.

I can't now, I'm meeting Timur for dinner, but I'll call you when we're done.

I'm still holding my phone when I hear his familiar voice behind me. I quickly tuck it in my purse.

"Lydia. Thank you for waiting so patiently." He stands tall and imposing behind me with an air of unapproachable strength. I turn to face my handsome fiancé, once more appreciating his features are sharp and defined with high cheekbones and a strong, clean-shaven jawline. Dressed impeccably in a tailored suit, he exudes confidence and sophistication, his demeanor composed but with an icy detachment that can be intimidating to those who don't know him. I know him, though. I know him well.

I stand and give him the full effect of my smile.

"Hi. How was your day?"

With a smile, he bends and kisses my cheek. My heart flutters at his nearness. Timur Yudin is all grace and refinement, a gentleman in every sense of the word. His hand rests on the small of my back for a brief second before he takes his seat. He always holds my chair out for me, so I stand a bit awkwardly before I realize he must've forgotten.

I clumsily sit in front of him.

"You're looking quite nice tonight, Mr. Yudin," I say flirtatiously. He smiles coldly when the waiter approaches.

Normally attentive and gentlemanly, his behavior takes me off guard. Timur addresses the waiter. *"Bonjour, je voudrais une sortie, s'il vous plaît."*

I cringe when the waiter looks confused. Timur's French needs a little work. He just accidentally ordered an *exit* instead of an appetizer. I don't want to correct him in public, but he's made a mistake.

I quickly amend. *"Je voudrais commander un apéritif, s'il vous plaît."* The waiter bows and takes his leave. Timur levels his gaze at me with an air of coldness so sharp I shiver.

"Do not ever do that again," he snaps.

"Do what?" I look at him in surprise.

"Correct me in public."

I laugh. "Timur, you ordered an exit instead of an appetizer. I was hardly correcting you, just making sure—"

His hand reaches out and snatches my wrist. "Are you talking back to me now, too?"

I blink in surprise. "No."

Sometimes, he reminds me of my father, and I *hate* that. Though Timur is handsome and polished and treats me well, he occasionally has a bit of a cold streak when stressed.

"What is it, Timur? You seem troubled," I say gently. I lay my hand on his. "What's going on?"

He shakes his head. "I'm guessing you haven't spoken with your mother."

I blink. "No. Why?"

He looks away, his jaw taut. "Oh, you'll see. Have you ordered yet?"

Why does my belly dip to my toes?

"Timur. What is it? What do you need to tell me?"

His gaze hardens. "I asked you if you ordered yet."

I shake my head. "No, I was waiting for you."

He blows out a breath. "Of course you were."

I look at him in surprise. My phone buzzes and buzzes in my purse. When Timur scowls at me, I silence it.

"What is wrong?" I ask, my anger rising. I don't like not knowing what's going on, and it seems like he's lying to me.

He only shakes his head. "It doesn't matter. Order. Something light, Lydia."

My cheeks color, and I suddenly lose my appetite. We've only known each other for a few months. Not long before my father's sudden and tragic death, he arranged for our wedding. Timur has been the perfect gentleman, attentive and generous, even if a bit cold sometimes. But he's never been like this before. He's definitely never commented on my food choices.

I look down at my full figure, my bust spilling out of the dress I wore to accentuate my curves.

I thought he liked my curves.

"You want me to choose something light?"

He smiles, but his eyes remain cold. "I'm teasing. Choose whatever you want. You know that." He mutters something under his breath.

What the hell?

"Timur," I say in a little voice. Who is this man, and what's become of the man I'd actually grown used to and was looking forward to marrying?

The waiter comes back with a wine menu.

"I worry about you, you know," Timur says as he butters a roll and places half of it on my plate. It's a lot less butter than I would use and only half the bread, but the gesture seems almost sweet.

"Oh?" I take a bite even as my stomach clenches. The food tastes like ash in my mouth. "Why?"

"We're getting married soon, and the weight of responsibility will fall heavily on you to manage our home, our social engagements, and eventually, our children. And the little hobbies you have aren't becoming of the wife I know you could be."

My *little hobbies?*

I drop the bread, my appetite gone. "I don't know what the fuck you're talking about," I snap.

"There you go again," he says, his eyes on me heated. "Losing your temper." He leans in and rests his chin in his hand. "I'm going to be your husband. I'm only expressing concern for you, Lydia. There's no need to lose your temper." He gives a casual shrug, but his tone is anything but. "I'd hate to have to lose mine."

Was that a threat?

I stare at him, my jaw slack.

The candle flickers between us. Beckoning.

"Look," I say in a low voice so as not to draw the attention of everyone around us. "I don't know what happened to you to cause you to behave this way, but I've had a few drinks and I need to use the bathroom. I'm going to just take a little break, and when I return, let's have a civilized conversation, shall we?"

It's hard to issue an ultimatum to a man who has more power in his left thumb than I do in my entire life, but I'm over this.

I stand, but he grabs my wrist again, even harder than before.

"Sit *down,* Lydia." When I don't, he gentles his voice. "I'm sorry. I had a bad day at work. Sit down and tell me about your day."

He almost convinced me. There's something about that suave, persuasive voice of his that almost convinced me it was only a slip-up and my real fiancé was going to come back. But I need a little bit of a breather.

I jerk my wrist away from him, getting the attention of several people nearby.

"I'm just using the restroom," I say. "Please let me go."

He reaches for me, but a waiter comes by, so to save face, he plasters a smile on his face. For once, I'm happy he's always more concerned with appearances than anything else. "Go. Come right back."

A crowd of women passes in front of me. I take the opportunity to step right into the middle of them and head to the bathroom before he can pull me back.

What's happened, and why is he behaving this way?

I feel sick to my stomach and wish, not for the first time, I had someone to confide in. I wish my sister and I were still close like we were when we were children, but now that she's married into the Romanov family, that's impossible. Timur has forbidden it.

I stare at my reflection in the mirror and take a deep breath.

He's *obviously* in a bad mood, but he's never been like this before.

I dab at my lips with lip gloss, trying to quell my rising nerves.

I reach for my phone, wishing again I could call Vera. I have no friends, and my mother and I were never close.

It doesn't matter. So he was... what, impatient? Crass? A man's entitled to the occasional bad temper, isn't he? I'm certainly not a ball of sunshine every waking hour.

Up until now, he's always treated me well.

Maybe I just have unrealistic expectations. It's a fluke—a bad night.

It will be fine. I'll go back out, and my charming fiancé will order dinner for me, and we'll forget this ever happened. I'm starving. Maybe I'm exaggerating things in my mind.

I tap the screen and stare at five missed calls and as many missed texts.

What the hell?

My blood runs cold.

> Vera: Lydia, you are in danger. Come home. I'm sending a car for you now. You have to leave. Please. I'll explain everything.

Come home? I'm two hours away from home.

I'm in danger? I look around the spacious, luxury bathroom. It's well-lit with marble flooring that gleams under soft, ambient overhead lighting. The walls are adorned with large, oval-shaped mirrors in gilded frames. The polished countertops boast bouquets of fresh flowers. It seems too elegant, too refined, for me to be here and in... danger.

Still, I walk to the stall and open it, sliding the lock in place behind me. I open my purse and eye the lighter and pepper spray I always carry with me. I have some measure of protection, anyway.

I check the rest of my messages.

> Lydia, please call me. It's urgent

And then another text from a number I don't recognize.

> Lydia, this is Nikko Romanov, your brother-in-law. It is imperative we secure your location and bring you to safety.

What the hell is going on?

I jump when the door to the bathroom opens, and I hear the click of heels on the tiled floor. I hold my breath as the footsteps approach. I reach into my bag and take out my pepper spray, my finger trembling on the trigger. But I only hear the door to a stall shut.

I'm losing my mind.

I put the pepper spray back.

I've made this into something much, much bigger than it actually is. I'm at a fancy restaurant. With the man I'm going to marry. Vera's being dramatic or influenced by her new husband.

With trembling fingers, I text Vera back.

> Okay what is going on?

> It's too much to text and something I don't
> want to communicate this way. I don't
> know if your phone is tapped. It's important
> to come home so we can chat. Are you
> alright? Are you safe?

I blink. My phone... tapped?

I'm hiding in a bathroom stall. My fiancé is acting strange, and my phone's blowing up with cryptic messages about my safety. No, of course I'm not alright.

> I'm fine, don't worry. I'll call you after
> dinner, okay?

I slide my phone into my bag and leave the stall. The door opens again, letting in another woman dressed in a silky ivory cocktail dress, but I barely notice her. Timur stands outside the door, leaning casually up against the wall, his hands in his pockets.

I go to him.

"I need to call my sister soon. She said she needs to talk with me," I tell him when I exit. The pinched expression on his face has vanished, and instead, he looks like the polished, civilized man who proposed to me while bathed in sunset hues on a beach in Maui. I breathe out a sigh of relief.

"Oh? Our first dish has arrived. Can it wait? You said you were starving. I'll expedite the delivery of the rest of our food, and we'll leave early so you can call her."

He ushers me back to our table, matching my strides as we walk hand in hand. I wonder if I imagined the grumpiness from before. This is the Timur I can't wait to be with.

"Thank you. I could tell she'd rather talk to me in person."

Timur leans in and reaches for my hand. "I'm sorry, Lydia. I shouldn't have been so rude before. I had a day from hell." He smiles at me, his warm brown eyes crinkling around the edges. A little dimple in his cheek flashes at me. I'm not sure why something makes my stomach dip with nerves, and a prickle of fear skates across the back of my neck.

This is Timur. My future husband. He's never hurt me. Maybe I had too much to drink.

"Forgive me?"

"Of course."

My phone buzzes again, and Timur scowls. He hates cell phones and especially hates being interrupted.

"Sorry. She's really worried."

"About what?" he asks as he takes a stuffed mushroom and slides one onto my plate. I'd rather eat two, but he's distracted.

"No idea." I reach for another roll to go with the mushroom, but he scowls disapprovingly.

"What?"

"The wedding's coming, and you said you were watching your carbs," he says with a shrug.

My cheeks flush pink. "Eating low carb made me feel like I had the flu. I hated it."

Why am I explaining this to him? Shouldn't he accept me for who I am?

When my phone buzzes again, Timur looks near apoplectic. His eyes burn into me, his cheeks flushed.

"What the fuck is—"

"It's fine, it's fine," I tell him, shaking my head. "I'll shut it off."

I polish off the wine in my glass to steady my rising nerves. In a normal situation, he would be sending me all kinds of red flags, but we're not a regular couple in an ordinary situation, and I know that well.

"She's just worried and said something about me not being safe."

He nods but doesn't look too bothered. "You're safe when you're with me. I stationed a guard here for you before I came. She should stop watching the news."

"She doesn't watch the news."

Timur's lips thin. He doesn't like being contradicted.

My food feels too dry in my mouth. I swallow with effort.

A chill shivers down my spine, and I don't understand why. I push my wine away. I don't want anything interfering with my ability to think straight. It's a strange, strange night.

I'm not in danger. I'm with my fiancé and bodyguards. "You'll keep me safe, won't you?"

Timur leans forward and holds my hand. "Of course I will, Lydia. Always."

CHAPTER THREE

Viktor

I CHECK my phone for video surveillance of Lydia. When I heard of her engagement, I did my best to get her out of my mind, but I might as well take my heart out of my chest and try to continue to live.

But now that Mikhail has given me the green light and my marriage to Lydia Ivanova is a go, she's taken up full residence in my every waking thought. The familiarity of my damn near obsession with her makes me breathe easy again.

I check the monitors in my office to see where she is—still sitting at dinner with that despicable asshole. I want to reach through the camera and pull her to me. Bring her home.

If her father wasn't already dead, I'd personally put him in a fucking shallow grave for allowing his daughter to be within ten feet of the fucking asshole. I check my phone, wishing I could have the accuracy of surveillance on the road that I do at home, but we had to move.

We were one hour out when the call came in from Nikko.

"Move. He knows. He's got her in a restaurant right now, and she doesn't suspect a thing, but she isn't safe. We have footage of him putting a large duffel bag, rope, duct tape, and gloves in his car. Not good, Viktor."

I've never driven so fast in my life.

"What's the plan?" Lev asks, sitting in the passenger seat as I weave in and out of traffic, driving over a hundred miles an hour with practiced ease. Aleks is in the back, blocking any police interference from catching our speed. We're ten minutes out.

"Fucking get her out of there."

"Vera texted her before Nikko realized what was going on."

"Shit."

"What did she say?"

"Said something cryptic about her being in danger and getting out of there."

Shit. If Yudin finds out, she's fucked. I shake my head.

"Tell her to stop. He could be tapping her phone."

"Of course he's fucking tapping her phone," Aleks mutters.

Jesus.

I need her to stay safe so I can bring her back home to me. It won't be the solution we need all around, but here is the best place for her. We'll deal with whatever shit the men of the *Ledyanoye Bratstvo* give us *after* she's here with me.

"She's tense. Vulnerable," Lev says, looking at the footage on my phone. "She knows something's up, doesn't she?"

"Who knows what the fuck he's saying to her."

"I do," Aleks says with a grin. He taps something on his phone, and Lydia's beautiful, sultry voice comes through the speakers.

"You'll keep me safe, won't you?"

"Always, Lydia."

A third voice joins the conversation. *"May I offer you a dessert menu?"*

"No, we don't need dessert," the asshole says. *"We're leaving."*

Fuck.

As long as there is breath in my lungs, Yudin will never touch her. I will protect Lydia with every ounce of my being. I will not allow anyone to inflict harm upon her. What happened to my sister will never happen to another innocent, fragile soul. Not while I'm alive.

Not *ever*.

I do a mental check of the weapons I've got—a sleek handgun and hidden blade.

I'm ready.

I can still see my sister's tear-streaked face. I can still see her broken body in my arms. I can still feel the way she clung to me as if clinging to life itself, and I was the only one who could save her before she drew her last breath. Every day, I remind myself of the vow I took because of her.

"When we get there, keep the car ready. We might need to move quickly. I don't know what kind of backup he'll have."

Lev nods while Aleks taps something out on his phone as fast as his fingers can move.

I bet she's scared. That bastard better not have said anything to hurt her. If he did, I'll fucking break his jaw for that. See how easy it will be for him to insult her then.

"They're getting ready to leave. Their car's been pulled around to get them."

Fuck.

"Got the car on our radar. We're closing in."

I hit the accelerator.

CHAPTER FOUR

Lydia

OUR MEAL'S come to an end, and I'm starting to get nervous about Vera's messages to me, but Timur seems in no rush like he was before. Instead, his moves seem almost... calculated. Planned.

The waiter brings us our check, and Timur pays.

"Listen, I need to speak to my sister right away. Can we go?"

"Of course." He doesn't meet my eyes, and a muscle twitches in his jaw, but when I give him a second glance, he's all gentlemanly grace as he puts his hand on my lower back and leads me to his car. A valet brings it to the curb. He opens the door for me, and I slide into the passenger seat as he gets into the driver's seat.

But something's off kilter as if there's a movie playing, but the reel is skipping, each second that passes a hair disjointed. The silence between us crackles with unspoken tension, the air thick with my repressed fears and whatever the hell is brewing with my fiancé.

"What did your sister say?" he asks as he unhurriedly pulls into the street. The car engine purrs, and it's almost reassuring.

Everything's fine.

There's nothing to worry about.

Still, my hands itch to strike the lighter in my bag. I can already hear the snitch of flame and see the flicker of measured fire. I swallow hard and look out the window.

I'm an adult now. I'm not the rebellious teen looking for something to control.

"Not much... just to come home."

"So she told you nothing."

"No," I tell him. "I don't know at all. It's a little odd; ever since Vera got married, she's been mysterious about things. She told me that I needed to talk with her in person." I don't tell him she thinks my phone's unsafe.

"Of course she doesn't. She fucking married a Romanov."

I look at him sharply. I didn't even know he knew a thing about her. Is this going to be an issue?

I trust Timur, but...

I'm looking down at my phone, trying to catch up on messages, when I see that my last messages to Vera never sent. Strange.

"Put it away, Lydia," he says cooly. "You know how I feel about that when we're together." His fingers drum impatiently on the steering wheel.

"I know, but she's worried." I'm distracted, trying to figure out if my cell phone service is working and don't notice the rising tone of his voice.

"She has no reason to be worried." He exhales. "I'm losing my patience. Put the damn thing away."

"I need to—"

The next thing I know, he snatches my phone from my hand, rolls down the window, and tosses it into oncoming traffic.

"Timur!"

His lips are set into a thin line as we drive even faster.

"How could you do that? That was my cell phone. Oh my *God!*" I clutch at his arm, but he shoves me off of him so hard I bang into the passenger door.

I open my mouth to protest further when I realize we're driving in the wrong direction. Ice pulses through my veins, my cell phone forgotten.

I draw in a deep breath. I have to stay calm. *I can't lose it.*

"Timur. Where are we going? I thought we were heading home." This is not the right direction.

"We are," he says, a hardness to his voice.

An uneasy feeling settles in my stomach. I glance around, the dark waters of the river glinting under the bridge lights as we speed across.

Before I can process the information or what the hell he's talking about, the car jolts to a stop. My heart leaps into my throat as I see a car in the rearview mirror gaining on us.

You're in danger.

Without missing a beat, Timur reaches under his seat and pulls out a handgun, his expression cold and determined.

"What are you doing?" I gasp, my voice trembling. "What the hell is going on? Oh my God. You know what she's talking about!"

"Yeah, I fucking knew they were coming." He shakes his head. "No matter what happens, stay in the car," he orders, his voice like steel. *"Don't move."*

Panic grips me. I've never seen him hold a gun before. And while I knew who he was, at least on paper, I've never seen him act any way but civilized and refined.

My breath catches as someone yells, and shots ring out.

The car lurches forward suddenly, hit from behind. I scream as Timur leaps back inside, slamming the door. "Get down!" he shouts, pressing on the accelerator. We're speeding down the bridge, the sounds of gunfire and shouting fading into the distance.

"What's happening?" I cry, fear clawing at my chest.

You're in danger.

Is this what Vera was talking about?

He doesn't answer, his focus razor-sharp on the road ahead. But when a loud bang rocks the car again, we swerve wildly. I scream, clutching the door as we crash into the guardrail.

The world spins, and to my horror, the car flips, skidding to a halt upside down. The airbag balloons out, crushing me. My head smashes against something, and pain ricochets through my skull. The metallic taste of blood fills my mouth.

I'm crying, dazed and disoriented, as I fumble with my seatbelt, the world a chaotic blur of noise and pain. I have a vague idea I should assess the situation, but I'm confused and can't figure out how. I somehow make it outside, my vision blurred and hazy. My dress hangs wildly off one shoulder, torn to shreds.

My eyes are wild with fear as I scream for Timur, but he's already gone, running toward the edge of the bridge.

A figure cloaked in darkness stalks toward him; something about his heavy, unhurried steps terrifying. His eyes are locked on Timur.

"Stop!" he barks, his words a harsh command. Timur turns, gun in hand, and I scream aloud.

Strong arms wrap around me. I struggle, trying to push them away, but I'm hurt, and my reflexes are slow.

"No! Let me go!" I yell, thrashing against my captor's grip.

The world around me seems to blur as adrenaline surges through my veins, heightening every sense to a fever pitch. I hear a sickening thud and a cry of pain. I scream and push, but it's no use.

Someone's got him. Whoever has come for us has Timur, and they're beating him.

"Stop! No!" I yell. "Help!"

Each blow feels like a physical blow to my own body, each cry of pain a dagger to my heart. I want to look away, bury my head in my hands and block out the nightmare playing out before me, but I can't tear my eyes away from the horror.

Why won't anyone stop to help?

A gunshot rings out. Timur takes off, hoists himself up on the bridge—and he's gone.

I scream and struggle, but it's no use; whoever's holding me has me secured.

"Let me go!"

"Stop fighting." The voice is deep, commanding, and unfamiliar. I look up to see a tall, hulking man with a shaved head and a scar running down his cheek. His strong, unyielding grip terrifies me, his presence overwhelming. He holds me easily as if my struggles are nothing.

An alarm clangs in my memory. Somehow, he looks vaguely familiar. I don't know him, but I've seen him before.

A hysterical scream is torn from my lips. "*No! Timur!*" I sob, my body trembling uncontrollably.

"Fuck!" one of the men yells. "Fucking get him!"

"Listen to me! You're safe now, Lydia."

How does he knows my name?

The fucking *liar*.

I continue to shove and scream, but I might as well be a mouse in the paws of a lion. With practiced ease, he deflects my blows, as if they barely register, before he bends and lifts me. He tucks me against his chest gently, but he's so much bigger than I am that I can't fight him off.

My vision clears slightly, and the bridge lights illuminate the intense eyes of my captor. His expression is a mixture of concern and steely determination.

He's holding me against him as if I weigh nothing. I'm sturdy and curvy... I'm not a petite little thing you might carry around like a doll. Only a man the size of a superhero would be able to hold me in his arms with such ease.

The thought only escalates my terror.

"I've got you," he says. "You're safe."

Safe? Of course I'm not safe. We were attacked. I saw one of them beat my fiancé with his own hands.

As I struggle, another man appears, younger and more clean-cut, his expression serious as he speaks to my captor in Russian. I can't fully hear their exchange, but the younger man's presence adds to my fear.

"Put her in the back of the car," a third man says, his piercing blue eyes locking onto mine. He's tall and imposing, yet as solid as the others. "Vera can explain."

Vera?

What?

"No! Let me go!" I demand, convinced they are kidnapping me. "Don't touch me!"

"Lydia, calm down," the one holding me says, his voice softer yet firm. "We're not going to hurt you."

But I'm too terrified to listen, my mind filled with my sister's warning and the sight of Timur fleeing.

Is my sister working with the enemy?

She fucking married a Romanov.

"Please," the big guy holding me says. "I'll explain—"

"*Fuck.*" Tires squeal as a car heads our way, driving at top speed. The big man holding me leaps to the side with me in his arms, crashing to the ground just in time as gunshots ring out. He cages me beneath him as if using his huge body as a human shield. From my vantage point, I can see the tall one stand and pull the trigger, one after another after another. Glass crashes, and one of the tires explodes before it slams head-on into the guard rail.

There's a hiss of airbags, and someone screams, but no one gets out of the vehicle. I'm shaking uncontrollably, and I have the sudden urge to vomit.

"*Ledyanoye Bratstvo,*" the younger one says in a growl.

Someone's opening a door. I struggle against his grip, but it's no use. I'm overpowered, lifted in his arms, and pushed into the car as if I'm a doll. I slap at strong hands, clawing and screaming. One of them wraps something over my wrists, and another buckles me in.

"I've got this," the younger one says. "Viktor, don't murder me." A roar sounds in my ears when something sharp pricks my skin. I scream, and the larger one tugs me against him.

"Enough," the largest one growls in a voice that makes my heart stop. "No one touches her but me." He slides in beside me.

"You're not thinking straight," the younger one says. "She's wild and unpredictable, and we don't have what it takes to keep her safe."

"He's right."

The huge one roars like an animal but holds me against him. "I've fucking got her."

"Jesus," the younger one mutters.

"You'd better fucking pray to him. I'm going to beat your fucking ass for that."

"He can't think straight," the tall one says to the younger one. "He's out of his mind."

What is happening? My head feels too heavy and strangely tight.

Oh God.

What are they going to do to me?

As we speed away, I glance out the window, the city lights blurring past.

They have to be the enemies of my fiancé. I have no idea where we're going or what they're doing, but I have to stay calm. I have to take in every detail so I can plan my escape.

But, he said Vera would explain—

I have to remain calm until I talk to my sister.

Even as we drive away, my mind races with thoughts of escape and the fear of what these men might do to me.

I've never seen these men before. I quickly assess the situation. It's three strong men against me, alone, and none of them look easy to get away from. The big guy, the one who carried me to this car, with the scar across one cheek, has a look in his eyes that tells me he's no stranger to violence. I shiver.

The tall one with black hair and those blue, blue eyes is the one driving, the younger one in the passenger seat. He looks over his shoulder at the man beside me. "I don't trust her. She's unpredictable."

I gawk. "I'm not going to do anything," I lie because I was absolutely planning on getting the hell out of here as soon as the car slowed down. But my words are already slurred, and my limbs feel as if they're weirdly detached from my body. Panic rises as I realize I've been drugged. My vision blurs, and a heavy numbness seeps into my muscles, making it impossible to move. The interior of the car spins, and I struggle to keep my eyes open, my mind racing with thoughts of escape that now seem hopelessly out of reach.

They drive in silence, the speed terrifying me. My head lolls. I fight to stay awake, to keep my eyes open.

"Who are you?" My voice trembles, the words barely coherent. I will it to stop. I want to stay in charge of myself and my emotions. I don't want to be a helpless, overpowered female. "Where is Timur?"

"Good fucking question," the driver growls. "I'd like to know that myself."

The driver and the man next to me look at each other in the rearview mirror.

"We are friends of your sister, Vera," one finally says. "Call her."

Vera.

When the men don't respond, I realize he's talking to me.

"I don't have my phone."

"Shit. You lost your bag in the crash?"

I look around me wildly as if it's somehow going to spawn into the interior of the car. Of course I don't have my bag.

"Yes." I don't tell them Timur threw my cell phone away before they came. It feels foolish to give them more ammunition against him when they already tried to kill him. The world goes in and out of consciousness as if someone's shutting the lights on and off.

It's warm in here, a stark contrast to the cold fear that had gripped me earlier. The man who captured me holds me against him with a tenderness that defies his rugged exterior, an unexpected gentleness that catches me off guard. I tell myself to be wary. No one is here to protect me.

My head rests on his shoulder, and instinctively, he wraps a protective arm around me, cocooning me in his embrace. I blink against impending sleep, but the warmth is soothing, a balm to my frayed nerves. I can't think beyond the threat of sleep lulling me into a reluctant surrender.

I can't... think.

Yet one word surfaces, intense and surprising in its clarity: *safe.*

CHAPTER FIVE

Viktor

I'VE GOT HER. She's with me. I feel like I'm dreaming.

Lydia Ivanova is asleep in my arms.

"I'm going to beat the fucking shit out of you once I've got her safe," I tell Lev. I can't believe the asshole had the nerve to drug her against my wishes. I haven't raised my hand to Lev since he was a dumbass teen who thought he was invincible, and I saved his ass from a rival gang he thought he could take. That was years ago.

Lev swallows. "I know."

She's mine.

Mine.

"Don't kill him," Aleks mutters, his eyes darting from the rearview mirror to mine. "If he didn't do that, she'd have fought you and probably opened the door or something."

I growl and look out the window, reluctant to admit he probably did the right thing. I could've handled her if she fought me. I might have even liked it.

"I told you I had her. It's easy enough to restrain her, you fucking asshole."

She stirs against me, and I lower my voice. "Now how will she trust me knowing we took her and drugged her?"

Lev shakes his head. "Don't overestimate how important it is to get her safe first, Vik. Look, you're not thinking straight. Once you—"

"I know exactly what I'm doing," I snap. I do. He doesn't understand how many times I've thought about this, about *her*. How goddamn determined I am to make sure that she's safe, secured, and well protected. "Let me make this clear. None of you so much as fucking *breathes* on her again."

"Jesus, Viktor, don't take your anger at Yudin out on us," Aleks says.

Rage claws at my chest when I think of what could've happened tonight, but it isn't misplaced. I breathe in to settle my fraught nerves the way Kolya taught me.

Aleksandr's phone rings, coming through loudly on the speakers. Lydia stirs against me.

"Shut it off," I snap. "For fuck's sake."

"It's Mikhail," Aleks argues. There's an unspoken rule that we answer Mikhail's calls immediately, without question, no matter the time of day.

"I don't care."

Lev and Aleks share a look before Lev takes the call. "Yeah. We've got her." He shakes his head. "No, he got away, but we had a backup crew below the bridge, and we're confident they'll get him."

They have strict instructions to find him and then deliver him promptly to *me*. No one gets to touch a hair on his head.

 They speak in hushed tones until, finally, he ends the call.

"Mikhail wants an update."

"Text him."

"Viktor," Aleks begins, looking at me in the rearview mirror again. "You have to be reasonable."

I hold his gaze for a few seconds before he snaps back to looking at the road.

"Let's pretend for a moment this were Harper," I say in a low voice. "Let's pretend you just fucking got her away from someone who not only planned on marrying her but fucking using her and then killing her."

A muscle tenses in Aleks's jaw. "I get it," Aleks finally says. "I just want you to be rational."

"I'll be rational when Timur fucking Yudin's no longer breathing and the *Ledyanoye Bratstvo* is destroyed. I'll see reason when I put a ring on her finger and secure her safely to me. Until then, I'll be the most unreasonable son of a bitch you've ever fucking met."

We lapse into silence, only broken by occasional updates from Lev, texting the rest of our brothers. She stirs against my shoulder as I make my plans. Until I get further updates, I have one goal: keep her safe.

"There's no word from our men," Lev says, shaking his head. "Jesus. I expected better."

It was more important to me to secure her than it was to get our enemy. I had to choose one or the other.

I chose her.

I will always choose her.

Yudin's a fucking dead man walking. I'll see to that.

She barely moves during the two-hour ride home. We pull into the drive to my home late into the night. I stay in the back with Lydia as my brothers run surveillance to make sure nothing's happened while I was gone, but I'm not surprised we find nothing. Timur Yudin will plan his retaliation, but he isn't a man who acts recklessly. He'll bide his time.

"Coast is clear, Vik," Lev says from my doorway, signaling for us to come. Lydia stirs but doesn't wake when I lift her from the car and cradle her in my arms.

When she wakes, she'll be ready to fight. I might be able to talk some sense into her when Vera gets involved, but it's more likely she'll fight even then. It's alright, though. I love that she's a fighter.

I love the way she feels in my arms.

So I take a moment to relish this. The warm, comforting feel of her in my arms, nestled up to my chest. The heat of her against me, her breath on my neck. The lingering scent of jasmine mixed with an earthy undertone, fiery but refined.

Her long, thick, wavy hair the color of tanned leather hangs down her back, an unruly strand across her face, some of it tickling my neck. Her dress, torn in the accident, barely clings to her. I turn her into me and hold her tighter so she doesn't get cold. The reassuring sound of her soft breath gives me a small measure of solace.

When I get to the entrance to the house, Nikita approaches, quiet and subdued yet alert. She's as concerned as I am. Her soulful eyes meet mine, and I give her a nod. "Yeah, baby. You'll protect her, just like I will." She gives a small, appreciative sniff of Lydia's foot before she follows us into the house.

She'll spend the night in my bedroom, where I can keep a close eye on her.

Vera's deep in the trenches of field study she's doing with one of her professors and likely won't be able to join us anytime soon. Zofia is currently leaving to travel abroad and head-up a series of high-profile charity events she's previously committed to. Our timing is absolute shit.

I am hoping the Ivanovs will be able to talk sense into her, but time will tell.

Behind me on the landing, Lev's phone rings. "It's Mikhail."

He answers immediately. "Yeah." Lev curses under his breath. This is not good. He shakes his head and hangs up the phone. "Yudin escaped."

CHAPTER SIX

Lydia

EVEN MY DREAMS are sluggish and confused. I wake a few times in the night, and every time I do, the fog lifts just a tiny bit more.

At first, I become aware of the fact that I'm in bed. Not just any bed, and definitely not a hotel because this bed is absolutely enormous, almost absurdly so. If a cruise ship were a bed, I'm sleeping on it. It feels like a vast expanse of luxury, with soft, plush pillows and a comforter that seems to envelop me in a cocoon of warmth and safety. The mattress is so wide and spacious that it could easily fit five people with room to spare. I can barely see the edges of the bed, the sheer size making me feel like I'm in a luxurious sanctuary, designed to offer ultimate comfort and security.

Another time I wake, I'm aware of the sheets, like the finest silk against my skin. My head is on a satin pillowcase.

What kind of captor do I have who puts me in a bed that would rival a luxury hotel?

At first, I think I'm alone but quickly realize I'm not. When I stir, the huge guy who kidnapped and drugged me looms beside me, sitting in a chair next to a desk. "Are you alright?" he asks.

I open my mouth to speak, but my tongue feels too big for my mouth, and I can't form words. Still, he rises, his large form blocking out any light from behind him as he makes his way over to me.

I flinch back from him as he presses something to my lips and I turn my head away. I don't trust him.

"Drink," he orders. "It's water."

I shake my head and press my head to the pillow. I'm vaguely aware of him cursing as I close my eyes and go back to sleep.

When I finally wake, I open my eyes. My vision's a bit fuzzy, and my head is *pounding*. It hurts just to open my eyes and try to turn my head. Where am I? Am I safe?

Other than my head, I seem okay.

The events of the night before come in a rush, and I stifle a sob.

Timur.

I was taken from my fiancé. Kidnapped. They're going to kill him.

What are they planning on doing with me?

I sit up with a start in bed and note that even though I'm covered with a blanket, I'm only dressed in my bra and panties.

"Shhh," someone says nearby. I blink into serious dark-brown eyes. I recognize him immediately as the man who attacked last night and choke back a scream. "I'm not going to hurt you," he says gently, shaking his head. "I promise."

Why would someone take me, attack me, and then promise not to hurt me?

Why is he so familiar? I wish I could piece everything together. I open my eyes and blink, trying to clear my blurred vision.

"Who are you?" I ask through thick lips, my words slurred.

He takes a bottle of water from the bedside table and twists the top off. "My name is Viktor Romanov." His voice is deep and gravelly, tinged with the faintest touch of a Russian accent.

Viktor Romanov.

Romanov... Vera married Nikko Romanov. I vaguely remember something last night about my sister, but my thoughts are muddied.

Still, I don't care. I've had no confirmation yet from anyone I trust, and so far, these men have done nothing to convince me to believe them.

I turn away from the water and shake my head. I won't take anything from a man who kidnapped me.

"Drink," he orders. "If you don't drink the water this time, I will be forced to call a doctor to come and give you an IV.

You are dehydrated." He speaks with that slight Russian accent, slowly and with patience, almost as if he's talking to a child. His eyes, cold and calculating, watch me intently as if he's waiting to be obeyed.

I gasp and pull the covers up, a scream trapped in my throat when I realize we're not alone. The largest dog I've ever seen is curled up in the bed a few feet away from me. When she lifts her eyes to look at me, she seems intelligent but powerful, muscle rippling beneath a glossy black coat of fur. She lies on the other side of the fully made bed.

Phew. No one else joined me in this bed last night. A crazy thought, but it's been a crazy series of events.

"Relax," he says. "This is just Nikita. She's here because she wanted to protect you."

He snaps his fingers, and the dark form of his dog, huge and muscular... not unlike *him*... obediently jumps off the bed and walks over to him.

"Go," he says, snapping his fingers again and opening the door. The dog walks out submissively. He closes the door and turns back to me. "Now drink, Lydia."

I hesitate, my gaze shifting from the bottle of water to his unwavering stare. There's no kindness in his expression, only a stern resolve that makes it clear he's not making an idle threat. My throat is dry, and I know I need the water, but the thought of doing what he says grates against my pride. And how am I supposed to know it isn't drugged to keep me in a state of compliance?

"No. I can't trust you," I whisper. "I don't know who you are."

"It's *water*."

I clamp my lips together. I expect him to lose his temper, but he doesn't.

"I will tell you who I am, though I'll be surprised if you believe me at first. But first, water, or I call the doctor."

I stare at the bottle. I feel like I'm dying of thirst. So finally, with a sigh of resignation, I reach for the bottle, my hand trembling slightly.

"Fine," I say with a frown because I've just realized my wrists are bound. I have a vague notion he wasn't happy when I was drugged, but he could've taken these restraints off. He wants me tied.

I take the smallest sip of water. It hits my parched lips and tastes so good, so I keep gulping. His eyes flicker with a hint of satisfaction as I lift the bottle to my lips. The water is cool and soothing as it slides down my throat, but the victory is his, not mine.

I set the bottle down and meet his gaze, defiance burning in my eyes. "There," I say, my voice hoarse but steady. "Happy now?"

"There," he says, his voice warm with approval. "What a very good girl." He reaches a hand to me and then pulls it back as if stung.

I wonder what makes him scowl like that.

My heart does a somersault in my chest.

I blame the drugs.

His phone rings. Looking down at the screen, he presses a button, and it stops. I watch him slide it into his pocket.

"What happened?" My voice is hard. Reserved. I don't trust him, and it scares me that I don't know where I am or why I'm here.

 I look to the bedroom door and see it's locked. I hate that my mind is muddied and hate that I'm not fully in control of myself. "You took me."

I wish my accusation didn't have that touch of petulance in it. I want to stay strong, but I'm depleted and hungry, and my head hurts so badly I cradle it in my hands.

The big guy—Viktor, he said his name is—bends down and brushes the hair off my forehead, but he touches me with utter tenderness as if I move too quickly, the moment will be lost.

My pulse ratchets higher, but my guard snaps into place. I know I can't trust someone who's gentle and careful. If you let your guard down… if you let yourself become vulnerable at all… that's when they swoop in to take advantage of you.

And he may be the most dangerous man I've ever met.

"What did you do to Timur?"

The man's eyes darken, storm clouds brewing.

"Not what I wanted to do, that's for damn sure."

A chill skates down my spine when I realize he's dead serious. He came for me and Timur. He captured me and Timur… a lump rises in my throat.

"Why?" I whisper.

His jaw clenches as he leans forward, his forearms resting on his knees. Last night, he wore a black leather jacket, but here, in the confines of this room, he's wearing nothing but a plain white undershirt that stretches across the expanse of his chest and bulges of his biceps. It makes him look only slightly more human, tattoos snaking around his arms and neck only adding to the look. "It's complicated."

I take another gulp of water, my strength returning. I sit up and stare at him. "I'm not going anywhere. I got a call from my sister saying I was in danger. My fiancé started acting strange, and then the next thing I know, we were attacked by you. You beat the shit out of him, and he disappeared." I shake my head, my hair falling onto my shoulders. I straighten them, trying to maintain some semblance of control. "I have all day."

He holds my gaze, an almost thoughtful expression on his face. "Timur was planning on hurting you."

I scoff, shaking my head. "You're going to have to start with a different angle than *that*. He is my fiancé."

I shift uncomfortably in the bed and realize I need to use the bathroom. I don't know if I trust myself to walk as I can barely see straight, and my legs might not cooperate. I want to get to the bottom of this, so I ignore the call of nature.

"In the back of his car, he had a duffel bag, rope, duct tape, and gloves."

I shake my head, not wanting to believe him. "It makes no sense that he'd try to hurt me. We are getting married."

"*Were*," he corrects. I blink hard, my eyes watering. I feel like everything in my world is spinning wildly out of control. I take in a deep breath and gather my wits about me.

"My family and yours have made other plans," he continues in his deep rumble of a voice colored with a Russian accent. "It is not in your best interest to marry into *Ledyanoye Bratstvo.* Your father made that choice when he thought it would benefit the Ivanovs, but it's clear that it was a poor decision that didn't take into account who you are and what is in your best interest."

I shake my head. "As if you know a thing about me."

Though his jaw tightens, he doesn't contradict me. Outside the window behind him, clouds shift, covering the sun. I half expect to see fog-swept moors behind him.

Where are we?

I hear voices in the hallway, but they grow quieter. He continues as if I said nothing at all.

"When your sister married Nikko, his primary job was to work with the Ivanovs to secure the alliance. The best way to continue doing so is for you to marry into the Romanov family."

I stare at him, my mouth agape. Am I still dreaming? Or is this some type of hallucination brought on by the drugs?

"What are you talking about?" I clench the bottle in my hand, and it spills over the side, splashing onto the bed.

"Stay calm, Lydia."

I *hate* when people tell me to stay calm. It's like trying to tell a sobbing child to stop crying. You can't just put a stopper on human emotions with a command.

"Stay calm? You ripped me away from my fiancé because it suits you, drugged me, and brought me here against my wishes. You're trying to blame my fiancé for this when you were the one who attacked. I don't know where I am or what you're going to do to me, and I'm supposed to just nod and go along with this? I can't possibly—"

He stands to his full height, and I have to admit, it's intimidating. The words falter on my lips as he unfolds himself, muscles bulging in places I didn't even know you could have muscles. The room seems to shrink, and still, even now, he looks at me with tenderness and concern.

I swallow hard and lick my lips.

"I knew this would not be easy for you," he says, his voice still placid. "But you're mistaken. I took you away from Timur because he was going to hurt you. He's an evil man, and there's no need for you to take my word for that. I can prove it. I didn't drug you—my brother did. And no, I don't expect you to just nod and go along with it, though the sooner you do, the easier it will be for you."

There's a sharp knock at the door. "Who is it?" he snaps. Apparently, patience is only reserved for me.

"Aleks."

He unlocks the door, "Come in."

The tall man with the black hair and blue eyes from last night steps into the room frowning, holding a tablet in his hand. He wears the same clothes he wore last night, as if he hasn't slept.

"I'm Aleksandr," he says to me, then turns back to Viktor. "I haven't been able to get Vera on the phone. Nikko is here, though. He says Vera is in a remote location doing field work and unable to get to her phone again until this evening."

Viktor's face registers mild surprise. "Is she alone?"

Aleks scoffs. "Of course not." He turns to look at me. "Lydia, how are you?"

They're surprisingly civil for captors, which is more than a little unnerving.

"Been better," I say, clutching the blanket to my chest.

"I'm sorry things were so clumsy," Aleks says. "And this is the first impression you get of our family."

I don't respond, staring at the two of them as if they don't speak the same language I do. Frankly, they don't.

"Who else has arrived?" Viktor asks, his arms crossed over his chest.

"Mikhail and Lev. Mikhail wants all of us downstairs for a meeting."

He shakes his head. "I'm not leaving her."

"Aw," I say under my breath. "I'm so touched." Viktor glances over at me but doesn't respond. There's something in his eyes that makes me shiver and look away.

"Mikhail says he'll put a guard outside the door—" Aleks begins when Viktor interrupts him with a growl.

"*I'm* her fucking guard."

CHAPTER SEVEN

Viktor

ALEKS HAS the fucking audacity to smirk. "Of course you are. Not sure why I expected any less. I'll relay your message to Mikhail, but you know how he is." He turns to Lydia. "Trust him. This will be okay. We'll get your sister or mother on the phone as soon as we can."

Lydia stares at me as if trying to figure me out, her beautiful eyes swinging from me to Aleks, then back again.

"Go," I tell Aleks. "I'll come once she's secured."

He clicks his tongue and shakes his head, muttering under his breath before he finally takes off, leaving me and Lydia alone. There was a time when I would've given anything to be alone with her, but now that I am, I want so much more. I want her to trust me. I want her to believe me. I need her to know that I'm not going to hurt her.

"Secured?" Though the tone of her voice is hard, I note the

way her breath quickens, and she clutches the blanket to her body.

"I'll have to talk to Mikhail. He's my oldest brother and the *pakhan* of our group. You know what that is, don't you?"

Swallowing hard, she's still scowling at me when she nods. "Of course."

I stand, pacing around the small room. "Then you'd know I have no choice but to obey him."

Her intelligent, beautiful eyes meet mine. "You always have a choice. Don't lie to yourself."

The starkness of her honesty surprises me, though it shouldn't. One of the things I love best about her is her refusal to placate anyone or talk bullshit.

"Yeah," I tell her while I check the locks on the doors and windows and make sure all surveillance equipment is on standby. "You're right. Allow me to rephrase. If I don't want him to murder me, I'll do what Mikhail fucking tells me."

With a frown, she gives a slight shrug as if to say *yeah, that's your choice, too.*

"Before you go, can you tell me as much as you can?" she asks. "Even though I don't like what you did to me, you seem kind of honest. Blunt. So before you meet with your brothers, what else can you tell me?"

I decide to go straight for the jugular. "Your mother's granted permission to dissolve the potential union between you and Timur Yudin, effective immediately. When she relayed this message to him, she was treated with a litany of profanity and a threat to both her life and yours."

She frowns. "You're lying. He wouldn't."

"I have video evidence to prove it."

A shadow crosses her face as if she doesn't want to admit to the truth. She trusted the guy, and now her world has been ripped out from under her. I get it.

"Alright then. Let's see it," she says.

I can tell by the tone of her voice and the flash of her eyes that she's trying to prove me wrong, that she wants to challenge me.

I nod and pull out my phone. We have a vault of videographic evidence we keep for my family, but I can access it to show her what I need to. I scroll through the files while she shifts uncomfortably in the bed.

I look up from my phone when I can't find it right away. God, she must be starving. What's wrong with me?

"Hold on. Are you hungry?"

She nods, still holding my gaze quietly.

"Yeah."

I've already gotten food ready for her but haven't brought it out yet. I know exactly what she likes to eat, but it depends on which version of Lydia is here with me. Is it Lydia, the good girl, trying to please whoever it is she's with? Or is it Lydia, the one who's comfortable in her own skin and owns it?

Sometimes Lydia will eat an egg white omelet and vegetables, or eat a protein bar, or maybe skip breakfast altogether when she's trying to diet her body into brutal submission.

Comfortable Lydia, on the other hand, will eat buttered toast, some fruit, or maybe a grilled muffin with a bowl of fruit salad or chocolate-frosted donuts.

To be safe, then, I've had all of those options brought here. I don't want to unnerve her by revealing how well I know her, though, so I've had an assortment of food prepared.

This room we're in is small. Normally, we'd eat breakfast in the eat-in kitchen. I love my kitchen with its huge, plate glass windows that overlook the front walkway and garden. I love watching the change of seasons from the kitchen table, whether we're heralding the coming winter with holly leaves and red berries, burnt orange leaves on my front yard maple in autumn, or early sunrise on a summer morning.

I've imagined what it would be like having her here with me at that table. I'd sit with her, just listening to her talk about whatever it was she wanted to. I carved the heavy kitchen table with my own two hands, and I have to admit I had her in mind when I designed it. I once heard her say she loved cherrywood and the memory never left my mind.

Right now, though, she needs to be kept in here. It's only for a while.

"Let me get you something to eat first." I stand and walk to the door, all the time thinking I need to watch her more closely. She has the run of the room, and Lydia is feisty as hell. If she could find a way out...

But I'll only be a minute. I quickly grab an assortment. When I return, she's sitting up in bed, the blanket clutched to her chest. .

"Here," I tell her. "Take a look and tell me what you want."

Eying me warily, she looks at the food on the tray. Mistrusting.

"You should untie me so I can feed myself."

"I'm sorry, I can't do that." There's no telling what she'll do when I do that. "I will once you've shown you're trustworthy."

She gawks at me, her jaw unhinged. "You think *I'm* untrustworthy? Are you out of your mind? You're the one who kidnapped me."

I grit my teeth and slide the food onto the bedside table.

"What would you like to eat?"

"Untie me, Viktor. I promise I won't do anything stupid. You're twice my size. There's no way I could if I wanted to. I just want to feed myself and get my clothes back on." Her voice lowers. "Please."

Goddamn, I have no power to resist her.

I reach for her wrists. "Alright, but if you try to hurt yourself or me…"

"I won't."

I untie her.

She sits back on the bed and chooses the plate with the omelet, hash browns, and bacon. She eats with gusto, obviously starving after being drugged. I've heard it can have that effect on people.

We sit in silence while she eats until she nods her head to the tray. "Are you going to join me or what?"

"I'm good. I ate earlier."

With a frown, she continues to chew before she swallows and nods. "So you're just going to stand there and watch me eat?"

I'd stand here just to watch her breathe, but I don't want to freak her out. I reach for one of the croissants and bite into it, crumbs scattering everywhere.

"Yikes. My mama would kill me." She looks down at the floor.

"Don't worry, I have house cleaners. They'll come by in a few hours."

"Ah." She presses her lips together and nods before she picks up her fork and takes another bite of egg. "Thank you for this. It's delicious. Now, please. Now that you've got me fed, can you tell me what's going on?"

I sit on the edge of the bed, eating a croissant as she continues to eat her breakfast. I pull out my phone.

"A recording of your mother's conversation with Timur. Fortunately for us, she had video surveillance set up where she was, so she had this evidence."

I tap my phone, and the screen pops up. Her mother, Zofia, sits primly in a chair in her living room. Her home is about thirty minutes from here.

The footage is grainy but clear. Timur shifts uncomfortably in his seat, his folded arms on his chest.

"Why did you call me?"

Something flickers in Lydia's eyes. I can surmise what it is—the friendly demeanor is a bit off putting, incongruent with the rough tone of his voice. He's laid it on thick for her, so it likely takes her by surprise.

"As you know," Zofia begins, "we've had a change in our family since Vera married into the Romanovs'."

She watches as Yudin stares implacably at her mother, his gaze stone cold, and she shifts uncomfortably.

"I'm not sure I understand. What does that have to do with me?" he finally asks, scowling.

Zofia clears her throat. "I have reservations about my daughter's marriage to you that my husband did not have. Leadership and I have decided it best that Lydia marry into the Romanov family. Please accept my apologies—"

"No." I wish I could reach through the screen and ring Yudin's arrogant neck.

"This marriage is in progress. I've already spent significant money on Lydia's dress." He scoffs. "It needed to be altered to accommodate her and was no small fee thanks to her size."

I forgot about that part. The fucker. Lydia's cheeks turn bright pink.

"Mr. Yudin," she says kindly. "I wish I could give my daughter to you with confidence, but recent developments make the situation unwise."

He stands. "I'll have Lydia, Zofia. You will not take her away from me."

Zofia gets on her feet as he turns to leave. "Please understand. This is a strategic decision that we must make—" He takes a step toward her, but two guards snap into position between them. He makes a fist.

"Watch your fucking back and stay out of my way," he snarls before he leaves, slamming the door behind him so hard the windows rattle. Fucking spoiled prick.

"Shut it off," Lydia snaps, looking away. "My mother shouldn't have intervened. My father was the one who arranged for our marriage."

Her father who's dead now.

I wonder if she really believes that, or is she only saying that as an excuse for Yudin's behavior?

She doesn't have to believe me. I know why I took her, and I know why she's marrying me.

When my phone rings, I glance down to see Mikhail's calling and stifle a groan. I turn away from her and take the call.

"Yeah?"

"Aleksandr tells me you're not attending our meeting. Our meeting I called *specifically* to make a plan with *you,* Viktor." The inherent disapproval in his voice sets my teeth on edge. I love my brothers, all of them, but I don't know if they have the first clue about what matters most to me.

"I know," I tell him. "She's scared. I don't want to leave her alone."

"She'll be fine. I expect you to join us. Immediately."

He ends the call. I shove my phone in my pocket when Lydia speaks up.

"I don't know what you think I'm going to do here," she says as she nibbles a ripe berry. "I have nowhere to go."

But there's a look in her eyes I've seen before... the look she gets right before she does something rash and dangerous. "Lydia," I say warningly.

"It bothers me how familiar you are with my name despite the fact that we hardly know each other." She tosses her head. "I want to talk to Vera. Go, have your meeting, and tell them I want to talk to Vera."

Turning away from me, she lies on the bed and gives me her back.

She's playing at something, but I don't know what. My phone buzzes with a text, though.

Mikhail: where the fuck are you

Jesus, Mikhail.

I shove my phone in my pocket.

I grab my jacket and head down to the office where my brothers are waiting. I'm halfway down the hall when the overhead lights flicker. I scowl, looking upward.

Strange.

Unlike my brothers' homes, mine is smaller but closer to my mother's. I like knowing I'm within walking distance of my sister and mother's house if they need me. So I settled for a home that was smaller than I wanted and instead made some modifications so it would be comfortable for a guy like me. Home gym. Gated yard for Nikita. Large doorways and sturdy furniture.

I also don't like staff milling about the place, so I hired a housekeeper but no one else. I vetted the fuck out of her background.

I stalk toward my office, every step igniting my temper. I'll kick Lev's ass for drugging her. I'm fucking pissed at Aleksandr for getting involved. I hate that Mikhail has made me leave when my place is with her. And if anybody else—

I shove the door open, and it slams into the wall behind it. Six pairs of eyes are riveted on me. Mikhail, Aleksandr, Lev. My brothers Nikko, Ollie, and Kolya.

Nikko gets on his feet, the largest one in the group after me and the one who's most likely to actually stand a chance against me. He heads toward me. I hold up a palm, trying to stop him before I kill him.

"Stand the fuck down, Nikko."

Kolya tries next, Mikhail and Aleksandr behind him. I shake them all off. Lev stands. I swing and punch his jaw. In one swift motion, I grab him by the front of the shirt and throw Lev across the room and onto the couch, where I know he'll land without breaking bones, but it won't feel good.

I shrug off Mikhail, kick Aleksandr back, and swing at Nikko. I'm breathing heavily. They're staring at me.

"*Viktor,*" Kolya snaps.

I blink. I start to come to my senses. *Shit*. If I had raised a fist to Mikhail…

"Do we have to fucking restrain you?" Mikhail spits out, his eyes storm clouds as he glares at me. Lev massages his jaw but doesn't say anything, probably knowing he got off easy. Kolya is fuming, his nostrils flared, but he gets to his feet and brushes his clothes off as if he's dusting himself.

"Sit down, Viktor," he snaps.

I stand my ground. "None of you know what it was like. None of you know what he was planning to do to her. She did not need to be drugged, and now I have to take a reluctant wife who doesn't trust me because my fucking family drugged her like she was an animal. I told you that I had it under control. I told you that I could handle her!"

My voice rises to a roar, and they are on their feet again.

"No one doubted that you could handle her, Viktor. But we needed to subdue her and get her back here safely," Aleksandr says. Mikhail is in my face, and so help me God, I'm going to knock his fucking teeth out, and then they'll all have the right to kill me.

No.

I step away from him only to land right next to Aleksandr. I shove him against the wall. His shoulder hits a framed print of the Louvre, and it crashes to the floor, glass shattering everywhere. Aleks rights himself and reaches for me, but I shove him back.

"When is the wedding?" I look at Ollie, the one in charge of international relations who knows exactly why we have to marry right now.

"Saturday."

I grit my teeth. She won't trust me by then. I have a vision of me dragging her by the hair to the altar. I will if I fucking have to, to save her. To save all of us.

"I need more time. Buy more fucking time."

Ollie and Nikko share a look. "I can make that happen."

The lights in the room flicker before they go off. An alarm wails, and that's when I become aware of the smell of acrid smoke.

"I fucking told you I had to stay with her."

Shit. I turn on my heel and run into the hallway. Smoke billows out from under the door, and all the lights are out. I run to the room and try the door, but it's locked, of course. She's jammed something up against it. What the fuck is she doing?

"Help me!" I scream to my brothers. "I can't open the fucking door."

"I'll get in through the window," Lev says. I snatch a fire extinguisher from the hallway and throw it to Ollie. I don't have that option, but he's small enough. "Go with him. When you get in there, you do not touch her."

I run around to the exit, into the garden, and around the house to where the window is. The window to my bedroom is wide open, smoke billowing into the sky, sirens loud in the distance. Lev and Ollie come up beside me, all of us scanning the grounds. How the fuck did she get out?

I stand still. Listen. She's got nothing with her. If she got out of that room, there's only one way out. She's either running or… hiding.

I scan. I haven't been gone long enough for her to get far. Even if she left the second she triggered the alarm, she hardly had any time.

"Get Aleks on surveillance immediately," I bark out to Lev. I walk with heavy footsteps around the perimeter of the house.

She's hiding. She hasn't had time to escape.

"I know you're here," I say, keeping my voice quiet. "You know I'm going to find you. There's no point in hiding, Lydia." I speak in a low voice, the timbre of it carrying through the garden. "There's no use hiding from me. You can try, but you're still going to end up right where you started—here, with me. And I promise it's not going to be as bad as you think it will be."

I smile to myself. It's a game. It's all a game. "Come out, come out, wherever you are." I stalk around the periphery of my garden, to my left, an area of thick rhododendrons. She's there. She's hiding behind the bush. Likely thought she had a hell of a lot more time than she did. Probably didn't suspect that the alarm would go off so quickly. Didn't know that there's no way she could get off my property without my knowledge.

She also doesn't know I have a tracker on her.

"If you come out now, it will go a lot easier for you, Lydia."

She doesn't move or respond in any way, likely terrified, unsure of what's going to happen with me, scared to be with a man she doesn't know.

I walk quietly toward where she is, aware of the fact that my shadow casts over every inch of this place. Sometimes I wish I could make myself smaller, less menacing. Sometimes I wish I could magnify it.

"Lydia, you need to trust me. I am not your enemy."

Something rustles in the bushes.

"Come out, Lydia. I know where you are, and I could reach out and take you. Or you can come to me of your own accord."

It feels somehow symbolic, offering her this small chance to surrender on her own. She can't escape; she knows that now. Even if she fled the premises, I'd locate her. "You can't get away, Lydia. You know that. Even if I walked away now and you sprinted for the exit, I would track you down. I would bring you back here, and you would still be mine. If you run, I will always chase you. And I will always find you. You have to trust me."

Someday... someday she will trust me. Someday, she will know that she's safest here, with me, but until then, I need to keep her with me in a secure way so that she doesn't hurt herself.

"Trust you?" Lydia stands, coming out of hiding, holding

herself apart from me. "After you kidnapped me? Bound me? You're insane if you think I'll trust you."

She turns her head away from me as fire engines approach my house.

Everyone exits as uniformed firefighters swiftly enter the building. One hooks up to the fire hydrant, and they efficiently get everything under control.

It's only a house. The house will be fine. What's important is that she's here with me.

I walk over to her, keeping my hands at my sides so I don't scare her. When I reach her, I stop short of touching her. "I know you're angry, but everything I've done is to protect you. You are in more danger than you realize." I crook a finger at her. "Come here."

She shakes her head and stands her ground. I take a step toward her, and when she looks as if she's about to run, I reach for her. Snatch her. Drag her to my chest and hold her to me.

I hold her shoulders and give her a little shake. "Listen to me, woman. For fuck's sake, Lydia, listen to reason."

I take a deep breath and stop myself. I brush my thumb along her shoulders. "Yudin was going to murder you. You're safest with me and with our family. Now that our families are going to align, we're going to bring peace to the situation. None of this went down the way I would've wanted."

"Do you have her?" Mikhail yells from a few feet away.

I nod and respond, "I do."

"Bring her the fuck over here."

I turn and stay and glare at my brother. He's all business, cold and authoritative, and I know why, but it doesn't make it any easier.

"I'm trying to talk with her. I won't have her treated like a prisoner. She deserves to know the truth."

It's a gamble. If I give her some freedom, if I let her know that she can walk away if she wants to, she might choose to stay.

Lydia looks from me to Mikhail, her fury giving way to confusion and fear.

Her large eyes go wide. "If what you say is true, then why not let me decide what I want to do? Why control me?"

I don't want to tell her the truth. I want time to get to know her. I can't tell her that I can't imagine losing her like I lost my sister.

Mikhail seems to understand we need to be alone now. He turns to leave, and over his shoulder, he speaks to me. "Make her understand, Viktor. We don't have much time."

I slowly release her and look into her eyes. She remains silent, a whirlwind of confusion and conflicting emotions in her beautiful gaze.

Nikko comes out next as the flames are put out and smoke rises into the air. As he approaches, Lydia takes a step closer to me.

"Lydia," he says, his deep voice resonating in the darkness. "My name is Nikko. I'm your brother-in-law." He looks next to me. "You've got her?"

I grit my teeth. "I've got her. She's not getting away, brother."

"Good. I've got Vera on the phone."

CHAPTER EIGHT

Lydia

AT FIRST, I want to ask him to give me a minute to prepare myself for seeing Vera. My hair is a mess, I'm wearing no makeup, my clothes are torn, and I wouldn't be surprised if there were smudge marks on my face or body from the fire.

I feel a little guilty about that. I wanted to take what I thought would be the one chance I had to get away, so I acted as quickly as I could.

Nikko marches over to me, tall and muscled and covered in tattoos. Phew. Nice job, little sis. His eyes burn into mine with an intensity that seems to run in this family. My heart thumps in my chest when I remind myself that I'm with Viktor, and he's already made it abundantly clear no one touches me but him.

"Lydia's safety is paramount, but she needs to understand the gravity of her situation."

"Oh, I understand the fucking *gravity*," I say, glaring at my new brother-in-law. "I was ripped from safety, drugged, held captive—"

"Nikko? Is that true?" I hear Vera's voice loud and clear on the line.

Nikko holds his phone up and shows me Vera's picture. It's dark where she is and hard to see her.

"Why would I make that up?" I snap.

"Here. Have a seat," Nikko says, gesturing to a bench in the small garden outside.

I sit and reach for the phone.

"Vera. What the hell is going on here?" Tears spring to my eyes. I blink them away. "I was marrying Timur. He got all weird at dinner, and *this* guy—" I stab my finger at Viktor— "says Timur was planning on killing me and has manipulated the entire situation to make it look like a rescue."

Vera, her large brown eyes magnified behind her round glasses, stares at me. "Do you have any reason to believe he's lying to you?"

Always pragmatic, my scientist sister. I blow out a breath.

"Do I have any reason to believe he's telling the truth?"

Vera nods eagerly. "Yes, of course. Because the Romanov family is much more reputable than the Yudins. Timur has a long history of fairly reprehensible behavior, Lydia."

I cross my arms over my chest. Whose side is she on?

"If that were so, why would Father sign off on my engagement then?"

Vera's gaze softens. "Because it benefitted him, Lydia. Because Timur may have protected you well financially, and you definitely would've been untouchable from any rivals as his wife. But the man has only served time *once*, and his record shows it was for a vicious assault on an innocent woman."

I feel like the man who I knew and the man who they are talking about are two different people. But I saw that video. I saw how he treated Mom...

"Nikko, how did he react when he found out she wasn't going to marry him?" Vera asks.

Nikko blows out a breath. "He took her out to dinner, and we have video evidence of him taking items that made it clear he planned on at least hurting and abducting her."

"Oh God," Vera says, her eyes wide.

"We have no way to prove that's what he planned," I snap.

"Lydia, these guys aren't going to hurt you."

I throw my hands up in the air. "They kidnapped me! Drugged me! Tied me!"

Vera bites her lip and looks over her shoulder. "Nikko?"

"It was essential to move quickly so we could save her," Viktor interrupts. "Lev thought it expedient to get her cooperation in a way that made sense to him."

I turn on him. "Is this how you gaslight all your captives? Hmm?"

"No, Lydia," he says in a low voice. "You have the honor of being the first."

That shouldn't tickle me in any way, shape, or form, but I'm not above a certain level of depravity...

"Listen, Lydia," Vera says. "I just want you—" The connection goes all gritty, and I can't hear for a moment.

"Vera?"

"Shit," Nikko mutters when the screen goes black. "We lost the connection. This is the last fucking time she goes to one of these things."

He shakes his head, shuts off the phone, and turns to me.

"Does that appease you at *all?*"

I look away. I still don't like how any of this went down, but it seems like I don't have much of a choice. What else will I do? Who knows where Timur is now and even if a fraction of what they said about him is true... *God.*

I don't want to go back to him.

But I don't want to be manipulated, either.

Maybe they put Vera up to this. Maybe they didn't.

The front door opens with a bang, and the tall man with tanned skin marches out straight toward us. Mikhail? I think they called him Mikhail.

Viktor bristles beside me.

"Are you going to deal with her?" he snaps, his attention on Viktor. "Or will I?"

Viktor stands, a low growl purring in his chest, and rises to his full height, which is impressively huge. He folds his arms across his chest.

"Lydia, meet my brother, Mikhail."

I glare at him and grit my teeth. "How nice to meet you," I snap, my voice dripping with sarcasm.

Mikhail ignores me and stares at Viktor. He's so close to us now I can see his flared nostrils. A vein throbs in his temple. "Don't push it, brother."

Viktor opens his mouth to retort when Nikko steps between Mikhail and Viktor.

I can feel the tension radiating off Viktor's body. Heat emanates from him in waves.

"Push what? My duty to protect the woman who I'm going to marry?"

My heart does a little twist in my chest. There's something about the way he says it that unnerves me.

Mikhail steps closer, Nikko a wall between them. I swear one of them is going to break a blood vessel.

"Alright, alright, settle down," I say, shoving my way in between the wall of alpha man chest. "No need to fight, boys. Geez."

Nikko's lips twitch, and his brows rise. "You look nothing like Vera, but there are definitely some similarities."

I shrug. "Yes, and suffice it to say, I could say the same exact thing about your brothers." I quirk a brow at him. "You all look nothing alike but seem to subsist on shots of testosterone and self-assurance."

I blow out a breath and roll my eyes. "Honestly. It's a shame Vera and I haven't chatted at length more recently." I turn to Viktor. "Can we go inside now?" I look at Mikhail. "So he can 'deal with me'?" I suffuse as much mockery as I possibly can in my tone.

Viktor hasn't hurt me, and I'm starting to believe he wouldn't.

"Guys." The younger one, the asshole who *drugged* me, stands on the steps outside. "Just got a call. We've got the captain of the *Ledyanoye Bratstvo* hostage."

"Where?"

"The Ironworks."

I feel Viktor's hand clamp on my arm. "You're getting dressed, then you're coming with me. I want you to see this. Every fucking second."

They spring into action while I stare up at Viktor. Mikhail's ordering things in Russian and obviously pissed, Nikko is busy on his phone, and the other guy is gone, probably because he doesn't have a death wish, and Viktor might murder him if he breathes the same air as I do.

I'd be lying if I didn't admit that it pleases me a little.

"I need clothes," I say to him, swallowing. Now that we're alone, I'm starting to get nervous about the whole "dealing with me" thing.

He looks down at me, at my tattered clothes, and his perpetual scowl deepens.

He looks from me to the house and back again.

"There's Harper, Aleksandr's wife. Aria is Mikhail's. Then there's Polina, my sister. We could borrow something."

I look down at myself. "Are they tall, curvy girls like me?"

The way his gaze glides down my body makes me swallow hard. His eyes smolder, and he licks his lips. We don't exchange a word, but the palpable thrum of erotic attraction is very evident.

Shit.

He licks his lips. "No one's like you, Lydia."

I ignore the way my heart thumps. "They're smaller?"

He shrugs.

Great. I'm marrying into a house full of supermodels. I cringe.

Viktor reaches his hand to my hair. A strand has crossed in front of my face, blurring my vision. He tucks it behind my ear. "Let them wait."

"Who?"

His gaze burns into mine. "All of them."

I stare, unblinking. "Your brothers?"

"The hostages. My brothers. We don't need to take all day, but we can go get what you need while they wait." He reaches for my hand almost casually. When our hands touch, a pulse of electricity skates between us. "I'll go with you."

"I can't go into a store like this." I shake my head. My mama raised me better.

"Then I'll take you home. Your mother's home is thirty minutes from here."

I look away, strangely emotional. My mother is nice enough, but she and I haven't been close in years. My father was the one who took me under his wing, for all the good that did. I suppose he fancied me the son he never had.

"I don't have anything of mine there anymore." I haven't in a long time.

He looks down at me, stroking his chin. "I could ask Polina… she's the closest and would be quickest at picking something out. Let me try her." He pulls out his phone and sends a text.

A minute later, he shakes his head. "That's not gonna work. She's out and won't be home for another hour."

I look down at myself. I only have to look the fool in the first place we go. After that, it should be easy enough for me to find something to pull on.

"Wear my jacket," he says at the very same time I say, "I could wear something of yours."

My cheeks flush, and he nods. "It's decided, then. Here." Shrugging out of his leather jacket with one fluid motion, he removes it and holds it out to me. He doesn't just hand me the jacket but holds it the way a gentleman would for a woman. He lifts it up so I can slide my arms in the sleeves.

It's warm and smells like leather, snow-capped mountains, and the smoky, woodsy scent of fire. I turn away so he doesn't see me inhale.

It feels so wrong to allow myself to be attracted to him at all, but I'm not a robot.

And he'll be... my husband. I haven't allowed myself to focus on what that will mean.

I walk side by side with him to the car. Wordlessly, he opens the door for me.

So many questions are teeming in my mind I barely know how to begin. Though Viktor scares me, and I have a feeling I haven't even seen the half of it yet, I'm starting to feel a bit more at ease with him than the others.

We drive in silence until he pulls into a parking space just outside a strip mall. "Any of these places look good?" He gestures to a few boutiques. "We know someone who owns this one here."

He points at a place with high-heeled shoes and purses in a large window. This shit's pricey. My family was well off, but nothing like some of the families I knew. More to the point, I've been independent and haven't taken their money in a very long time. I thrust my chin out.

"It looks fine, but I'm going to pay you back. Just because I don't have money on me right now doesn't mean I don't have any."

"Like hell, you'll pay me back," he says, shaking his head. He opens the car and comes over to my side, but I quickly open it before he can get the satisfaction of doing it for me. I still don't trust him.

I step quickly out of the car and walk with him toward the little boutique. I'm nervous about what will happen next after I get dressed, and I want this part over with.

It feels a bit strange to be walking into a boutique with him. He isn't the type who fits into a place like this. Men who go boutique shopping with a woman should be pretty and refined, well-manicured and shellacked. He's so big he has to duck to walk through the door. A five o'clock shadow ghosts his chin already, and when we enter, a woman with a baby in a carriage draws in a sharp breath and takes off without a backward glance.

Yeah, he's that terrifying.

"Mr. Romanov." A tall, older woman, who could be my grandmother, approaches us on silver stilettos. Her hair's trendy and short, a bit spiky, and she wears diamond studs that accentuate the crisp navy of her tank and pencil skirt. "Rosa told me to expect you. I hope you don't mind that I've already taken the liberty of pulling out some clothes that might suit the occasion, as I know you're pressed for time." She holds out her hand to me. "My name is Opal. So pleased to meet you."

I take her warm, confident hand and return the gesture. "I'm Lydia."

"Pleased to meet you, Lydia," she says with utter grace, as if I'm the Queen of England and didn't just walk into her high-end boutique in a tattered dress covered by a man's worn leather jacket.

"Rosa's a family friend," Viktor says in a low rumble. He places his hand on my lower back and escorts me to the back of the shop. "She's the owner and a friend of ours. I texted her. She's in Boston but said Opal will take good care of you."

I nod, allowing myself to be escorted, as I do a quick sweep of the boutique and the kinds of clothes they have.

It's filled with racks of beautifully crafted garments that smack of sophistication and comfort. They're chic and timeless, with soft, high-quality fabrics and an array of earthy and neutral tones. These are not factory-made or fast fashion designed for skinny mannequins but garments that hint at understated luxury made for real women.

My kind of place, honestly.

In the back, the fitting rooms are roomy and private. There's a small area with a coffee maker and mugs and a beverage fridge with chilled drinks. Viktor reaches in wordlessly and takes out two bottles of water. He twists the top off the bottle before he hands it to me. "Drink."

"No wine? I'm disappointed."

He only narrows his eyes at me. I'm not a fool, so I drink. I'll need it.

"Please choose whatever else you wish," Opal says. "You'll find our clothing features a natural blend of luxury, comfort, and versatility, featuring diverse sizes and styles. I'll leave you to it and be right outside this door if I can help in any way."

My cheeks flush when she says *diverse sizes.*

We have plus sizes.

I sigh. Fine. There's no need for me to try to squeeze into something that isn't made for me.

I stare at Viktor, waiting for him to step out of the changing room.

"Well?" I say with a shrug. "Should I try these on or what?"

"Of course," he says, holding my gaze with challenge in his eyes as he folds himself into a sturdy chair in the corner. I half expect it to snap in two. He looks like he's trying to fit into a chair made for a child.

"Viktor."

"Mmm?" He polishes off the water in the bottle. I must be out of my mind because the way his Adam's apple bobs and the sight of his huge hand dwarfing the small bottle is so unapologetically *masculine...*

I look away.

"I don't want you in here."

I jump at the sound of him crushing the water bottle before he tosses it into a small wastebasket.

"I thought you might say that," he says, his eyes as dark as storm clouds on a winter day. "I've been lenient with you, Lydia. I've given you lots of freedom. Unfortunately, you lost the privilege of privacy by setting a fire in our house."

Not *my* house.

Our house.

He's chosen his words deliberately.

"It's not appropriate for you to watch me get dressed."

"You've made it clear it's not appropriate for me to step away." He crosses his massive arms across his chest, his biceps bulging. "We're wasting time, and it's pointless. We're getting married."

"For God's sake," I curse. "*Fine.*"

I shrug out of his jacket and whip it at him as hard as I can. He catches it mid-air and casually shrugs it back on, his eyes never leaving mine. I swallow and turn to the mirror.

I hate these places. Mirror upon mirror under bright lights seems to highlight every flaw and bump and lump. I cast my eyes away and reach for a pair of jeans and a pair of black leggings. Black is forgiving.

"What was that?"

I turn in surprise to look at him.

"What?"

"That face you made. You looked in the mirror and made a face then turned away."

"Did I?"

I'm focused on removing my fucked up clothes and not looking at him when I stand in front of him wearing only my underwear.

"Yeah."

I shrug. "Don't know. Maybe I'm uncomfortable getting undressed in front of a man I hardly know?"

"Mmm."

He isn't buying it.

I rip off the rest of my clothes and throw them into a heap. We'll have to toss them out. I turn to face him. I want to take back some measure of control, and maybe standing in front of him wearing only panties and a shitty push-up bra under my ample breasts is one way.

I'm not wrong.

I intentionally bend over and pick a hanger off the floor. When I look up, his gaze is heated, his eyes half lidded, and a flush of color spreads up his neck, darkening his already rugged features. His jaw clenches, a subtle hint of his loss of control, and his breathing grows a hair heavier. The air around him seems charged. He shifts, his large hands flexed on his elbows as he seems to struggle to maintain his composure.

My heartbeat thunders.

It worked.

I do my level best not to wilt under the heat of his stare, fixated on me with raw, unhindered desire.

"You're fucking gorgeous. Now put those on before I do something that makes us even later than we are."

Oh God. Why does a part of me wish he would? Why does a part of me *want* him to?

I slide into the jeans, turn to the mirror, and try to button them. Too tight. My belly bulges, and the button doesn't snap.

I turn away, mortified, and step out of them.

He watches me silently.

I reach for a second pair, and the same thing happens.

"Fuck those. Leggings," he growls, handing me the pair of black leggings. "We're out of time. I'll pick out what you'll try on."

I'm not sure how that's going to make us choose any quicker, but fine. I toss the jeans in a pile and step into the leggings. They're soft and luxurious and fit me as if they were created for me.

"Alright, I'll reluctantly give you that point," I say with a huff. "But leggings are hard to fuck up."

"That's not what Polina says."

I reach for a top when he smacks my hand away. I pull back as if bitten, my jaw unhinged.

"What'd I say? I told you I'm picking them out. Behave yourself."

I open my mouth to protest, but instead, that isn't what comes out. "Who's Polina again?"

Am I jealous?

"My sister. She's particular about things like leggings. She went on a rant about it a few weeks ago." He chooses a dark, brick-colored fitted blouse for me to pair with the leggings. It's sleek with long sleeves and would almost be conservative if not for the deep vee that accentuates my bust. The fabric is thick but has a hint of stretch.

I slide into the top and turn this way and that, checking myself out. "Damn, I look hot. Like, CEO-of-kickass hot."

Wow.

Viktor nods, his eyes still intense and on fire. Approving. "This will do."

"It better. We're getting more of these." I watch his reaction.

"I'll be the judge of that. You can submit your requests, but I'll handle procurement."

I scoff, hands on hips, as his phone rings. It reminds me that Timur tossed my phone out the fucking window, and I need a new one. Why'd he *do* that?

He quirks a brow at me. "You can put in some requests, but I get the final say."

"What is this, the 1920s? Should I light up a Pall Mall and wear some heels? *Sir?*"

Viktor takes a step closer to me in the small interior of the dressing room. Though it's roomier than most I've seen, he's the size of a bear, and I'm no pixie, so there's not exactly wiggle room.

"We'll skip the cigarette, but heels? Yeah. I'll add those to the list." He leans in and whispers in my ear. "You can wear *just* those heels and repeat that *sir*."

Gawwd.

He glances at his watch. "But not now. We need to go. Wear the clothes out." Leaning over, he plucks the tags off and answers his phone. "We're on our way."

CHAPTER NINE

Nine years ago

Viktor

"HE DOESN'T KNOW his own strength, Stanislav," my mother said, her voice trembling as she held both hands up in front of her. "Listen to me. *He doesn't know his own strength.*"

My father was in pajama bottoms, his robe cinched around his waist. All he needed was a pipe to complete the look. This was a man who had been dragged from his sleep to meet the police. One more year. All I needed was one more year, and I'd be a legal adult. The second I was, I'd be gone.

The flashing lights faded away.

"He's always used that excuse," my father sneered. "He's known his strength for years."

"It's not an excuse!" my mother pleaded. "Listen to me!"

I was sitting on a chair, staring at the blank wall of the fireplace. We never lit a fire in it because my father didn't like it. I wanted to think he didn't like warmth either. My father's eyes locked onto mine, his neck veins bulging as he clenched his fists by his side. He wanted to hurt me, but the last time he did, I deflected his blows.

Now he was wary.

Instead, he'd bait me. He looked at me, his eyes filled with disdain. "What was it now? Someone interrupted you when you were talking? Someone took your parking space? Someone kissed a girl you liked?"

I clenched my fists and remained silent. He was baiting me. He knew I wasn't petty with my violence. The truth was, he used me when it suited him, justifying his own brutal methods. I was his secret weapon.

I didn't respond because that's what he wanted—a fight. If he could get a rise out of me, he could hit me. It was easy to justify punishment when I reacted. It was harder when I stayed silent. I looked away from him, my eyes resting on the cold fireplace.

"Stanislav," my mother said, her voice pleading.

"Answer me!" my father roared. His footsteps thundered closer. My brothers, Mikhail and Nikko, had heard what was going on. I could see them hiding on the stairway, ready to defend. My heart swelled in my chest. They were prepared to defend me if necessary, but we all knew how complicated things got when we defended each other over something trivial. Still, they had my back.

But I didn't need them. I was completely at peace with what I did today.

I took revenge on the teenage boys who hurt Lydia. I had absolutely no regrets. The person who started it was only the first on my list. The news had already spread, whispers circulating among the teenagers at school and even rumors at the local church.

Some called me a demon, others an angel of vengeance, a harbinger of justice. I embraced it. I would eliminate evil.

"Out of my life," my father said, his voice trembling with fury. "You're nothing more than a curse. A scourge to punish me."

A curse.

A scourge.

I didn't reply.

"Answer me!" he thundered.

My father took a step toward me, and my mother stepped in front of him. "No! No more," she said, her voice cracking. It was only last month that he put Aleksandr in the hospital with a broken jaw because of a trivial misunderstanding that could easily be twisted by a narcissist.

This time, I saw the determination in my mother's eyes.

I didn't blame her. My mother, a woman of firm resolve, was so diminished she needed to choose carefully when to intervene. If she didn't, it would come back on her, and the rest of us would suffer.

"Get out of my way," he sneered.

She shook her head, and her hair fell from the clip holding it together. It cascaded over her bare, thin shoulders as she stood her ground.

"Move."

My father raised his hand to strike her.

I leaped to my feet and grabbed the front of his robe. It took everything in me to hold myself back from throwing him bodily into the cold, empty fireplace.

My father's eyes widened with fear. I dropped him. He stepped back, stunned.

The realization hit me like a punch to the gut—I was someone to be feared. My sheer size made people cower.

It filled me with a mix of pride and sadness. I didn't fully understand why.

"I'm done with you," my father spat, his voice laced with contempt. "You're dead to me. Let Kolya deal with you."

Relief and sadness entwined, even as the blood pounded in my veins, and I wished I could hit him, just once, without losing my hand and my position in this family.

My father's rejection stung, but I welcomed the change. This was my path now, one I would walk with pride and resolve.

CHAPTER TEN

Viktor

WE WALK OUT of the shop with a few bags. She sits in the passenger seat beside me, doing some kind of magic to her mane of hair and applying lip gloss she found at the checkout.

"What's happened with your brothers?" she asks.

I don't want to take her to where I'm about to go.

But she needs to see. She needs to know.

"There's a secluded warehouse that's one of our secure locations. Only family's allowed there. We need it quiet and off the grid."

Nodding, she looks out the window.

"And why am I coming with you?"

"Because I can't trust you at home."

The cars zoom past us as we take the exit that leads us to the warehouse. "So I accompany you everywhere you go, then? That's your big plan?"

"Until I can teach you to behave yourself." The truth is, once we're married, she'll be a lot more secure than she is now. The *Ledyanoye Bratstvo* will have less of a claim on her, and even our rivals would know she's off-limits.

"Indefinitely?"

"Yeah, Lydia. Indefinitely."

She drums her long fingernails on the dash. "I need a phone, Viktor."

"I know. I'm on it."

We drive in silence. We're only a few minutes out.

"What if I promise you I won't try to escape again?"

I shake my head. "Talk is cheap. I don't give a shit what you tell me. I won't let up until I know you're not going anywhere."

She frowns, shaking her head, and curses under her breath.

"You're a fucking liar," she finally says. "You know that, don't you?"

I'm not a liar. I tell the truth even when it hurts. She's baiting me, trying to get some measure of control back—a last-ditch effort to rattle me.

I won't be baited.

"I don't. So why don't you fill me in on why you think I'm a liar?"

Her eyes flicker with surprise, momentarily thrown off. She shifts, crossing her arms over her chest defensively. The air between us is thick with tension, unspoken words, and unresolved anger.

"You keep telling me you won't hurt me. You keep hinting at the fact that you know me. But if you *really* knew me, you'd know that the number one way of hurting someone like me is trying to control them."

Ah. Well played. But she's still missing a piece of the puzzle.

"Mmm. When someone makes choices that could endanger them, sometimes the only option is to ensure their safety by exerting control. You ought to know that." I give her a sidelong glance as I exit the highway and make a quick turn toward the warehouse. "Your parents sent you to boarding school for that reason, didn't they?"

They sent her to boarding school because she was a danger to herself and her peers. They sent her to a place with strict rules and an authoritarian structure in an effort to give her the guidance and supervision she needed. Like most attempts at controlling defiance, it didn't work well.

"You don't know the first thing about me," she seethes.

"Settle down. We'll pick this conversation up later. For now, we have a job to do."

The secluded warehouse is grim and shadowy. There's only one other car here—Mikhail's. I know Nikko, Mikhail, and Lev are all waiting inside for us.

I don't want her to see what I'm going to have to do, but I have no choice. The only way forward is through this.

She hesitates when she sees the heavy iron door and dim setting.

"What if I promise to stay here? You can lock the doors or... or something."

I shake my head. "No. I won't take the risk, and I need you to know what's at stake here." When we reach the doorway, I turn to her and place my hands on both of her shoulders. I massage them with my thumbs and hold her gaze. "These men here have information that we need to have. They will not willingly give it up. They might even be willing to die before they do. But we must have it. Your mother's life is at stake and so is yours. We need to find out what they are planning to do. I want you to understand the gravity of this situation. You don't want to admit it yet, but Timur Yudin is an evil man who had the intent to kill you. We don't have him in our possession, and we'll stop at nothing until we do."

The door opens, creaking on its hinges, and Lydia's breath hitches. I reach for her hand on instinct. It feels small and warm in mine, and my heart swells in my chest.

I will protect her no matter the cost. No matter the risk.

I take a moment to quickly observe what's going on. Mikhail stands in the corner of the room, his hands on his hips. Several men, bound and gagged, sit in folding chairs, obviously bloodied and beaten. Nikko wears nothing but a tee. His hair is slicked with sweat, and his fists are covered in blood. Lev stands in front of one of the men, staring dispassionately at them. He holds a baseball bat in his thick fists.

Lydia stifles a gasp. "Holy shit," she whispers. "*Viktor.*"

I squeeze her hand. "You'll be fine. You're a strong woman. Remember who they are. They're pieces of shit unworthy of the bottom of your fucking shoe."

Her eyes widen, and she stares at me. She licks her lips and finally nods.

"Alright."

"Here. I want you to stay here. You're going to see me do some fucked up shit, Lydia, and I won't pretend otherwise. You'll stay here. You'll watch me, and you're going to survive just fine." She nods. I lean in closer. "You were raised by Petr Ivanov. You've witnessed shit no woman should ever have to see." I know she has. I was there for some of it, only she doesn't know that yet. "And here you are. Strong. You're a survivor, Lydia. A fucking survivor."

"How do you know that?"

"You'll see." I bend and kiss her cheek. The touch of her skin to mine lights a fire in me. Rage courses through my veins like molten fire. I'm going to fucking kill these sons of bitches, and she's going to watch me.

I'm on deck.

I turn and lock the door from the inside, underscoring the confinement and gravity of the situation. I turn and face them.

"What have we found out?"

"Absolutely fucking *nothing*," Nikko says.

"Not totally true," Lev responds, shaking his head. He jerks his chin at the one in the middle. "*This* one has a thing for

Lydia. I've got video evidence of him stalking her. I even found videos he took of the two of them—"

"*Stop.*" I take in a deep breath through my nose and let it out slowly. I do *not* need to talk about her and Timur fucking Yudin together. My breathing's heavy, my rage at a low simmer. "Do you mean to tell me that he's a fucking creeper?"

"Ohhh, yeah," Lev says, his jaw tight. I can tell he wants to beat the shit out of this guy for me, but he won't. He'll leave it to me. "Caught him jerking off to the video."

Motherfucking asshole.

I stand before the men, my gaze assessing each of them in turn. One of them is already breaking, tears streaking down his face, and I haven't even laid a finger on him yet. Whatever Lev and Nikko did was only a prelude—the scolding before the storm. Their fear is palpable. They understand this is their endgame and that if they don't cooperate, they'll die right here.

I take a step forward. "So you're prepared to die for your cause?" I ask, stroking my chin. "You do know that if you don't cooperate, you'll never see the light of day again?"

No response.

I slowly walk over to the most visibly frightened one. I lean in and whisper in his ear everything I'm going to do to him, right here, right now, if he doesn't cooperate. He closes his eyes, and tears fall.

I'm unmoved, but Mikhail wants to drive this home.

"Remember, they're loyal to the man who would fucking destroy her, Viktor. Remember who they are."

My brothers like to... *encourage* me with a reminder of the depravity of the men I punish. It helps.

I reach out and grasp the chin of the man in front of me. He's terrified, but I don't fucking care.

I snap my fingers at Lev, who hands me the baseball bat.

"We'll start slow. You'll tell me where your leader is, or I'll break both of your knees with this baseball bat. Are we clear?"

He shakes his head from side to side. "I can't do that. I don't know!"

"He knows," Nikko growls. "He's lying."

I snap the bat against one kneecap with a vicious swing. Bone cracks. He screams, pleading for mercy, but he won't get it here. Lydia stifles a scream.

Good girl.

The other man, the fucking son of a bitch who defiled Lydia, will get special treatment. He glares at me defiantly, daring me to touch him.

"Tell me. Where is he?"

The man beside him curses at him in Russian, daring him to defy their orders. He promises him he'll burn in hell if he divulges anything, and his family will suffer a brutal, vicious death.

It's a bluff, though. Neither one of them will ever leave here again.

"Do you understand the gravity of lying to me?" I ask, my voice a low rumble in the quiet warehouse. I capture his attention. "Imagine a slow, excruciating pain that only starts with the warning. Broken kneecaps. Let's discuss facts, gentlemen. The human body is a masterpiece in its capacity to withstand pain. Take, for example, your broken kneecap. It isn't just the broken bone, is it?" I tap his kneecap with the tip of the bat, and he screams until he's hoarse. "The pain is about a nine on the pain scale. Severe enough to cause shock or even cloud your vision."

I lean in, allowing him to truly process this. Sometimes, the threat of torture and pain magnifies the effect of a brutal beating. "But the true agony is what comes after. The way every movement causes unbearable pain to shoot up your leg. How a simple act like a cough or a shift in weight becomes unbearable." I stand up straighter. "And I'm about to break your second. So I urge you to consider your next words very carefully. Are they worth so much pain you pass out until I cut you into strips and you bleed out on this floor? You know we chose this place deliberately because it's so easy to mop up the blood and mute any noise."

I tap my palm with the bat. Lev watches me. Nikko's eyes are burning into our enemies' with the heat of a million suns. Mikhail watches all of it go down, unmoved. Lydia is a statue.

I slam the bat into my palm, welcoming the burn. The man tied up cries out.

"Alright, then." I lift the bat and rear back.

"Okay!" he screams. "Alright, okay, I'll tell you! *God!*"

I lay the bat on the floor and look over at him. I nod to Nikko.

"You got Aleks on the phone?"

"I'm here," Aleks says. Nikko nods.

The man beside the traitor rocks his chair, doing his best to get at his pussy traitor of a brother. He writhes and squirms, screaming at him in Russian.

"Manhattan!" He says, weeping. "He's at Midnight Wharf."

"Did you get that?" I ask Aleks.

"Yeah. I know where that is. Privately-owned port on the East River."

The other one curses, spittle flying out of his mouth. I nod to Nikko. "Give him his rewards."

Nikko presses the gun to the man's temple and pulls the trigger. He slumps in his restraints.

His companion meets my eyes, unmoved.

I look at Mikhail.

"I've changed my mind. I don't want her to see what I'm going to do to him." I don't want her recoiling from my touch. Reliving what I'm about to do.

Mikhail nods. "We'll leave you to it, brother."

"Viktor," Lydia says, her voice choked. "You don't have to do this. You're still fucking *human.* Just... just end it quickly."

I meet her eyes and shake my head. "I'll get there. Take her out, brother."

Her eyes water, and for some reason, she looks like she's going to cry. I don't understand.

I walk over to her and brush my finger along her cheekbone. I draw it back, wet with her tears. "Why don't you want to leave?"

"I don't know," she whispers. "I don't know, but I—I have to stay."

Fuck.

I don't want her to see me and see a monster. But I have to honor her request.

"Alright. I'll allow it. But you stay behind me," I concede, a heavy reluctance in my voice.

As Mikhail steps aside, Lydia takes a deep, shuddering breath, steeling herself against the violence she is about to witness.

And there... in the dark, cold warehouse with her eyes staring into mine, her commitment not to walk away or shield herself from who I am and what I do—something shifts between us. I know who she is. I've seen her demons. I know the darkness she battles and the darkness she revels in.

She's about to see mine.

I turn back to the man bound before us, his fate sealed by what he's done. I whip the baseball bat against the wall with all my might. It splinters into pieces. I won't need weapons for what I'm going to do next.

I flex my hands.

Lydia doesn't flinch.

"Get behind me."

CHAPTER ELEVEN

Lydia

"NO."

I don't know why I need to see him do this. I don't think it has anything to do with that piece of shit he's got tied to a chair.

This is about Viktor and me.

When he nods, power surges through me. He's... agreed. He'll let me.

I swallow hard and face him. It's not about the violence—it's about him... trusting me enough to let me watch it. To know that I'm not going to dissolve into a puddle and lose my shit.

He turns back to the man, who seems to not be showing a lot of fear. If it were me, I would literally be wetting my pants. Viktor is the biggest, most powerful man I've ever met in person. He just knocked the kneecap out of another man before he ordered him shot and killed. And now this asshole was some kind of creeper for me...

I don't know how he's still sitting there, staring at Viktor with a look of sheer challenge.

He must not be right in the head because any normal human who saw Viktor just splinter a baseball bat into matchsticks in one hard throw can't possibly be still sitting there without a single trace of fear or remorse on his face.

Viktor stalks over and grabs this guy by the hair. With a vicious pull that makes me cringe, he yanks his head back, bares his neck, and stares into his eyes.

I half expect him to scalp him with a knife, bloody and brutal.

"Tell me what you did," he snarls. I hold my own. It isn't easy.

The man in front of us has the gall to spit at him. "Yudin promised me that he would share. So he did. He gave me pictures of her. He took videos. And he was planning on letting me have her fucking pussy."

I gasp and cover my mouth with my hand.

He *wouldn't*.

He *didn't*...

How could I have been so fooled?

Viktor takes the man's head and slams him bodily against a wall. His prisoner screams, then falls heavily to the floor. It's astonishing to me that the pile of limbs and sinew, muscle, and blood cells that constitute the human body is somehow both fragile and soft yet remarkably resilient.

Viktor bends, lifts the man by the shirt with his left hand as if he weighs no more than a toddler, and brings his right fist back. The punch lands with the force of a judge's gavel.

Blood spurts from his nose. Bone breaks. He hits him again and again. Nausea blooms in my belly with every sickening thud.

"And you took it. You fucking let him do it."

The man spits on the floor, spitting teeth and blood and bile onto the concrete. I take an involuntary step back.

"I fucking did because she's nothing to me. She's a sack of bones and holes. I was going to use one of those fucking holes, you son of a bitch—"

I've seen evil things in my life. I was raised by Petr Ivanov, one of the cruelest men I've ever known. I've seen what my father and his men were capable of. But somehow, staring into the face of the man Viktor is destroying, I feel like I'm staring into a pit of darkness.

Sack of... bones? *Holes?* I think I'm going to vomit.

For the first time, I think I *want* Viktor to hurt him.

Viktor kicks him. Throws him against the wall.

My heart pounds like a drum in my chest, my breaths shallow and rapid as I stand in the dimly lit warehouse. The stench of oil and rust is heavy in the air, making it hard to breathe. I idly wonder if there's a car shop nearby. I watch, transfixed and terrified, as Viktor, a tower of rage and muscle, drags the man who dared to lay a hand on me back in front of me to face him. The man's feet barely touch the ground, his face contorted in fear as Viktor's iron grip holds him aloft so he can punch him again.

Viktor's face is a mask of fury, the scar on his cheekbone stark under the harsh light. He throws the man into a chair, the sound of wood scraping against concrete echoing through the space. That's when I notice more ropes coiled like a snake in a shadowed corner. Viktor, with precise, practiced movements, ties the man to the chair, his large, calloused hands moving with an efficiency that chills me to the bone.

Viktor doesn't seem to know I'm even there. His focus is solely on the man before him, the man who was going to hurt me. He leans close, his presence so overwhelming that the air seems to thicken around him.

His accent is heavier. He's angry.

"You tried to touch what is mine," Viktor hisses, each word dripping with venom.

The man whimpers, his eyes darting around, seeking escape where there is none. I watch as Viktor straightens, and in one swift motion, he pulls a knife from his boot. The glint of the blade is sinister, the intent behind it even more so. My stomach churns as I watch, my feet rooted to the spot, unable to move, unable to stop the scene unfolding before me.

Viktor places the cold metal against the man's cheek, the threat clear. "This is the last face you'll see before you learn the price of your actions," he says, his voice low and dangerous.

Relief swells in my chest. Will he end this violence? I want to walk away, move on with whatever happens next.

Tears prick my eyes, my conflict palpable. I know this man deserves punishment, but the brutality—the power and cruelty that Viktor personifies—is almost overwhelming.

He is my protector, yet in this moment, he embodies every dark nightmare I've ever had.

Viktor turns to look at me, his eyes searching mine for a moment. There is a question there, a silent asking for my approval, my sanction to continue. My heart aches, torn between my desire for safety and my fear of the man before me.

With a heavy heart, I nod slightly, my silence giving him the go-ahead he waits for. Viktor's expression hardens, and he turns back to his captive, the knife now poised with deadly precision.

The scream that tears from the man's throat is cut short as Viktor works, his actions efficient and ruthless. I turn my head away, unable to watch, my ears ringing with the man's cries.

Just because he deserved what he got doesn't mean he wasn't a human who will never breathe again, who will never walk this earth and have a chance to repent.

The body falls to the ground. Blood splashes on concrete. I don't need to look into the face of the man he killed, but I do have to look into the face of the man I'm about to marry.

He turns to me, his face spattered in another man's blood. I realize he's done this before because he's good at what he does. His skill comes from practiced experience.

"That's nine down," he says in a low growl as he reaches for my chin, his hand rough and warm against my skin. "One to go."

CHAPTER TWELVE

Viktor

WE DRIVE BACK HOME in silence for the first half of the trip. The weight of what just happened lingers in the air. Lydia's usually vibrant eyes are clouded with a mix of confusion and something I can't quite place. Maybe acceptance? I don't know. But I know I need to make this right for her.

"Do you have a doctor you could see?" she asks, her voice breaking the heavy silence.

"I don't need a doctor."

She reaches for my right hand and lays it gently in her lap. It's bloodied and bruised from delivering a beating that had to happen. She doesn't flinch or pull away, and that steadiness in her touch unexpectedly grounds me.

Today, Lydia watched me beat a man before I sliced his throat right in front of her. It was brutal. It was vicious.

It was necessary.

I saw the shock in her eyes, but she didn't look away. Why isn't she more disturbed? Why isn't she running from me?

I glance at her, blowing out a breath. "Alright, then. I'll clean you up myself. Tell me you have a first aid kit."

"Yeah, baby," I respond, the term slipping out naturally.

She shivers and moves a little closer to me, that small gesture sending a wave of warmth through my chest. Solidarity I didn't expect and never hoped for.

"What happens now?" she asks, turning to me, uncertainty evident in her eyes.

"I will take you home. We get cleaned up, we get some dinner, and we go to sleep." I shrug, trying to sound nonchalant. "And tomorrow, we plan our wedding." I let go of her hand and scrub it across my brow, feeling the adrenaline still pumping through my veins. "After a night like this, I need to let it bleed off."

"What do you mean?" she asks, her voice soft but probing.

My eyes are focused on the road. "When I fight, when I let that part of me take over, it's not easy to just turn it off. It's like... it's like an engine that's been running at full throttle and suddenly slams to a stop. The energy, the power—it doesn't just disappear. It has to wear off, or it consumes me."

She swallows hard, trying to grasp the weight of my words. Her acceptance of this part of me brings a strange sense of relief.

"Makes sense. So what do you need to do?" she asks, her voice steady.

"I need to come down slowly. *We* need to come down slowly. That means I don't want to talk much or do anything outside of routine. It's how I cope, how I keep it all from spilling over."

"You need aftercare?" she says, a hint of teasing in her voice, trying to lighten the mood.

I growl softly. "How the fuck do you know what aftercare is?"

"Okay, alright, don't change the subject," she says, sobering quickly.

Her understanding sends a chill through me, but she continues. "Okay, Viktor. I get it. After something intense, I need to go for a walk or something. Though, I mean, to be clear, I've never done anything like that."

I nod, a glimmer of something—gratitude, maybe—warming me before I turn away, feeling the tension in my shoulders slowly easing.

"I'm honestly... well, I've never done what you did, but I've had intense moments of..." She looks away and doesn't give me details, but I know exactly what she's talking about. I know she's been arrested, and her time in boarding school was more like a reform camp than school because of her vices.

"What do you find helps?" I ask her.

She sighs. "A hot shower. Sometimes a drink, but that's my least favorite way of handling it. Weed." She looks out the window, pausing. "Sex. You?"

My vision momentarily clouds, but I shrug it off. *Sex.*

Fucking sex.

Her openness surprises me, but it's exactly what I need. I grip the steering wheel tighter, knowing that tonight, we'll both find our ways to cope—to come down slowly and face whatever comes next together.

"Some of that, or sometimes I lift. Sometimes, I just need to sleep for hours and hours." I don't tell her that sex isn't part of my toolbox.

It's been at least five years. Yeah, some people would call it a dry spell for guys like me. But sex with anybody else would be like licking pavement to try to satisfy my appetite. *Never.*

"I want to tell you that I'm sorry you saw that," I begin. "But I don't want to lie to you, Lydia."

She nods and swallows. "Do you think he was lying, though?"

"I do not. I wouldn't have killed him otherwise."

"Oh," she says in a little voice. "Right."

I have the sudden desire to break something.

If she's even entertaining the slightest notion that Yudin was even the least bit redeemable...

Fuck.

When I get my hands on him... I don't think she'll be able to look at me that time.

By the time we get back to my house, it's late. She's tired and I am too, but I'm fucking starving.

"I don't think we've eaten anything since breakfast, and I'm famished. You?"

She nods. "I could literally tear the legs off one of your tables and eat it with a little ketchup right now. Maybe even *without* the ketchup."

I smile. It feels good to smile. It feels good to become human again.

"You like pizza?" I just told her I'm not gonna lie to her. Is this a lie? I'm trying to be polite and not freak her the fuck out. Because I happen to know for a fact that pizza is one of her favorite foods in the entire world. Especially New York style, with all the meat. It's almost unfair how much I know about her and how easily I will be able to use that to my advantage.

I look over at her. Her hair is disheveled, her face streaked with tears, dirt, and blood. She needs cleaning up as badly as I do.

"How the fuck did you get blood on yourself?"

"You did a lot of... splattering?"

I grunt under my breath but don't reply.

"Alright, so we're gonna order food, and then you're gonna get your ass in the shower."

She gives me a sidelong look. "Are you going to personally wash me, sir?"

Shit. What happened back there?

"Maybe I'm an old-fashioned man. Maybe I don't think I

should touch you until we're married." I pull up in front of my house and park the car. "Don't touch your door."

I think I've earned at least this one little crumb.

I wonder if she'll push me. I watch as she sits with her hands in her lap. When I get around to her door, she reaches for the handle. I stand on the other side of it. Our gazes lock, but she doesn't open the door. She seems torn, unsure of what to do next.

Good. I want her to at least keep guessing about contradicting me.

I open the door and reach for her hand. In this short time, it's already become my thing.

I like the feel of her hand in mine. She doesn't trust easily, but it's the slightest gesture and gives me no small measure of comfort. For this one brief moment in time, when her hand is connected to mine, her fingers entwined, she's not going to get away from me. And no one's going to take her away.

It's quiet here, set apart from everyone else. My little sanctuary in the city. From my front door, I can see the bright lights of Manhattan in the distance.

My family owns this area of New York known as The Cove. Businesses pay us to keep them safe, and we employ over two-thirds of the residents. It's a power move that has served us well.

I wonder what it's like being back in New York for her.

Her family home is thirty minutes from here, but she didn't spend her childhood there.

I open the door and touch the app on my phone.

"New York style pizza," I tell her. "I like it with a lot of meat. Sausage, bacon, pepperoni. Red sauce, none of that white sauce bullshit. You order anything you want."

I'm not just trying to appease her this time. The truth is, I've been eating it this way since the first time I saw her.

I place it in the cart and hand her my phone.

It's dark when we enter the foyer. I don't bother to flick on overhead lighting. I know from my distance surveillance that this house has been undisturbed, just how I like it. I had a cleanup crew sent to where she set fire, but luckily the damage was contained and you'd never know what happened.

"I don't need anything else. That looks fine," she says quietly. She doesn't want to admit it's her favorite.

"They're kinda known for their handmade ice cream. It might help... the bleed off."

She fucking adores ice cream more than any chocolate or baked goods or anything like that. She gives me a sidelong look. "You want to fatten me up?"

No, baby. You're fucking perfect. You don't need to change a fucking thing.

"Don't be ridiculous. Fine, I want ice cream; I'm getting it." I take the phone and add two hot fudge sundaes to the cart, an extra large order of french fries, and a salad, just to appease her conscience. I know what she likes. I tap the button and order it.

"It'll be here in thirty minutes. Let's go shower."

She heads to the shower, but her shoulders slump. I wonder if her bravado has failed her. Before she gets to the bathroom, she turns and sits on the bed and buries her face in her hands. Her shoulders shake, and I can't tell if she's crying.

I stare and look at her, unsure of what to do. Adrenaline still surges through me. I haven't crashed yet.

"Are you all right?"

I don't know what to think of this. I don't know how to help her. I reach tentatively to rest my hand on her shoulder.

This time, she doesn't flinch or turn away, but she also doesn't answer my question.

"You go first," she says shakily. "Go shower and I'll go after you."

Is she playing me? Is she trying to get out of this room so she can attempt to escape again? I doubt it, but I'm not taking risks either.

I shake my head. "No. You either come with me, or you go alone."

Her shoulders sag. I want to make it better. I hate that she's distraught, and I know that I had something to do with this.

"You'll feel a lot better after a shower and some food."

Finally, with a deep sigh, she gets to her feet. "I guess that's sensible. I don't know how I feel about you showering in the same room with me. I know we're going to get married, but I don't trust you. We hardly know each other."

"I know. I didn't say I was getting *in* with you. Go. Get in the shower. But I'm not leaving you alone. We're getting married in a few days, Lydia. The sooner we get comfortable with each other, the better."

"Fair." She stands and stretches before she starts taking her clothes off. I turn my head away, but her voice arrests me.

"No. We're going to be married, right? Why turn away? That's only a waste of time and playing games. This is me. This is what you're marrying. Let's see what you think."

Her voice is hard. Challenging. I stole a woman who's constructed of sheer fire and ice and should have expected nothing less.

Holding my gaze, she lifts the pretty brick-red top, now wrinkled and smudged, over her head. "I hope that all comes out of this. I would very much enjoy wearing that again."

Doesn't matter if it does or not. I'll get her another. I'll fucking hire someone to sew her another one if I have to.

She stands in front of me, her full, curvy body making me fucking hard. Maybe I *don't* need to bleed anything off. Maybe just watching her is enough for me to let that shit go.

Her blush-colored bra pushes up her full breasts. She's got the sweetest little dimple in her belly. I imagine laying her down and tonguing it before I taste even more of her.

We'll get there.

I take a step toward her before I realize what I'm doing. I freeze, her gaze still locked on mine.

Next, she reaches for the waistband of her leggings. Her fingers, adorned with long, blood-red nails, hook into the waistband before she begins to slide them down. I swallow hard as she pushes them over her luscious hips and shapely thighs. A hunger gnaws at my core, a craving that food won't satisfy.

She folds the leggings and places them next to her top. I'm standing in front of her, staring at her perfect body. I can't believe that she's mine.

Mine.

I reach for her shoulder and stroke it with the pad of my thumb. "You're a fucking masterpiece. The most beautiful woman I have ever laid eyes on." When she opens her mouth to likely protest, I shake my head. "And don't you dare contradict me. If you say one fucking self-deprecating thing about your body, I'll put you straight over my knee and spank you until you beg me to stop and you're ready to admit you're fucking gorgeous."

"You wouldn't," she whispers, but the heat of her gaze tells me there's a part of her who hopes that I will.

I stare into the depths of her eyes and comb my fingers through her hair. I lean in and kiss her temple. "I promise I would, so I wouldn't test that theory. Let's clean you up. Our food will be here soon."

"So sex isn't in your arsenal of tools to come down after a high like that?" she whispers.

I kiss her cheek and turn her around to face the bathroom. "I guess we'll have to see."

In the bathroom, I turn the shower on. "I want you to trust me. I'm not going to take advantage of you. I promise. You are getting in the shower, and you're not leaving this bathroom until I take a shower, too."

She looks over at where the clothes are. "Does your housekeeper do laundry?"

I shake my head. "I don't trust people to do shit like that for me."

"Very nice. A man who can take care of himself. I'm impressed."

I don't take the bait. I open the shower door and jerk my head. "Go."

As she steps into the shower, the doorbell rings. I can hear it from here and quickly pull up the monitor on my phone. I can't see Lydia except through the frosty glass, but she is trying to look at me. "Food?"

I nod and tap a button on my phone. "Leave it at the door. Thanks."

She looks for me again. "I need a few more minutes. Do you want to go get the food?"

I feel a corner of my lips quirk up. "Nice try, Lydia. Nice try."

"Seriously, pizza's no good cold." She's totally fucking testing me. She'd eat pizza cold straight from the fridge. It's one of her favorite things.

"It'll stay hot for a while longer."

"You still have to shower. And I am dying to shave these legs." She looks down. "Fine. Listen, Viktor. You're going to be my husband whether you want to or not, and we're both starving. Come shower with me already."

Lydia isn't like other girls. Others would be shaking in terror being alone with a man she hardly knows. But Lydia likes to live on the edge. She likes to be scared. I'm going to use that to my advantage.

"Are you sure about that?"

My voice is low, husky. I can't help the raging hard-on I get with the suggestion of being near her nakedness and sharing a shower with her.

Lydia frowns, turning so that the shower water cascades over her shoulders and back.

"Is there anything I can do to prevent our marriage?"

"No."

Her voice is hard. "So we're going to share a name, rings, and a bed. Then, yes, I'm sure. We can share a shower."

There's that edge again. My cock throbs. I can't wait to fucking tame this woman.

"This shower is big enough for all of your brothers to fit in here."

I growl before I realize I'm even responding, and she laughs out loud. It's music to my ears.

"I'm not saying I *want* to share the shower with your brothers any more than you do. I'm not saying they should. I'm just saying they *could*. So relax."

I strip my clothes off and throw them into the hamper.

"I like a man who keeps his things tidy."

"Is that right?" I ask, opening the shower door. Steam billows out at my skin.

"So my house fits your needs? Is it clean enough for you, your majesty?"

She's extremely neat and tidy and hates anything out of place. Even before she gets to work, she always has to clean up her space. Her car is impeccable.

When I found out she was coming here, I hired an entire team to clean my house from top to bottom. Even though I already have a housekeeper, we did a complete deep clean all the way down to the basement.

"It does. I like that." She finishes rinsing her hair and turns to face me.

"Dear God," she says, shaking her head. "How much do you lift?"

"Like, how often? Or how many weights?"

She shakes her head. "Never mind. I don't think it would make sense to me anyway. I wouldn't know what it looks like to bench press fifty or a thousand pounds. Your body speaks for itself."

"Is that right?" I look down on my body. "What does it say?"

All traces of humor leave her. She looks from the top of my head, down my neck, and over my shoulders. The heat of her gaze skates down my skin to my massive erection, my strong thighs, all the way down my legs.

"Your body looks like it's been honed into an instrument of torture. Perfection." She licks her lips and swallows. "It says you're trained to kill."

She's not wrong.

I step into the shower. "It also says that you are incredibly turned on by me," she whispers, almost surprised.

"Did you seriously need to see my hard-on to know that?"

I'm going to go to bed tonight with the worst fucking case of blue balls I've ever had in my life.

Jesus fucking Christ.

"Honestly? No. Of all the things I've doubted about you and me so far in this short time that I've known you, your attraction to me has not been one of them."

Yet she lets me hold her hand. She's let me comfort her. Lydia may be afraid of me, but if she is, she hides it well.

I reach for the bar of soap and scrub it on my back. Quickly wash and rinse.

I'm aware of her watching me. I'm aware of the way her breath hitches, and she looks away.

I want to touch her. I want to feel her. I want her to touch me.

She leans over me, reaching for the conditioner that Polina bought her. Her arm brushes mine, and I have to hold my breath to keep myself still. To keep myself from grabbing her and ravishing her right here in the shower, hours after I've taken her into my captivity.

I swallow hard, the rise of adrenaline making the blood pump in my veins.

"See? It's easy to read." She turns and looks at me, her thick lashes dotted with droplets of water. She moves closer to me. "God, so many things I wish I knew."

"You can ask me anything you like."

"Really?"

"Mmm."

"Do you speak Russian?" she asks in Russian. "I've always wanted a man to speak Russian to me."

"Konechno, ya delayu."

Of course I do.

"Why do you want me to speak Russian?"

She hangs her head and takes a step closer to me. "I think it's hot. I've always imagined my husband would speak my native language to me. I think it's my Russian blood. Something about that calls to me."

"Then why aren't you speaking Russian now?"

She shrugs and doesn't answer.

"Have you been with a lot of women? It seems like a reasonable thing to ask someone who's going to be your husband."

She takes a step toward me and reaches for the bar of soap in my hand.

"No. Some, but they didn't need anything from me." I sink a world of meaning into that response, unsure of how she'll take it.

Without a word, she washes my shoulders and my neck and my chest.

"Aren't you going to ask me if I've been with a lot of men?" I shake my head.

"I don't need to. All I needed to know was that you thought fucking Yudin was worthy of your time and attention. I'll remedy that. He didn't love you and wasn't worthy of you."

Her eyes flash, and she snorts.

"And this is what real love looks like? This is the real deal, right? Who are you kidding, Viktor?"

I shake my head.

"You need to know that I fucking hate him, and I'm going to kill him. And I'm not going to lie to you about that. I thought by now you would've seen who he was."

She shakes her head and turns away. "I'm starving. Let's get out of here and get something to eat." I'll have to remember she changes the subject when she gets uncomfortable.

We rinse and towel off, not saying a word to each other. I show her where Polina left some clothes, and I pull on a pair of boxers. The whole time I'm wondering, what does she think of me? Does she still think that asshole was worth her time?

I show her to the kitchen. She wears soft flannel pajama shorts and a little tank top. They fit her perfectly.

"These are nice. I'll have to thank Polina. Do you have a dining room?"

I shake my head again.

"I eat in the kitchen. I'll show you."

In silence, we quietly get paper plates and napkins out.

"Do you like pink lemonade and Diet Coke?"

I shake my head. "I don't give a shit. My housekeeper got those."

They are her favorite drinks. She's smart enough to know why they're there. She eyes me curiously and takes a bottle of water, leaving the lemonade and Diet Coke there. It feels like a moment of calm before a storm of emotions is about to hit. Lydia burns as hot as the fires she sets.

She's grateful right now. She had a shower, and I ordered her favorite foods. But she doesn't like the control over her life, and that's going to come to a head eventually.

We sit at the kitchen table, the food spread up before us. Lydia takes a large slice of pizza and eats slowly, her eyes fluttering closed.

"Oh my God, this is so good," she says, savoring her food. I watch her. I love making her happy.

We eat until we're full.

"Soon you'll meet Aria, Mikhail's wife. These were her favorite when she was pregnant."

I put the rest of the food away as she throws the paper plates in the trash. It's simple and comforting, but we're both mostly just tired. When our eyes meet, an unspoken understanding passes between us. Maybe she's trying to reconcile the fact that I know so much about her, and yet I'm still a complete stranger.

My phone buzzes with a text.

> Mikhail: They lied or he was warned. No Yudin.

Lydia shifts in her seat, drawing my attention back to her. Her gaze is intense, her lips slightly parted. "Who was that?" she asks, her voice soft but probing.

"Mikhail," I reply, my voice low.

Her eyes narrow slightly. "Do you always handle your problems with violence?"

I step closer, the air between us charged with tension. "I do what needs to be done to protect those I care about."

Her breath hitches, and she doesn't back away. Instead, she stands, closing the distance between us. "And what about me, Viktor? What do I need protection from?"

"From anyone who would hurt you," I say, my voice rough with emotion. "Including yourself."

Her eyes flash with defiance. "I don't need a protector."

"Maybe not," I murmur, reaching out to tuck a strand of hair behind her ear. "But you have one anyway."

She shivers at my touch, a mixture of anger and something more in her eyes. "You think you know everything about me," she whispers, her lips inches from mine.

"I know enough," I reply, my voice husky. "Enough to want to keep you safe. Enough to want *you*."

Her breath catches, and for a moment, we just stand there, the tension between us electric. Then she steps back, breaking the spell.

"We'll see," she says, her voice trembling slightly. "We'll see if you really know me, Viktor."

I shoot Mikhail another text.

Keep looking

CHAPTER THIRTEEN

Lydia

I LIE in bed staring at the wall. I slept well for a while, my belly full after a hot shower and a human hot water bottle beside me.

But now I'm wide awake, my mind buzzing with fear and possibilities.

I'm starting to see the wisdom in staying because if I leave... Where will I go? My family is entwined with the Romanovs. If I want anything to do with my mother or my sister, I stay here. If I leave, if I try to get away, I don't trust that my former fiancé won't come after me. And after what I've seen, I don't know what he'd do to me.

What if that man Viktor killed yesterday was telling the truth? What if Timur did intend to use me and share me with his men? The thought of it disgusts me. I wake up with a heavy heart, my future husband next to me.

"Are you awake?" he asks.

I nod. "You?"

"Yeah," he says in a low voice. Everything about him is so heavy and big and masculine, even his voice.

"What time is it?"

"No idea. Time when you should still be sleeping, anyway."

"Thank you, Captain Obvious."

I feel him tense beside me before he sits up, tossing the covers to the side. My heart leaps into my chest.

What the hell—

"That's it," he says, shaking his head. "I've had it. I've been as understanding as I possibly could be with you, Lydia."

I stare, my jaw unhinged, as he reaches for my wrist. I pull away, but I don't stand a chance against a man as big and as powerful as he is. "I am *done*."

I gasp as he sits heavily on the bed and drags me over his lap.

"What the hell?" I protest, even as my pulse skyrockets. "Viktor, what the fuck—"

His hand slams against my backside hard and fast.

"I've been gentle. I've been understanding," he continues, as his palm connects against my skin. My cheeks flame, but there's something about the way he overpowers me that sends arousal coursing through me. I can hardly speak or think as heat blossoms in my belly, and a delicious warmth spreads between my legs.

I want to see what he does when I protest. When I fight him. When I don't cave and roll over and show him the underside of my belly.

So I kick. I claw at his legs and yell, throwing my head back and hollering with everything I've got.

"You son of a bitch! You *bastard.* Let me up, or I'll *scream!*"

He fists my hair, gathering the crazy lot of it in his massive hand before he tugs my head back. "Do it. If you don't scream, I'll get my belt and whip your perfect, pretty little ass until you do."

"You *bastard!*" I scream. "Let me *up!*" I scream until I'm hoarse and my ears are ringing, earning me a low, dark chuckle from my captor.

"That's what I was hoping for," he says approvingly. In one fell swoop, he divests me of my clothes and bares my ass to him. The feel of his hot, heavy, calloused palm on my screaming hot backside sends bolts of arousal to my lady parts. My mouth is dry, and if he were to touch me right now, he'd find me sopping wet.

Something deep, deep inside me of I can't quite decipher whispers with delicious satisfaction... *this.*

This.

Him.

This.

I want to be taken. I want to be controlled. I want to be dominated and pushed, and when I push the fuck back, I don't want him to crumple.

His palm slaps hard against the underside of my thigh, and it stings way worse than it did before. I whimper and squirm, trying to get away, but he pins me in place and spanks me again.

My breath catches in my throat, a mixture of fear and defiance surging through me. I struggle against him with everything I've got, my hands pushing at his strong, sturdy thighs, my body twisting in an attempt to break free. I almost actually wriggle out of his control, but he catches me, pins me in place, and growls, "You naughty little thing," before he gives me three hard, stinging slaps in rapid succession.

"Viktor, no!" I scream, my voice trembling, even as a part of me thinks *Yes, yes, THIS.*

But his strength is overwhelming, his grip like iron as he holds me in place. Without a moment's pause, he brings his hand down on my naked ass again, the sharp crack of the spank echoing in the room and mingling with my cries.

We've been dancing on the periphery of something, and I didn't know what until this.

I fight harder, my struggles becoming more frantic, and somewhere in the dark recesses of my mind, I think I should tell him to stop, but I don't want to. It hurts like fuck, and I'm humiliated beyond belief, but I've never, in my entire life, been more turned on than I am now.

When the spanking continues, my defiance begins to wane, replaced by the utter need for pleasure.

"Viktor," I plead, my voice softer this time. "Oh God. Okay, alright, I'm sorry."

His palm pauses, poised above my ass. "Sorry for what? *Say it.*"

"Sorry for mouthing off at you." His hand stills, his fingers lingering for a moment before gently rubbing my aching ass, soothing the sting his own palm inflicted.

"Are you going to mouth off to me again?" he asks, his voice dangerously low. "Or do we need to continue this?"

I pause only a moment before I reply. "Do you want the truth or a lie?"

"Lydia," he growls.

"Okay, okay! I am absolutely going to do it again," I admit, cringing for the next swat of his palm, but to my surprise, he chuckles and lets out a breath.

"You were honest. I fucking love that, baby," he whispers. "You're a good girl, Lydia. A good girl who needs an occasional reminder to behave herself. And good girls get rewarded, don't they?"

I squirm on his lap. My breasts are pressed between his lap and the bed, my nipples dangerously hard.

"They do," I whisper. "They totally fucking do."

Leaning down, he whispers in my ear, "It's a good thing I don't punish you for that potty mouth of yours, or you'd be toast."

"I so fucking would," I agree with a nod. Because I'm a good girl. His good girl.

"Do you want to see what happens when you're honest with me?"

"After you dominated me and spanked my ass? *Ooohhh, yeah,*" I whisper. "Please, please, *please.*"

He swats my sore ass. "Come here, baby. Give me that pussy. I'll bet you're wet for me, aren't you?" When he pushes my legs apart and touches my pussy, my pelvis convulses at the first touch of his finger.

"Oh fuck," I moan. "Holy shit."

"Someone liked her spanking."

I moan. "Liked? More like loved. I *loved* my spanking."

"Jesus. That means I'll never be able to actually teach you to behave yourself," he says, but the sly grin on his face tells me he's not all that broken up by it.

He lifts me as easily as if I weigh nothing at all, lays me on the bed, and kneels before me.

"Oh God," I whisper, my voice shaking.

"These are the rules. I'm going to eat your pussy. You earned this climax, and I fucking earned eating you out. You're going to come on my tongue. If you decide you're going to come before I give you permission, you'll get spanked again, and I'll make you wait. If you move your hands out of the position I put them in, I'll tie you up and whip you again until you're begging for mercy. In other words, if you want to come, baby, you'll do what I fucking say."

He fists my hair, his strong, masculine, utterly handsome face making my heartbeat racket higher. "Are we clear?"

"I don't know about this," I start, squirming when his eyes narrow on me. It was only seconds ago I was sprawled across his lap, getting my ass handed to me, so I'm more than a little afraid of that happening again.

"Don't know about what?" he snaps, his gaze burning into mine with such ferocity I gulp.

"You... doing that... to me."

"What the hell are you talking about?" As if to punish me, he bends his head to my thigh and bites.

Bites me.

I scream and try to push him away when his tongue licks the place he just bit. I sit up and stare, half expecting to see blood. Why the fuck does that make me skate to the edge of climax? I try to push him away again, but he smacks my hands away and glares at me.

"Put those hands above your head and don't fucking move them," he growls, getting to his knees. "You like it rough, baby. I know that now." He grins wickedly. "Lucky for you, so do I."

I squeeze my eyes tight because even though I'm inexplicably scared, I want this. I want this so damn badly. It takes effort to keep my hands in place. I remind myself of what he said he'd do if I moved them.

I'll tie you up and whip you again until you're begging for mercy

Do I want that?

What?

I'm still aching from the spanking he gave me but more than

a little curious about what being tied up and whipped would look like.

Gah.

I think I might swallow my tongue in the effort of shutting the fuck up.

"Good girl," he says, his gaze locked on mine tells me he knows exactly what I'm tempted by, and he knows how hard I'm trying. "Keep them right fucking there."

His hands come to my breasts, and he gives my nipples a hard tweak. I scream out loud, but just in time, remember to keep my hands where he put them.

"That's a girl," he says approvingly. "That's right, baby."

He pushes himself on the bed and bends his mouth to my nipples, laving one at a time with the warm, wet, flat of his tongue while he fingers my pussy. I squirm beneath him, but my hands stay in place, even when his teeth clamp down and he bites my nipple.

"Ahhh!" I scream. "Viktor!"

"Mmm, you taste so fucking good, and I haven't even tasted your pussy yet." He shakes his head. "Jesus fucking Christ, I did something good in my past life to deserve a woman like you," he says reverently.

"Good thing I'm not punishing *you* for your mouth. You swear like you're in a gang."

He smirks at me. "I'd like to see you try."

And then he's gone, and I'm scared because all I see is the

breadth of his shoulders casting my body into shadow and the top of his head between my legs.

And then I'm drowning, dying, finally actually *living* when his tongue meets my aching, throbbing clit. It feels like the heat of hell and the perfection of heaven all at once. I close my eyes and shiver as waves of pleasure consume me.

He growls and fists his cock, jerking his massive erection as he lazily drags his tongue along my swollen slit. My thoughts fizzle into vapor at the hot feel of his breath on my inner thighs. When his teeth graze my clit, I wriggle my wrists, but a swift slap to my thigh makes me pause.

"I told you what would happen," he warns. "I'm eating you out, girl, and you're obeying me. You got me?"

I nod, stifling the need to whimper or smack him. I swallow, my mouth dry. "Mhm." I nod, eager for him to continue.

And then he's back at my pussy, worshiping me with his tongue until I feel like I can hardly stand the pleasure. I've never come on a man's face like this, and it somehow both terrifies and thrills me, but I couldn't stop now if I wanted to.

"Tell me when you're close," he growls, pausing to scrape my thighs with his stubble. The prickles feel like a million little needles. He drags his chin just on the very edge of my swollen clit and I scream.

"Atta girl," he says, his hot breath on my thighs. "That's what I like to see. You have my permission, my good girl. Come on my mouth, baby. Let yourself go."

And then he sinks back down to the floor and fists his cock. Somehow, hearing him give me permission makes the first spasm of pleasure course through me, but I'm scared. I hold my breath, unable to move past the need to come and actually allowing myself to get there.

I've never had a man bring me to climax before.

I've had sex and felt... passing pleasure... but I never felt that earth-shattering, freeing, absolute bliss I've read about in those romance novels my sister gave me.

I don't even know what it's like. I don't even know what it is I'm chasing.

I feel so tightly wound I'm a string about to snap, but I can't seem to get there. Every time I think I'm going to, I can't seem to get there.

"Come, baby," he orders. I sniff and shake my head. I didn't even know I was crying.

Why am I crying?

"Lydia." My eyes snap to his. "You can come. I gave you permission."

I sniff hard. "I... I can't."

"Of course you can." he says, lowering his mouth to my pussy again. "Relax, baby. Breathe into it. You need to get out of your head."

I shake my head. "I can't, Viktor."

Staring at me, he finally asks me, "Why not?"

I look away. I don't know how to answer that question.

Because I'm not worthy? Because I'm not pretty enough? Because letting myself climax means surrendering to him?

All of those things, maybe? I don't know.

I can't put it into words.

He strokes my inner thigh. "This is about trust."

I shake my head. My breath hitches, my anger momentarily ebbing when I see a flicker of vulnerability in his eyes. "If I didn't trust you, at least a little, you wouldn't be kneeling in front of me with your mouth on my pussy."

"Close your eyes, baby. Breathe with me."

Hesitantly, I do what he says. I close my eyes and take a deep breath. His voice is a low, somehow soothing command.

"Imagine yourself powerful. Unstoppable. Imagine yourself in control of your body and your life and your happiness. Can you do that, baby?"

I nod, licking my lips and swallowing. My hips jerk when I feel the warm, wet press of his tongue on my clit again. He suckles hard and grips my thighs. My clit *throbs*.

"Now let yourself go. Let yourself surrender without shame. You deserve to feel pleasure. You deserve to let go."

I feel his hands on my waist, a grounding touch that somehow makes my reserves crumble.

"I don't know if I can."

"You can, baby. Imagine yourself surrounded by fire, but this fire isn't destructive, it's warm. It's your safe place. Let it burn away any insecurities and fears you have. Let it consume everything but *you*."

I nod.

"Alright," I whisper as he bends his mouth to my sex and sucks again. A spasm of pleasure lights me up, its warmth and intensity making me squirm in delicious anticipation.

"Let it consume you. Trust in it. Trust in *yourself*."

I feel a little of the tension I'm holding onto begin to ebb away. "Good girl. That's it, Lydia. Let yourself go."

I close my eyes and breathe. I imagine the room is filled with flames licking at us on all sides but not burning us. There's something about the flicker and heat that calms me.

He grips my hips, lifts my legs, and straddles them over his shoulders. If I wanted to, I could crush his head with my thighs.

This, too, is an act of trust.

I close my eyes and focus on relaxing. Focus on the sensation. Something shifts in me, and I feel like that match to tinder. My low smolder grows to something more, something hotter, and I know I've reached the point of no return when my whole body goes up in flames.

"Oh God," I scream, "yes!" Pleasure floods my limbs, and I'm totally consumed in the perfect feel of his mouth on my sensitive parts. I moan in pleasure as flames completely consume my body until I finally sink to the bed, spent.

He stands, fists his massive cock, and holds my gaze as he throws his head back and comes. Hot spurts of come paint my breasts, my belly, my thighs as he marks me as his, and for once... for once in my life, I think, *he loves my body*.

He loves what he sees.

He hasn't been lying.

He loves my body.

 I blink, coming down from my high as he leans over and presses his lips to my cheek. "You're mine, Lydia," he whispers in my ear. "You're mine. Stay right here. I'm going to clean you up."

The man who spanked me, scratched me with his stubble, and bit my nipples was a different side of Viktor I hadn't yet seen. He's been nothing but tender to me, even when I pushed him until he finally snapped.

I stifle a whine when he gets up off the bed and walks to the bathroom. He comes back later with a small hand towel. When he wipes me with it, I'm reminded of the hot towels they wrap around my legs when I get pedicures at Mom's. It's warm and damp and feels incredibly soothing, smelling faintly of lavender.

I reach for it to help him, and he shakes his head with one curt nod. "Let me."

After what he just did to me, I've somehow lost the ability to push back. I'm putty in his hands.

"You'd better enjoy this while it lasts," I say. My voice sounds like it's distant, out of my body, coming from someone else and not me.

"What?"

"My compliance."

He grins at me. "Oh, I seem to have figured out a way to deal with this."

My eyes are heavy and my body boneless as he lays me back on the pillows. "Get some rest, Lydia."

I close my eyes and fall into a deep, dreamless sleep.

"You should get out of bed and get ready."

"Why?"

"It's getting harder and harder to lie next to you and not fuck you," he says, his teeth gritted together.

I've never had this power over anyone before.

"You don't trust yourself with me? That's interesting, isn't it? We should observe this as part of human nature." I lean over and push myself up on one elbow.

He grunts and makes some sort of sound that is half between a growl and acquiescence before he slaps my ass. I squeal.

"Get dressed."

"Do you say please, Viktor? Or do you just order people around?"

He quirks one eye open. Last night's stubble grew to a dark shadow on his chin. I remember that stubble quite well...

In the morning light, I see the silver scar that runs from his forehead down his cheek.

"Let's try. Please, get ready, my love," he says in a sappy, unrecognizable voice. "Before I pin your wrists to this headboard and fuck you. I don't know how much longer I can last, so I'm warning you. Stepping away from me would probably be in your best interest. I'm not sure if you remember anything about yesterday, but I only have so much self-control." His eyes narrow. "Was that better, doll?"

I actually swallow a giggle. "Much."

Am I letting him get to me? I walk to the bathroom, grab some clothes, and quickly change.

My hair is crazy from the day before, but I'm starving. I blame the adrenaline. So I pin my hair up in this crazy bun on top of my head like a ballerina, wash my face with some of the excellent skincare products Polina picked out, brush my teeth, and slap on some quick makeup.

I chose a little white peasant top that accentuates my curves in all right ways, slimming my waist and accentuating my breasts. Comfortable, stretchy jeans that are wide and go all the way to the floor. I'm still wearing these slippers because they're so comfy, but I guess I'll have to wear shoes, too.

Viktor's changed into gray sweats and a white tee. Hot damn. What is it about a white tee and gray sweats that just do it for me? There's something just... manly and sexy and raw about it. Especially the way he fills those out.

"We have a couple of interesting developments. We'll talk it out over breakfast." Frowning, he reaches for my hand. "Did you cut yourself?"

I look down. I think I did it yesterday at the warehouse, but I don't want him to feel bad.

Why? Why the hell do I care whether he feels bad or not? It was his fault that I was at the warehouse.

I shrug. "It's fine. I don't know how I cut it."

"Does it hurt?" he asks in a gentle voice that makes a lump rise in my throat.

I swallow it hard. God, I'm fucked up.

"No, it's fine," I lie. Because when he brushes the top of his finger against it, I wilt.

"Liar," he says, his tone rough. "Sit on the bed."

He stalks off barefoot to the bathroom and comes back with a Band-Aid and some type of cleansing wipe.

"Viktor, I'm fine," I say. Jesus, what would he do if I actually hurt myself? This is practically a paper cut.

Quietly, he bends on one knee, reaches for my hand and frowns, his eyebrows flashing together as he cleans little cuts on my skin before he opens the Band-Aid carefully and slides it on my hand. When he's done, he crumples the papers and lifts my hand to his lips.

But he doesn't stop there.

He kisses the top of my wrist. My forearm. He keeps going

until he's kissed the length of my arm, the warm, erotic touch of his mouth making my belly squirm deliciously.

"You're so gorgeous," he says reverently before he says the last thing I expect him to.

"Marry me?"

I can't help it. My heart turns in my chest. I'm only human, after all. And there's something about this powerful, dangerous man who only goes soft for me that's making me swoon a little.

Timur wouldn't have put a Band-Aid on my wound.

Goddamn, I can't think of that asshole now.

"I suppose you'll do," I say in what I attempt to be a haughty tone, but instead, it comes out all breathy. I need to change the subject. "What are these developments?"

"I'll tell you after coffee."

"Ah, so you're one of those guys who's a bear until he's had his coffee."

He growls as if he's incapable of speech until that caffeine hits his veins.

I love this kitchen. I won't tell him because I don't want to give him the satisfaction. It's all stainless steel appliances, high-end stuff like a chef might have, immaculate, clean, and filled with bright light, possibly the brightest room in his whole house. He walks over to the counter, on which he has set up with a little coffee station. I squeal. This is perfect, like something you'd find on a Pinterest board.

"This thing makes caramel vanilla lattes? Are you kidding?"

He shrugs. "I'm well stocked."

He knows my favorite things. Is he trying to seduce me?

How much does he *really* know about me?

 He grunts, takes out the cup, and slides it under the Keurig. "I got that for you." He doesn't look at my eyes.

I take it from him gratefully.

"What do you drink?"

"Espresso."

"Straight black?"

"Mmm."

Of course.

If he has my favorite coffee creamer in that goddamn fridge —he opens it, takes out the matte-white creamer bottle, and slides it across the counter to me. "Vera told me what you like. It's good stuff. Of course you like it."

I'm not sure what that means. He hands me my latte and makes his espresso.

Nikita comes up to me and licks my hand. "You're such a pretty girl." I bend to scratch her ears. She does that thing that dogs do, unable to hide this near bliss she has when I scratch her ears. Her eyes go half lidded, and her ears go back. "Such a pretty, pretty girl," I croon. I love her.

Viktor sips his espresso, his eyes burning into me.

"What? I can't scratch her ears?"

"You have to stop putting motives behind my looks; it isn't fair, and you don't know me."

When he turns away, I snort. "Oh, that's right. Hello, pot calling the kettle black."

Frowning, he walks over to a white pastry box on the counter and takes out a pastry bigger than his hand, drizzled in white sugar and sliced almonds. My mouth waters.

"What? I'm not doing that to you. I mean, isn't that what you're doing to *me?*"

"Assigning motives to someone and understanding what they're thinking are two completely different things, Lydia."

I stand and walk away from him to assess the situation.

I take a frying pan and slide it onto his stove. He has one of those fancy flat induction things. Heat instantly springs to the pan. I throw a pat of butter in, and when it's nice and hot and sizzling, I slide bacon into the pan. I fry eggs and bacon, drain it all, and put it on a plate with a sprinkle of kosher salt and fresh pepper.

He watches me, sipping his espresso. "Don't get used to this," I warn him. "I'm just starving, and I like your kitchen."

He only shrugs.

He takes the pastry out of the box and puts it on a plate. We eat in almost amiable silence. Almost.

The food hits my belly, and it's delicious. I eat until I'm full then push my plate away.

"Now, are you ready to tell me about the new developments?"

He eats an egg with one bite, chomps, and swallows, as if it's his life mission to eat with efficiency, slaps butter on four slices of toast, eats all the bacon on the plate, and then reaches for my discarded plate and finishes everything on that.

Shit.

But I guess you have to feed a man like that well. He's a big guy.

Viktor wipes his mouth and looks at me, his gaze intense. "We couldn't find him."

My heart skips a beat. "What do you mean you couldn't find him?"

"Our contacts, everyone we have on the ground... He's gone. Disappeared. No trace."

I stare at him, processing the information. "Isn't that good? He can't hurt us if he's gone."

Viktor shakes his head slowly. "It's not that simple. The fact that he vanished means he might have powerful help. And he might come back when we least expect it."

Fear coils in my stomach, but I try to keep my voice steady. "So what do we do now?"

His eyes darken. "We stay vigilant. I'll increase security around you and Vera. We can't afford to take any chances. I got you a new phone, and you'll keep it on you at all times."

I nod, feeling the weight of his words. His protectiveness is overwhelming, suffocating, but a part of me is grateful. For now, I'm under his watch, and there's a twisted sense of safety in that.

"We'll heighten security. I'll train you in self-defense."

I swallow. "Alright. And what if it doesn't work?"

"What do you mean?"

"What if you don't find him? What if he…"

I can't say it aloud.

What if he kills me?

"That won't happen because it's not an option."

He threads his fingers through my hair. "I promise."

CHAPTER FOURTEEN

Seven years ago

Viktor

"WHERE IS SHE?" My voice sounded too low, too weak to counteract the inky darkness, to give me the answers that I needed.

"She's gone, Viktor. I am so sorry," the doctor in the white lab coat said. His facial expressions didn't match his words, though. Even then, I understood that people lie to get what they want and to make their own lives easier.

"What do you mean?" I asked, my fists clenched at my sides. My brain refused to comprehend his words.

He took two steps over to me and put a heavy hand on my shoulder. "We did everything we could."

I shook my head. "If you had done everything, she would be here!"

"I promise you, we tried," the doctor continued. Another lie.

I knew my sister was sick. I *knew it.*

"I brought her here two days ago. I told you she was sick. You sent her home and told her she needed some over-the-counter meds and sleep!"

My sister didn't need more sleep. She coughed up *blood.* But we had no money for a doctor. I came here, offering them anything I could give, but they had no use for a young man like me.

"I told you," the doctor said, his voice hard. "When she came here the other day, she was fine. She had a little bit of a cold. Tonight, she was in great distress, yes, but we did everything we could. Now, if you'll excuse me, I can send someone out to talk with you—"

I lifted him by his coat and threw him against the wall so hard his skull cracked against it. One of the nurses screamed while someone else frantically called for security.

I advanced on him. "You asshole. You could've saved her, and you did *nothing.*" I punched him again and again, and when he fell to the floor blocking his face, I kicked his ribs.

I knew how this would go. This wasn't my first rodeo. I had thirty more seconds before a team of "security guards"—half-assed, skinny dudes who couldn't cut it in real law enforcement—would come here and tell me to put my hands up, tell me to leave, and threaten to stop me.

I had just enough time to impart the lesson I needed to. I lifted the doctor and shook him. "I don't know why you're here or who the hell you think you are, but you let a little girl die, and it's all your fault. I want *that* on your fucking conscience."

I could have killed him right then, right there. I could have ended him, but I didn't want his life on my own conscience.

I marched out of that hospital, everybody stepping out of my way. I was already too big for anyone to stop me, even the security guard.

No. It was just me now. All alone. And I was going to find someone who valued me, who could use my fists, my strength. I would never, ever let anyone weak or vulnerable suffer again.

CHAPTER FIFTEEN

Lydia

I AM DEFINITELY nervous about today. While I might come across as a confident woman, it's something else entirely when you're about to meet your future husband's family.

What if they hate me? What if they've already formed preconceived notions about me? His brother certainly seems to have done that. There's hope, though, because I haven't met his sister-in-laws, his sister, or his mother.

But as a woman, those are the ones I am most afraid of. What if I don't fit in here? I've never fit in anywhere.

Who the fuck cares? Since when have I really cared about the opinions of other people?

I blow out a breath and look at myself in the mirror.

Yeah, I've cared about that since I took my first breath as a human being. Sure, I'm at least outwardly confident, and

I've *mostly* gotten over the need for approval from others. But I still have an intrinsic need to belong.

How do I put this makeup on, anyway? I look at the array of makeup on my counter. While I thought I was pretty confident using it, I wonder if I could learn something new.

I pick up the new phone Viktor gave me, sleek and beautiful, in a soft purple matte case. I've never owned anything like it before. When I touch the screen, it springs to life, vivid colors filling the display so quickly it feels almost space-age.

I notice a tiny dot in the top right corner of the screen, barely noticeable unless you're looking for it. It's a subtle but persistent red blink.

"What the hell is that?" I mutter to myself, my curiosity piqued. Leaning closer, I squint at the dot. It looks like a small camera or a tracking device, but I can't be sure. I tap it lightly with my finger, but nothing happens. It's just a tiny, blinking dot.

My heart rate quickens. If Viktor has been watching me, what else has he done without my knowledge? A mix of anger and fear churns in my stomach. Determined to find answers, I pull up a browser and type in, "What does the little blinking dot in the upper right corner of my screen indicate?"

The search results are filled with technical jargon and troubleshooting forums. I glance at several articles, looking for confirmation. Then, I find it—an article discussing surveillance software that can be installed on personal devices to monitor activity.

My blood runs cold. Viktor is tracking me.

Why would I think any less of him? Why would he hand-pick this high-end phone if not to install something to spy on me with?

Future husband, my ass. Protection, *my ass*.

Well he can *fuck. Off.*

I lift the phone over my head and smash it to the ground. Nothing happens. Goddamn, these things are indestructible now. I look around the bathroom for something heavy to destroy it with. I see a ceramic vase, so I lift it and drop it as hard as I can on my phone. The vase shatters, but the phone is fine.

Jesus.

 For the love of God.

"Lydia? What the hell are you doing in there?" Viktor's voice is sharp through the door. He turns the handle, but I've locked it.

"I'm shocked you don't know," I snap back at him. "You don't have cameras riveted on my every move in here?"

"Lydia," he warns outside the door. I stare at my reflection as if my monster of a future husband isn't pounding on that door to get in and continue to apply my makeup. That's when I feel the little bump under the skin on the back of my neck.

What is that? It's a little itchy. I turn and try to look, but I can't see it properly. I assume it's a bug bite or something similar.

Oh my *God,* if he's installed a fucking tracker *on me*—but when I look in the mirror, it just looks like a bug bite. Okay, maybe I'm overreacting. Maybe I've gotten way in my head about this.

"Lydia, if you don't open this fucking door..."

I smirk at myself in the mirror and give myself a little shrug. "What are you gonna do?"

And that does give me the upper hand with him. He could march in here and dominate me, but it will only turn me on. He can't control me that way.

"Open it," he snaps, but he's clearly gotten the memo.

I finish getting myself ready, irritation rising with every second that passes. Finally, I open the door, and he stands in the doorway, filling it entirely as usual. He's wearing a black leather jacket that hugs his muscular frame, a fitted black shirt that accentuates his broad chest, and dark jeans. His shaved head and the scar running down his cheek only add to his intimidating presence. My pulse quickens despite my annoyance at the flash of anger in his eyes.

Ping.

"What was that crash? What the fuck are you doing?"

"Me? You don't know? Haven't you recorded the bathroom?"

"Of course not. You can have some measure of privacy."

"Oh, that is rich coming from you," I tell him. "Jesus, Viktor." I pick up my phone from the floor. "You tracked my phone."

He has the nerve to shrug. "I never pretended I wasn't tracking you. Of course I am. How the fuck am I supposed to keep you safe?"

"So, smothering me, keeping me immediately by your side, marrying me, and not letting me out of your sight isn't good enough?"

He scowls. Of course it isn't.

"You were trying to break your new phone?"

"Yeah. It didn't work. What did you get me, some military-grade whatever?"

"Yes."

I throw my hands up in the air. "Jesus Christ! I was exaggerating. I didn't think you actually did that!"

"Of course I did. You just threw your phone out the window, remember? I knew the chances of you losing your temper and destroying it were pretty high."

"I wasn't the one who did that!" I snap.

He shakes his head. "What if you had something important on that phone? Somebody throws this phone out a window, at least you get to keep your pictures or whatever else you have on your phone."

"You're snooping on me!"

"I have no interest in snooping on you, but I do want to know where you are at all times. And that is never, ever going to change." His frown deepens. "So you better get used to that."

"*You better get used to that,*" I mimic, my hands on my hips. He takes a step toward me as if to intimidate me, but I'm unfazed. I'm starting to think that Viktor couldn't hurt me if he tried.

"Don't mock me," he snaps. "God, you're such a brat."

Fury claws at my chest, an angry, untamed beast. My voice shakes with the effort of controlling it. "I'm not a *brat*. A brat acts out over stupid things. I don't lie down and let people tell me what to do. Those are two very, very different things, Mr. Romanov."

He's in my space, his breath tickling my hair. I'm breathing heavier, and so is he. He loves fighting with me. I love getting a rise out of him. We're a match to tinder.

When he doesn't respond, I try to drive the memo home. "Get this through your head. I'm someone who doesn't like to be told what to do."

"Oh, I am *well* aware," he says, his voice low and dangerous.

His eyes darken as he steps even closer, crowding my space until I'm forced to back up against the sink. "You think you can push me, and there won't be consequences?" His voice is a low, dangerous rumble, sending a shiver down my spine.

I lift my chin defiantly. "You don't scare me, Viktor."

A slow, predatory smile spreads across his face. "Oh, I think I do. But it's not fear I see in your eyes right now, is it?" He leans in, his lips brushing against my ear. "You like this, don't you? The challenge, the danger. It excites you. It's like that first strike of a lighter. You can already smell the flames."

I try to hide my reaction, but I can feel my heart racing. He's too close, too perceptive, too in my head. "You're wrong," I whisper, but my voice lacks conviction.

His hand snakes around my neck, firm but not painfully, forcing me to look into his intense gaze. My heart twists in my chest. "Lying to yourself won't help you, Lydia. I know you better than you know yourself." His thumb strokes the side of my neck, sending an involuntary shiver through me. "You want someone who can match you, who can handle your fire. Someone like *me*."

I try to twist away, but his grip tightens just enough to hold me in place. "Let go of me, Viktor," I demand, my voice shaking.

"Not until you admit the truth," he murmurs, his breath hot against my skin. "Admit that you feel something for me, something more than just hate."

I glare at him, refusing to give him the satisfaction. "You're delusional."

His other hand slides down my arm, igniting a trail of heat. "Am I? Then why are you trembling?" His lips ghost over my neck, making it harder to focus on my anger. "Why does your heart race every time I touch you?"

"Because you're a controlling bastard," I snap, but the words come out breathless.

He chuckles softly, a sound that reverberates through me. "You need control. You crave it. And deep down, you know I'm the only one who can give it to you." He pulls back slightly, just enough to look into my eyes. "Submit to me, Lydia. Not because I force you to, but because you want to."

I feel my resolve weakening, the intense pull between us too strong to ignore. My breathing is ragged, my body turning against me as I lean into his touch. "Why should I trust you?" I whisper, a last attempt at resistance.

"Because I will never hurt you," he promises, his voice fierce and sincere. "I will protect you, cherish you. But you need to let go, to trust me."

His words break through my defenses, and I close my eyes, letting out a shaky breath. "I have no choice," I whisper. "But don't think for a second that this means you've won."

He releases his grip slightly, his thumb brushing my cheek. "This isn't about winning, Lydia. It's about us finding our way through this together." He leans in, capturing my lips in a kiss. He's already made me climax, but this is the first kiss we've ever had. It feels like we're sealing the unspoken agreement between us.

As the kiss deepens, I wonder if submitting to Viktor might not mean losing myself but rather finding a new kind of strength in our twisted, complicated bond.

He pulls away and stares at me, his pupils dilated.

"We have to go. We're already running late."

"God forbid we leave your family waiting," I say sarcastically.

"Lydia," Viktor warns, his voice a low growl.

"This argument is unresolved, Viktor. But I will go with you." I turn away. "Not because I'm conceding, but because you told me they're serving brownies. And I'm fucking starving for a brownie."

I have to admit, I'm starting to like our little tiffs. It excites me when he gets in my space. It feels like that first scratch of a match, the excitement rising in my chest in the same way. He is like fire, danger, always skirting the fucking edge.

We walk to the car parked outside.

"Aren't you going to tell me what you expect of my behavior, sir?" I ask in a mocking tone. The way his eyes turn to fire when I call him sir...

"Yes, that's an excellent idea," he says, opening the door for me. I climb into the seat, and he watches as I buckle up. Almost absentmindedly, he reaches over and smooths a crinkled part of the belt. I look away. That doesn't mean anything. No, I'm not going to soften just because he's doing that tender thing with me again. Nope.

When I glance back, he's looking at me with a mixture of awe and surprise.

"What?" I ask, immediately self-conscious.

"I just..." His words trail off, his voice husky.

"Just what?"

He swallows. "Sometimes it feels like I'm dreaming, like this is all an illusion."

I look away so he doesn't see my eyes watering.

He starts the car and pulls away from the curb. We drive in what I have to admit is amiable silence. It's a gorgeous day, sunny and bright out. I roll the window down, the wind ruffling my hair. Without a word, his hand comes to rest on my thigh.

"How far away are we?"

"Not far. We could walk there if I wanted to, but I want to drive today."

"Why?"

"This is why," he says, tightening his grip on my thigh. "I sometimes feel like I'm in a dream. I'm going to blink, and you'll be gone. It's just hard to believe that you're actually... here."

His mouth opens as if to say something else, but then he thinks better of it.

Meanwhile, I am trying my best to get my shit together.

I'm going to marry him. We know what this means in our families. I will not ever truly belong to Viktor Romanov until I submit my will and my heart. And neither of those will ever happen.

Still, I'm not immune to the connection between us, that erotic vibe that makes me want to be closer to him. I'm not immune to being treated like I am the absolute focus of someone's desire. I am not immune to being loved.

Love me? How can he? He doesn't really know me.

Then why does it feel like he does?

"You want to listen to some music?"

"Yeah. Whatever you want."

It seems like that's going to be a theme between us.

Whatever I want to eat. Whatever I want at the wedding. Whatever I want to do... except walk away.

I flip through the different stations, trying to find something to listen to. Nothing seems right, fitting. I shut it off and look out the window.

I can't stop thinking about him touching me. His touch is possessive, his thumb gently pressing against my skin, his fingers firm.

"I don't think I can ever be who you want me to be," I blurt out, feeling unexpectedly emotional. Why do I feel this way? I don't want to be who he wants me to be. I want to be my own person.

Why did I just say that out loud?

"And who do I want you to be?" he asks in a tone that suggests he thinks I have no idea.

"Submissive. Docile. You want me to have your kids, be a homemaker, or whatever the hell. You want me not to have a mind or will of my own."

His muscles tense, and his eyes stay focused on the road, but his hand on my thigh suddenly feels heavier.

"Is that really what you think I want?"

I swallow. Is it? Or is that just what I'm telling myself so I can keep my defenses up?

"Of course. What else would a man like you want? Sex? Well, you'll have that, but I like that too." Okay, that sounded petulant. Borderline bratty. I hold my chin up so he doesn't get any ideas or solidify his position on my brattiness.

"It doesn't matter what I tell you. You've already made up your mind about what I want, haven't you?"

Have I?

"No," I lie. "I want to hear you say it. Do you think I'm so ignorant that I don't listen to what someone has to say, and I make up my mind before they speak?"

Maybe I do. Damn it.

He blows out a breath, doing that thing where he strokes his thumb on my bare skin. The touch is almost platonic and gentle. But it never ceases to make my heart race, and whatever reservations I had about the two of us burn to ash.

"I've only wanted one thing my entire life that I can remember, Lydia."

I give him a sidelong look, my heart hammering in my chest. My hand rests atop his on my leg, and I don't remember moving it there. I know what he's going to say before he does.

"What?"

"You, Lydia. You are all I've ever wanted. I know that's hard for you to understand; it might even scare you. But eventually, I hope you will understand." He strokes his thumb along my thigh again, and I don't understand why my eyes are watering. It's just a normal possessive thing to say... isn't it?

"Oh, you're just saying that," I say teasingly. "You really do care about what I do and how I behave. Obviously, you've shown me that."

He shrugs a massive shoulder. "Baby, you want to skydive, paint the house purple, or become a circus performer, I don't care. I literally don't give a shit about any of that. I know that I want you, and I want you safe. Every single goddamn thing I do is for that. No more, no less. Even my home? I barely decorated it because I don't care. Once we're married, you can pick out a place to go and I'm there."

I shake my head because this doesn't make sense to me. "Why me?"

He smiles then as if he has a secret that no one else knows, his very special little secret.

"Eventually, I hope you understand that too."

I blink, surprised when we stop outside a large mansion.

Oh God. It's go time. It's his family's home—it must be.

"Are we here?"

CHAPTER SIXTEEN

Lydia

"YES. Don't worry, they're going to love you." He reaches for my hand and kisses my knuckles.

"How do you know that?"

"Because anyone who gets anywhere near you is helpless to fall in love."

Before I can respond, a little blonde-haired girl, about four years old, comes running out with Aleksandr sharp on her heels.

"Ivy!" he snaps. "Get over here!"

"Uncle Viktor! Uncle Viktor!" She holds her arms up. Viktor opens his arms, bends to one knee, and the little girl leaps into them.

Oh my God. My heart. Goddammit.

He rises with her in his arms, his grip protective as he stares at Aleksandr. "What did you do to her?" he snaps.

Aleksandr rolls his eyes. "I didn't do anything. I told her she had to eat her dinner before she could have dessert. Don't you see how she plays you?"

A petite woman with light brown hair and freckles on her nose appears behind Aleksandr in the doorway. "That's not exactly true, Aleks. You told her she had to eat her peas before she got dessert, not her dinner. And she hates peas."

"They're good for her," he says, shaking his head with a frown.

"They could be the elixir of eternal life for all I care," she says, her eyes twinkling. "But she doesn't like them, so we're not going to make her eat them." She looks over at the little girl in Viktor's arms. "Ivy, Daddy's right. You have to at least eat some of your chicken and something green before you get dessert."

Ivy is sobbing in Viktor's arms, huge crocodile tears streaming down her cheeks. I hide a smile because she is being so overly dramatic, it's adorable. And Viktor looks like he'd give her damn near anything she wanted.

He whispers something in her ear, and she giggles, her grip around his neck tightening. I don't care if I have a wall around my heart as strong as Fort Knox and made of stainless steel and diamond. No woman is impermeable to seeing the man she's attracted to and about to marry, holding a little girl and making her smile with that tenderness and be immune to it.

I fall like a ton of bricks.

Viktor walks over to my side, opens the door with his free hand, and reaches for mine.

"Ivy, I want to introduce you to someone."

Ivy gives one last dramatic sniff before she turns to look at me. "She's pretty," she says to Viktor in a little voice. His lips split into a grin, such a rarity. It feels like I'm seeing the sunshine for the first time in my life.

"She's beautiful," he says to her, his voice strangely choked. "And she's going to be my wife, Ivy. Do you want to be the flower girl at our wedding?"

Oh my God. My heart.

"What is a flower girl? I like being a girl."

His lips twitch, and the woman behind Aleksandr, who I'm guessing is his wife, giggles from the doorway.

"It means that you get to have a basket with flower petals, and before we walk down the aisle, you get to throw the petals in front of us," I explain. "Do you like that idea?"

"I think so. Is there cake at a wedding?" Ivy asks, her brows knit together.

"Not at every wedding, but I can promise you there will be cake at mine," I tell her. "I love cake. Cake is my favorite thing."

Ivy's eyes widen, and she looks at me in awe. "Mine too."

"You must be Lydia." The woman walks over to me and extends a hand. "Pleased to meet you. My name is Harper. I'm Aleksandr's wife and Ivy's mom." She glances at Viktor.

"Your mother is in there with the photographer, and she wants to talk to you about what you want done."

"She can talk to Lydia about what she wants. You know what I want."

Harper laughs prettily. "Yes. Lydia on your arm. A wedding ring that you can slide on her finger. And a name change that makes Lydia a Romanov."

I swallow. She knows, too?

"He's a little possessive," she says to me. "But you're going to see really soon that that kind of runs in the family."

Why does that not surprise me?

"We are so excited to meet you. These guys all have each other, but every time one of them gets married, we gain another sister." She smiles warmly. "And we love Vera."

It feels strange that they know my sister better than I do.

"She isn't here, is she?"

Harper shakes her head sadly. "Not yet, but they moved mountains to get her here. She'll be here tomorrow for sure."

A lump rises in my throat. "Great. And my mother will be here, too."

"Yes! We love Zofia, too, of course! Let's go inside." We walk into the house. It's imposing and majestic, just the way I would imagine Viktor's family home would be. In another room, I see Mikhail talking to a man with gray hair and a beard. Uniformed staff walk around with trays of appetizers and bottles of champagne. I close my eyes, listening to the strains of music, and take a deep breath.

Viktor comes up behind me. "I told them you'd like that."

There he goes again, revealing that he knows something about me I never told him. I'm still not sure how I feel about that.

"You must be Lydia." A woman with elegant silver hair walks into the room. "My name is Ekaterina. I am Viktor's mother."

"I'm so pleased to meet you," I say softly. I am. This woman helped mold Viktor into the man he is today, for better or worse.

"Is Mikhail in the other room?" she asks over her shoulder.

"I've heard a lot about Mikhail, too."

"Yes, let me introduce you."

She quirks her head at Ivy and Viktor. "Ivy, why do you have your arms around Uncle Viktor's neck as if you're trying to strangle him to death? What's the matter, little one?"

"Aleks was mean to her," Viktor says soberly. My lips twitch.

"Aleks," Ekaterina says, turning on her other son.

Aleksandr rolls his eyes.

"He told her that she has to eat good food before she gets dessert," Viktor says. "Imagine that, telling her she can't have cake for dinner?"

"So old-fashioned. Never would've expected it, Aleksandr." Ekaterina shakes her head.

"I'll tell you what," Viktor says. "If you eat your chicken, you can sit on my lap, and I'll get you that ketchup you like."

"Ketchup?" Aleksandr scoffs. "It's half sugar, Viktor."

"Says the man who used to put ketchup on his fries, mac and cheese, and filet mignon."

Aleksandr huffs. "Operative word, *used to,*" Aleksandr retorts.

"You act like you grew out of it when you were five years old," Viktor says. "You were twenty."

I snort and Viktor winks at me. My heart does a little flutter in my chest, and I quickly turn away; I'm so unaccustomed to how this feels.

Aleks shakes his head but caves. I watch as Viktor holds Ivy to his chest with one arm and talks to his brothers. I stand at a distance as she nestles her little head on his shoulder. She's found rest with the gentle giant.

I get it, girl. I really do. And I'm not sure how I feel about it either.

"We all need to discuss something," Viktor says as we sit down for dinner. Ivy remains perched on his lap, clinging to him like he's her personal fortress. "We should put the wedding off."

CHAPTER SEVENTEEN

Viktor

EVERYONE STARES, especially Lydia. Her hand is frozen on the fork in her left hand and the knife in her right. Wordlessly, I reach for a roll, open it, and spread it liberally with warmed butter.

I hand it to her. "Eat."

"What do you mean, put off the wedding?" Lydia asks. "Did you finally realize that forcing me against my will doesn't exactly make for a romantic love story?"

I respond with a smirk. "Oh, believe me, romance was never the point."

My mother has the grace to stand and ask if anyone wants a refill of wine while Lydia and I continue.

"Then what *is* the point? Why drag this out?"

"The point is, you're mine. Whether the wedding is tomorrow, next week, or next year, our vows to each other aren't going to change any of that. But I want you to understand what this means."

"Understand what?" she hisses. I know exactly why she's touchy. She thinks I'm not eager to marry her, that somehow my putting this off is a criticism of her. "That you're someone who wants to control me?"

I lean over and chuck a finger under her chin. "Careful, baby. You're skirting really close there."

Her cheeks flush, and I suspect she's remembering something like my stubble against her thighs or my palm against her ass.

Good.

I continue. "This isn't about control but inevitability."

She scoffs and tosses her head. "I'll never be *yours*. Not in the way you want."

I reach out, gently tucking a strand of hair behind her ear. "We'll see about that." I clear my throat and raise my voice so my brothers look over at me.

"I've been thinking about this. We know that Yudin wants her. He's hiding, and nothing we've done has brought him into the open, which means he has friends in high places. We need to draw them out. If we put off the wedding, he's going to circle us. It will give us time to prepare. Make no mistake, I'm going to marry her. But if we delay, it will make him anxious."

I look at Lydia. "Would you describe him as a patient guy?"

She huffs a little but finally responds.

"Hell no," she says. "He's one of the least patient people I've ever met."

"Exactly. When he sees that we're not making a move, he's going to snap. He thrives on revenge. Let's get all our ducks in a row first. We'll put off the wedding and set a new date later." My eyes lock onto Lydia. "In the meantime, I'll teach you self-defense."

Aria's eyes light up. "Oooh. I get it. You'll use Lydia as bait."

Heat rises in my chest, and I clench my fist. I hate that idea, but I like Aria, so I have to be careful with how I respond. I grit my teeth but keep my voice calm.

"No," I snap, my tone so harsh it startles Ivy, who jumps on my lap. "She will not be bait. The situation will be. I'll be waiting."

Aleksandr looks at Ivy. "We need to discuss the details, but with only adults present."

"Does that include me?" Lydia mutters under her breath.

"Depends on the day," I mutter back.

"I think this is a sound plan," Mikhail says. "We should follow Viktor's lead."

I nod. Lydia frowns but doesn't reply.

I watch as she plays with her roll but doesn't eat it. We pass the food around, and she takes the smallest bit of chicken and a bunch of lettuce, her gaze darting nervously around the room. I've watched how she gets self-conscious when she's going to eat in front of a crowd of people. I wonder if she holds any of those memories of her school days and the relentless teasing of her classmates.

Ivy reaches for her glass and spills it on herself. Harper helps us clean up. "Alright, I'm sorry to tear you away from Uncle Viktor, but we need to clean you up." She stands up and takes her away from the table.

I move closer to Lydia.

"Why aren't you eating?" I ask in her ear.

"I lost my appetite," she whispers back, but I know it's probably a lie. She hasn't eaten much since she arrived, likely because she's uncomfortable around everyone here.

"Stop it. You're perfect, Lydia. Eat."

She rolls her eyes at me, but I can see a smile tugging at her lips. I reach for the food and put more on her plate.

I eat while I talk with my brothers, and we form a plan. I'll teach Lydia self-defense, and we'll ensure the wedding is postponed and held in the safest place possible, surrounded by our men. "And the good thing about this," Harper says thoughtfully, joining us again, "is that it will give us time to secure everything."

"Alright." Lydia seems reluctant to agree. "How long?"

"Another month. Make him wait. That's plenty of time for me to teach you, and by then, Vera will be at the end of her program and able to come home."

She still isn't eating.

"Excuse me," Lydia says. "Where is the restroom?" Something is troubling her.

I stand. "I'll show you."

"You can just tell me where it is," she says, her tone sharp.

"I'll go with you," I insist, my hand on her elbow. I guide her into the hallway, and as soon as the dining room door closes behind us, I push her up against the wall, leaning on my forearm to cage her in.

"Viktor," she hisses, her cheeks flushed. "This isn't the time or place."

"It is always the time," I counter. "And I can always find a place. Now. Tell me what the hell is going on." I take her chin in my hand, tilting her face up to mine. "You're holding something back. What is it?"

She tries to look away, but I grab her chin and bring her gaze back to mine. I bend down and touch my lips to hers. She tastes like honey and sunshine, evoking memories of warm summer days. She tries to push me away, but I don't let her. I wrap my hand around the back of her neck and deepen the kiss. Our tongues meet, and she moans into me, softening.

When we finally break the kiss, we're both panting.

"Tell me now, Lydia," I warn her, "or I'll drag you into the office and fuck it out of you."

"That's supposed to stop me? Maybe I want you to. Maybe I want you to take control and show me that you actually want me instead of talking about it, skirting the issue, treating me like I'm made of glass, and then announcing to everyone that you don't want to marry me."

"What the fuck are you talking about?" I temper my anger so I don't snap. I will not let it consume me. I will always, always be careful around my Lydia.

She juts her chin out defiantly. "You say you want me, and then at the first opportunity, you put off our wedding. Why don't you fucking show me you want me?"

Ahh. There we go. There's the truth.

"Is that what you want?"

My dick is painfully hard. I want her. I want her so fucking bad.

Her eyes blaze into mine. "Prove it."

Her voice is a mixture of anger and challenge, and I can't resist any longer. I grab her wrist and yank her to me. The shock in her eyes only fuels my desire.

When she digs in her heels and tries to get away, I lift her up and toss her over my shoulders. She screams and pounds at my back, so I step out the first exit that takes towards the garden.

"Let me *down!*" she yells. I know now that her protests and screams are part of our dance. She pushes, and I don't yield. I push back, and she melts. She's at my mercy.

It's better than I ever fucking imagined.

I stalk out the back door into the garden. It's turned into a cool evening, in stark contrast to the heat of her temper. She's so cute and would probably hate it if I told her so. She's like a little petulant kitten who didn't get her way, trying to claw in retribution with barely there claws.

I stop near a large oak tree, its branches providing a canopy that shields us from onlookers. I push her against the rough bark, my body pressed into hers, trapping her in. "You want me to prove it?"

I capture her mouth in a bruising kiss, one hand gripping her hair while the other slides down the length of her curvy body. I groan into her mouth, my dick throbbing as she gasps against my lips. She bites down, the taste of copper in my mouth.

I growl and move my hand under her dress. I rip away her panties in one tear.

"Viktor!"

Her voice is breathless, but there's no turning back now. I lift her, wrapping her legs around my waist, and press her harder against the tree. The rough bark bites into her back when I pin her wrists above her head with one hand, the other undoing my belt. I yank it out of the loops and loop it in my fist.

"Tell me you want this. Tell me you need it."

She glares up at me, her chest heaving. "I hate you."

I snap the belt across her thigh. My dick throbs when she yelps as I lower my mouth to her ear. "Liar."

With one hand still holding her wrists, I yank out my cock and position myself at her entrance. Teasing her. Relishing the way she squirms. Her body arches as if subconsciously begging me to come closer, but I hold back.

I want to savor this. Her frustration. Her need.

"Damn it," she says, her voice almost a moan. A plea. "Just do it."

"You want me?"

I tease her entrance with the head of my cock. Her wet heat is driving me wild.

"Yes, fine, fucking *yes*," she growls, shaking her head at me. "*Do it,* you jerk."

I slap her again with the belt. "Watch that mouth before I give you another use for it," I growl in her ear. I whip her again until she's whimpering and needy, clinging to me.

I thrust into her, hard and deep, drawing a cry from her. I set a punishing rhythm, each thrust marking her as mine. "Feel that? Is that fucking clear enough? Do you *feel* how much I want you?"

Letting go of her wrists, she moans, her nails scraping into my back. I relish the taste of pain as I bury myself inside her. I close my eyes and groan. I've imagined this, imagined having her, but it felt so out of reach, and it never felt this fucking good.

I wrap my hands around her hips, yanking her to me to pull her closer. Deeper.

Her hands grip my head, her legs tightening around me as she meets my thrusts. The garden muffles the slap of our bodies colliding.

"Viktor... I... I can't," she pants.

"Let go. Let yourself fucking go."

With a shuddering cry, she breaks. Submits. Yields. Her body convulses around me as she reaches her climax. I follow on her heels, muffling my own cries in her hair as she rests her head in the crook of my neck.

"You see?" I whisper. "You're mine. You'll accept that eventually. Now, get over my move to bring out our enemies. The only purpose is to keep you safe. You're already mine, Lydia. *Mine.*"

I kiss her, and the world fades. She trembles slightly as if she's crying, but when I pull away, her eyes are only shining brightly on me, and there are no tears.

I know she feels it—the pull between us, the twisted bond that holds us together.

"When we get back, everybody's going to know that something happened," she says, tossing her beautiful hair. I'm hit with a faint floral, seductive scent that is all Lydia.

I shake my head. "They don't know shit. They know you're going to be my wife. And they know that I want you. They know we have things to discuss. Don't overthink it."

I entwine her hand with mine, still high from what just happened. I suspected that Lydia liked sex like this. I've known for a long time that she and I are well-suited for each other. The possibilities that lie before us...

"If you say so," she says. And for the first time since she came into my custody, Lydia is almost... demure. Quiet. It's like the raging storm inside her has settled to a simmer.

I bend down and kiss her forehead. "You're a good girl, Lydia. I know sometimes I scare you. But I don't want you to be afraid of me." I bend and kiss her cheek. "I know that talk is cheap, and you may not believe that I want you—that I want you more than anything else in the entire world. I get that. And that's okay. You'll know."

"What?" she asks, her eyes wide with curiosity and a hint of fear.

I hold her gaze, my voice low and intense. "You'll see how much you mean to me… and why."

When we get back to the house, the dining room is cleared, and everyone is in the living room. My mother has large trays of pastries and chocolates laid out for us.

I lean in close to Lydia as we walk in. "You see this?" I gesture to the spread. "When we were little, my father had strict rules. Everything had to be eaten in the dining room. No snacking in bedrooms, no casual breakfasts in the kitchen, and absolutely no dessert in the living room."

Lydia raises an eyebrow, intrigued. "And now?"

I smirk, nodding toward my mother. "Now, she's in charge. Things are different. She likes to break his rules."

Lydia smiles, understanding the subtle rebellion. "I like her already."

"And if something spills, we clean it up," my mother says, smiling warmly. "Lydia, let's talk about what kind of cake you want. Now that we have more time, we can actually plan this wedding." She practically rubs her hands together with glee.

"Honestly," Lydia says, "I like all kinds of cake. Well, I *don't* like vanilla."

A corner of my lips quirks up. "Me neither, baby," I whisper in her ear. Her cheeks color, and she continues as if I didn't say anything, "Red velvet, carrot cake, chocolate cake with vanilla frosting, chocolate cake with chocolate frosting…"

She looks down at her curvy figure and her hips. "Maybe that's my problem."

"Oh, stop," my mother says. "Who doesn't love cake? Let's go take a look at some options."

"With me, Mom," I tell her. "I want to plan this with her."

As we walk over to the side table, where my mom has an array of catalogs and her laptop, I lean in and whisper into Lydia's ear and pinch her ass. "If you make one more self-deprecating comment about your body, you're going over my knee when we get home for that."

"Viktor," she says, her cheeks flushing, but a surge of power courses through me. I may have just had her, but I want her all over again. And she absolutely is getting a spanking for that.

"Take a look," my mom says, spreading the glossy catalogs out. "How can we make it so that we have a variety of different cakes?" Lydia asks, stroking her chin thoughtfully.

"Oh, that's easy," Harper says. "You do cake shooters. Like these little glasses with a variety of different flavors so we can try different ones. You have your own wedding cake in your favorite flavor, and then we have a groom's cake in his favorite flavor, and then we have trays and trays of cake."

"I'm already getting a sugar rush just thinking about it," Mikhail says.

"That's fine," Aria says, her eyes twinkling. She winks at Lydia. "More for me."

As Lydia peruses the catalogs, I walk over and put a variety of desserts on a plate.

We sit in the living room, eating dessert, drinking cocktails, and planning our wedding. But what I really want is to take her home with me, so it's only the two of us. What I really want is to make sure we have a plan in place for self-defense. What I really want is for her to be married, safe, and by my side.

Mikhail walks over to us and shows me his phone. "Interesting development. You have a minute?"

I glance at Lydia, then back at him. "Yeah, let's talk."

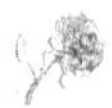

CHAPTER EIGHTEEN

Lydia

"I'VE SPOKEN with the Ivanov captain. He's got some interesting data, but it's all encrypted, and there's foreign language embedded I don't know."

Hope surges in my chest.

This. This is something I can do. Finally, instead of being a damn wallflower waiting to be protected or rescued, I can actually help.

"Let me look? I'm good at this."

Mikhail's eyes widen in surprise. He looks to Viktor, who nods.

"She is. Let her look."

Back in Mikhail's office here at headquarters, with a few of the brothers present, they've laid out a series of maps, surveillance photos, and weapons. Mikhail opens up the largest iPad I've ever seen and flips the brightness up.

"Here. Take a look."

I've always been good at deciphering patterns and intricate puzzles. This one takes me a moment as I look at the notes they've used.

"Dmitri," I say, my heart beating faster as I start piecing things together. "It's his middle name. Super original to use that as his screen name, isn't it?" I shake my head. "It looks like they're not far from here, planning to take over a warehouse in Manhattan, but there's no telling when."

"Mmm." Viktor nods. "Of course they don't divulge the when in case their intel was intercepted."

"How much do you trust the Ivanov captain?" I ask, frowning as I look things over. "This sort of looks like a trap."

"Fuck," Lev mutters. "Let me see."

I hand him the map, and after a moment of perusing it, he nods, frowning.

"She's right. The timing is off. If I were setting up an ambush... well, this is how I would do it. The routes they've highlighted funnel us into a choke point, perfect for an attack. It's too convenient."

I shake my head.

Viktor's eyes narrow as he scrutinizes the details. "You're right. If we take his word for it, this could be a setup. We can't take that risk."

"I would suspect that either he's in on this with them, or they know he's going to report to you. In any event, it's dangerous, and I'd be careful."

Aleks curses under his breath, running a hand through his hair. "So we just let him do his thing? Don't pursue it?"

"We will absolutely fucking pursue when the time is right."

"Right. Agreed. And when the time is right, we can create a diversion. Let them think we're falling into their trap."

"I have an idea," I tell them. "Maybe send a decoy team through the highlighted route while backup circles in from behind. Catch them off guard."

Viktor nods appreciatively. "I like how you think, doll."

I grin and pop a cocoa-dusted truffle in my mouth and groan.

"Oh God, get a room," a tall blonde who must be Viktor's sister says from the doorway. She winks at me. "I'm Polina. I kid, I kid. Any friend of chocolate is a friend of mine."

Viktor's arm snakes around my waist. "When we do counter, we'll show them who we're dealing with when we're paired together."

I grin. "Yup."

"For now, we're heading back," he says to Polina. "We'll be in touch about the wedding details."

"So soon?" Polina asks with a pout. "I need to get to know your bride, though."

"We'll have time," he says, but he's obviously a million miles away, completely preoccupied with the threat against us.

The ride home is intense, fraught with need and want and innuendo as he kneads my thigh with his huge palm and tells me every wicked thing he's planning to do to me.

"I have a surprise for you outside," he says when we arrive.

My heart beats a little faster, but I manage to brush it off. "Dude, if it's more sex… we might consider a bed next time."

He only growls and narrows his eyes.

Do I want this? I don't want to lose control to anyone.

But when he insists… it makes my heart expand in my chest.

I feel *wanted*.

"Alright, alright…" I walk where he gestures. I haven't really explored the grounds outside his house yet.

"This. Over here."

I turn the corner and cover my mouth with my hand when I take it all in. "Viktor."

He knows me. How does he know me so well?

Nestled in the secluded, lush gardens that surround his estate, there's a fire pit area, an oasis that looks as if it were designed specifically for someone who… likes fire.

No. *Loves* fire.

It looks somehow gothic and enchanting here like it was lifted straight out of a fairy tale. The fire pit itself is a large, intricate design made of black iron, resting on a base reminiscent of gnarled tree roots. The iron is carved with patterns of flames and runes, giving it a mystical, timeless appearance.

The pit has built-in compartments for kindling and logs, as well as a custom grate for controlling the intensity of the flames. A wrought iron poker and tongs hang from the side, ready for use.

Surrounding the fire pit are heavy, dark wooden benches cushioned with deep, wine-colored velvet. Gothic-style lanterns hang from wrought iron posts, casting a warm, flickering glow across the space. String lights are woven through the surrounding trees, their soft twinkle making it feel magical.

"Viktor... is this for...?"

"You? Yeah. Of course it is."

I swallow, a mixture of honor and fear warring within me. "I... I don't know how to feel."

Leaning in, he kisses my cheek. "That's alright."

"How did you know?" I hold his gaze. "Tell me the truth."

With a casual shrug that almost makes him appear boyish, he looks away. "I've been following you for a while. I know you were sent away to boarding school when your father couldn't keep you in control, and you were booked on charges of arson. I know even your mother tried to stop you, but her methods involved trying to marry you off to the next suitor who would help you." He shakes his head. "There's sadly a shortage of people who understand your need."

I swallow. "My need?"

He strikes a match. "Your need to set fire, baby."

He takes a step toward me. "Let your wall down. Stop fighting, Lydia. You're safe here." He gestures. "Look. The fire won't go beyond these brick walls." I look around and notice for the first time the space filled with candles and match-sticks, a stack of firewood, and a flame thrower.

I can already feel the way my pulse races when I strike a match. The way my breathing regulates at that first smell of smoke. The utter control I have watching flames wreak havoc, devastation just there, at my fingertips.

I look away and don't respond.

"What is it? Why the hesitation?"

Why do I feel so much more confident with him than I've ever felt before? Like he *knows* me, really, truly knows me.

I wonder if making love to one another the way we have—the way he tears down my walls and splits me wide open, making me feel vulnerable and exposed—is why I feel like finally, for the first time in my life, I can actually be myself.

"Lydia. What is it?"

"I was always told that something was wrong with me. That I was broken. That I should avoid anything that had to do with fire…"

I look away from him, the weight of his gaze too much to bear. "It's troubling to me that you know so much about me."

"Accept it. I've been looking for a very, very long time. I've always been obsessed with you, Lydia. That might frighten you, but I don't want it to because I am going to protect you." He strokes my hair down the length of my back. I step closer to him. "You're going to be my wife."

Something surges within me, a confusing mix of fear and excitement. He gets me. It feels like he really gets me. A part of me is freaked out, but another part of me feels… relief.

"So what do you know about me? What do you know about my past?"

"I know that you were sent to school away from home because you were convicted of arson," he says, holding my gaze without fear or hesitation. "I know that you were labeled a pyromaniac, and people feared you. But I know you aren't someone to be feared. I suspect you're a victim of being labeled and misunderstood."

My breathing hitches in my throat. It scares me that he knows me so well.

"Listen. I've noticed your fascination with fire, Lydia. I built this for you—a place where you can indulge in your passions safely. Fire can be beautiful and controlled. It doesn't have to be destructive." He reaches for me, cupping my jaw in the palm of his hand. "I like to think that we're alike in this way."

"How?" I swallow hard, trying to keep my voice steady.

"We're both attracted to fire, baby."

He bends and captures my mouth in a kiss. My toes curl at the feel of his warm mouth on mine, need thrumming through my body. I feel alive, energized. I feel like I've fallen out of my mind and fully into my body, every vibrating, living cell of being.

When he pulls away, a faint smile touches his lips.

"Go ahead, Lydia. Do it."

Taking my hand, he leads me to sit next to the fire pit. He strikes a match and holds a candle up to me, the scent of warm vanilla toffee filling the air around us. His voice hardens, his words a command. *"Do it."*

My hands tremble as I light the match, but excitement courses through me at the first lick of flame. The addictive smell of the lit match fills my senses. I light the candle and watch it burn, the flame dancing between us.

I want more. I lick my lips and swallow. "Give me another one."

"Say please," he teases.

"Please, Viktor," I breathe, holding my hand out.

"Remember," Viktor says as he lifts another candle from the large array before us, this one in a light-pink matte, smelling faintly of strawberries. "There's a difference between fascination and compulsion, Lydia. Pyromania is an uncontrollable urge to set destructive fires. But here, you can explore that fascination without harm. Control is the key."

I light another match and shake my head, adrenaline coursing through me at the beautiful way the light flickers in the dark.

"Control? I've never felt like I had control over it. It just... took over."

"Really? When was the last time you set a fire? A real fire, not a candle or something small."

"It's been a long time." I lower my voice, ashamed. "I've learned to suppress my primal urges. The need to burn things, to consume everything when I'm stressed and anxious. I'm better now."

"Maybe you don't need to get better. If you were a real pyromaniac, you wouldn't have been able to do that." He lifts up a beautiful cylinder box of long, thick matches. "Light them. Throw them in the fire pit."

I sit beside a camping chair in front of the fire, take out one of the long matches, and strike it. I watch it lick up the thin wood until it almost reaches my fingers before I toss it into the pit. I do it again and again, watching the flame with exhilaration and the slightest hint of fear.

Am I like an alcoholic who just took a sip of a drink? Or have I mislabeled myself all this time?

As the growing line of lit candles fills the space with a warm glow, I walk between them. My feet are so light I practically feel like I'm dancing, free in the mesmerizing, intimate light they create.

Viktor stands, his huge arms crossed over his chest, nodding approvingly. "You're in control, Lydia. Feel the power without fear. It's not about destruction. This is about understanding and embracing what you love. You're safe."

I swallow the lump in my throat when he says that.

I'm secure.

Sheltered.

Out of harm's way.

My entire life, I've never felt safe, and I knew that when I lit those fires as a child and then as a teen—all that time I spent in juvenile hall, I was trying to gain some control. My mother had little interaction with me when I was younger, thanks to my father's grip on me. And Father didn't love me; he was only trying to mold me into the person he wanted me to be. His heir, the son he never had.

As the firelight casts shadows on our faces, highlighting the intensity of my emotions, I feel a sense of liberation. My fear melts away as he moves closer, his hand caressing my cheek, his touch tender and possessive. My breath quickens, my eyes darting from flame to flame, reveling in the reflection of the flickering flames in his eyes.

"I've never felt this way before."

Viktor kisses my cheek. "You're safe with me, Lydia. Always. Let the fire be part of you, not something to fear."

His lips brush against mine, the evening warmed by the firelight. The connection is intense, fueled by the shared moment of vulnerability and understanding... maybe even love. Safety is a beautiful, powerful mutual attraction.

He bends me back so he can kiss my neck. I let myself melt into the heat that consumes me, surrounded by flames, when he lifts me into his arms, and my legs encircle his thick, muscled torso. I never in my dreams imagined being with a man who could carry a curvy woman like me in his arms like this. But Viktor's no ordinary mortal.

His footsteps unhurried, Viktor kisses me like we're the last people on earth, the only two standing while the world around us burns to rubble. My tongue meets his, the sound of his deep, manly growl making my own need for him amp higher and higher with every second that passes.

This time, I didn't bite or claw. This time, he doesn't spank my ass or dominate me. This time, he's slow and seductive, and by the time he sits us in the chair by the fire pit, I'm so wet and eager to have him inside me, I can't think beyond being filled by him.

He lifts my skirt and puts me bare-assed on his lap while he kisses my neck and scrapes his teeth along my collarbone. I whimper when he sucks and licks, flames of arousal growing between us. He moves me to his knee for seconds while he unfastens his buckle and pulls his hard, firm erection into his fist.

"We haven't talked about birth control," I whisper, a little afraid of where this will all take us.

The head of his hard cock meets my core, and I move involuntarily closer to him. I want him in me so badly I can hardly breathe.

He shakes his head, his eyes intent on mine. "Nothing between us, Lydia. Fucking nothing. You'll have my babies, woman." I half expect him to pound his chest and fist my hair, but he only holds my gaze.

I nod. "Yeah."

I want children, too, when it happens naturally. I couldn't walk away from this marriage—I tried, and I'm starting to realize... I'm not sure I want to.

With the first thrust, I throw my head back, anchoring myself on his shoulders, my arms wrapped around his strong neck. With the second, he's splitting me open, and I whimper with need and want, my pleasure building as he thrusts in and nearly fully out of me before he plunges in my heat again and again. My head tips back, and he tears my dress down the middle so it pushes my full breasts up.

His mouth is on my nipple, his teeth grazing the tender bud while he thrusts in and out, his thick cock pulsing inside me. I'm losing myself to him as I near climax, as I near surrender. My need builds and grows until it encompasses my entire being. My eyelids flutter closed. The flames around us flicker and ebb as my ecstasy erupts.

I scream as I come, pleasure flooding me. I throw my head back as his hot seed lashes into me. His bite becomes savage, his grip nearly painful.

"I love you, Lydia," he growls, more of a fiery claim than a flowery whim. "I love you, whether you know it or not, and I will continue to tell you this until one day, someday, you actually believe me." He thrusts again as we climax in unison, joined in our pleasure.

There's some kind of cognitive dissonance to his words and my ability to accept them.

How?

When my breathing begins to steady, he settles me in a chair and reaches for a blanket. He wordlessly kisses my temple before he rises. A few moments later, he returns with a warm washcloth and a dry towel. First, he inspects me with a frown, likely looking to see if he's broken skin or bit too hard.

"Not this time, tiger," I say with a wink. "You'll have to try again. I love the way you clean me up after you've defiled me," I say, only half teasing. "The way you're so gentle with me after you've fucked me hard."

"It's the least I can do. I'm blinded when we make love. I worry I'll hurt you when I unleash on you."

It's only been minutes since I came, and still, hearing him say *unleash* makes my pulse race all over again.

"Eh," I say with a shrug. "I can take a lot more than that."

His gaze on me intensifies. "Oh, really?"

"Mhm."

"I'll keep that in mind."

I'm too languid to build a fire, so I watch him do it. We sit in silence until the flame dies to glowing embers. I feel a profound sense of peace and acceptance.

"I had no idea I needed this." I look at him. "Thank you, Viktor, for showing me that I can have this without fear."

"You're stronger than you know."

I wonder as I sit before the fire encased in brick...

Am *I* something to be controlled? Something to be held back? Or will I be consumed in the flames?

What if I lose myself to him?

I reach for another match, the question hanging in the air between us, waiting to be answered.

CHAPTER NINETEEN

Lydia

CAKE. I need cake.

Deep, dark, rich, chocolatey cake with thick icing.

Or marble. Maybe lemon. I mean, beggars can't be choosers.

I need to get away from myself. I need a distraction. And while a small part of me knows that nibbling myself into a diabetic coma may not be the most responsible thing to do... I need cake.

It's the middle of the night, Viktor's dead asleep, and even Nikita only opens one lazy eye to see what I was up to before she falls back asleep and starts snoring.

I walk down to the kitchen in Viktor's tee. It billows around me because he's the size of a lion. I have no idea where his mother must've gotten his shoes or clothes from when he was younger. Did she make them herself?

I'm bare under the tee, and it feels nice walking around the house barefoot like this.

The tee smells like him.

When I get to the kitchen, I open the fridge. I've opened it to cook for both of us a few times now, but I haven't really taken the time to *look* look. Like, really get in there and see.

At first, when I open the door, I note my favorite beer, the craft kind you can only buy in Upstate New York because they hand make it in small batches and don't widely distribute it.

Interesting. Did Viktor buy this for me? Or does he somehow miraculously like the same things I do?

I finger the cold bottle.

I still want cake, and while beer and cake together are a thing according to some people, I'm a bit of a purist.

I reach for the carton of milk and pause, my hand on the carton. "Huh," I say out loud.

How does he know I only drink organic milk? While I'm hardly a natural foodie, I've only had organic milk since I was in high school and read an article that hinted at the correlation between a woman's boob size and hormones in milk. While I have no idea if the claims were true, I did anything and everything I could to *not* let my boobs get any bigger, so I started drinking organic milk.

I frown, staring at the fridge. Well, he doesn't know me that well. If he knew me that well, he'd know that when I drink milk *without* cake, I don't drink it plain; I always—*oh*. Oh, interesting.

Well, everyone has chocolate syrup in their fridge.

Right?

I pour myself a glass and go to shut the door when something else catches my eye. There's a tray of chocolate-dipped strawberries, garnished with an artsy little swizzle of white sprinkles. There's also a package of handmade macarons, light and airy, their rainbow hues hinting at an array of flavors. Oh my God, temptation fell from heaven and is sitting right here in front of me.

When did he get these? We met with his family a week ago, and I admitted my love for cake. Though… something tells me none of that was news to Viktor.

I peek in the freezer out of curiosity and shake my head. I swallow. There are three different types of hand-packed ice creams from a local dairy, all in my favorite flavors—moose tracks, peanut butter swirl, and cookies and cream.

That can't be a coincidence. *It can't.*

I shut the freezer, my mouth watering. Now I'm legit starving.

So he has my favorite ice cream.

My favorite desserts.

Even the damn chocolate syrup and milk I drink.

Out of curiosity, I walk over to the pantry.

There's no way—

I yank open the door. It's huge and well stocked, the kind of pantry that could make a woman who loves cooking lose her mind.

The first thing I note is the tubs of protein powders and shaker bottles in here, obviously because Viktor can't magically grow to his size without some intentional decisions. Fair, fair.

But when I scan past the protein powders and shakes, I stifle a gasp. Gourmet, kettle-cooked chips. Sourdough pretzels. Jars of my favorite peach salsa and lime-flavored corn chips. A variety of flavored nuts. The honey-roasted peanut butter I slather on buttery crackers and Italian chocolate-hazelnut spread that I eat by the spoonful.

He has *everything*.

I shut the pantry and head back toward the fridge.

I'm eating the damn cake.

I open the door and remove the large white pastry box Polina brought over, along with a canister of whipped cream. I grab a spoon from the drawer and prop myself up on one of the stools.

Just one bite. I'll just take one bite.

I will die of mortification if he comes in here and sees me. I don't eat the shit out of dessert in front of anyone.

I take a dollop of the red velvet first and a generous taste of the cream cheese frosting. I squirt whipped cream on it, and boom, down the hatch.

I moan, savoring the taste of it. I've been so damn *good* on my diet, and I've missed this so much. I lick my lips and swallow before I reach for a taste of the marble cake.

I swirl a good-sized bite onto the spoon, top it, and eat it. Oh, yeah, that's even better than the chocolate. This is perfection. If the best sex known to man were magically converted into a cake, it's right here.

Next up, strawberry with vanilla bean icing. I stifle a snort to myself.

I don't like vanilla, I said, right in front of his family and everything. *God.*

I take a bite of the spice cake with cream cheese icing and another of the red velvet. My belly is content. I swing my legs on the stool and swipe my finger right through the billows of whipped cream frosting on a strawberry short-cake layer cake.

"Did you save some for me?"

I drop the can of whipped cream to the floor with a bang.

Viktor stands in the doorway, leaning against the doorframe, bare-chested, but still wearing his jeans slung low about his waist.

"You can't just sneak up on me. You scared the shit out of me!"

"You should pay more attention. I'm not exactly a small person who sneaks around the house. Seems you were too busy with the cake samples."

My cheeks color, and I toss the spoon in the box as he walks up and stands behind me.

"Don't be embarrassed."

"I'm not." My cheeks burn hotter.

"Liar."

He walked in on me totally binging on cake straight out of the box, licking whipped cream from a spoon. Timur would berate me.

"I'm not embarrassed," I insist, shaking my head.

"Woman," he says, his hands on either side of my hips. "I love everything you do. I'm not going to judge you. I came in here because I want to try the fucking cake. But if you want to get freaked out, I'm happy to give you a reason to blush."

"*Viktor.*"

"*Lydia,*" he mimics as he leans over me, his back flat against my torso and his hands on either side of the counter. "Relax."

He reaches into the box and takes out a spoon. "But I'm the one who feeds it to you."

"Is everything about sex?" I tease, my heart beating faster. I swallow.

"Of course. If it wasn't, how would humanity continue?"

I snort and shake my head. "I'm done anyway," I tell him, eying the rest of the flavors with regret. I am definitely not done.

"Did you even try the lemon coconut or the German chocolate?"

I shake my head.

"Hands in your lap, please," he orders. I obediently slide my hands into my lap as he lifts the spoon and scoops out a generous taste of lemon. "Open for me. The only rule is, *I* get to feed you, and then I get to do whatever the fuck I want to you."

"Is that all?" I ask teasingly.

"I promise you'll like it."

I nod and lick my lips. My mouth waters. "Alright."

He stands in front of me and places the spoon on the counter before he reaches in and lifts me bodily. I squeal as he slides me into the middle of the corner. The tee skates up my leg, baring myself to him.

"Fuck, woman," he says, shaking his head before he kneels down in front of me.

In front of me.

He leans in and inhales my scent. My pussy clenches. I close my eyes when the feel of his hot mouth on my sex makes me squirm with need and desire for him.

The first touch of his tongue to my pussy makes me whimper. By the second and third, I'm drowning in sensation, and he's suckling my throbbing clit. With a reluctant sigh, he gets to his feet.

"I could do that all fucking day."

"Oh, *really?*" I tease, shaking my head. "I'll remember that."

"But first… cake."

"You sound like a placard you'd find in a bakery."

He shrugs a shoulder and puts my hands behind my back. "Keep them there." The sound of his voice sends a shiver down my spine, and when he reaches for his belt, my pulse skyrockets.

"Viktor—"

"Shhh."

He tugs the belt through the loops in one motion, leans back, and loops it around my hands. When he cinches it, his body's pressed up against mine, and it's instant fire. I swallow hard, trying to get a grip, when he adjusts me so I'm leaning back on the counter.

Leaning in, he lifts the whole piece of lemon cake in his hand and offers me a bite. "Where are your manners?" I ask teasingly.

"Ladies first," he says as if that's the only rule that matters.

I lick my tongue out and scoop the lemon icing into my mouth. "Mmm," I moan. "Oh God, this is delicious." I take a bite. The cake is light and fluffy, with a thick layer of lemon filling sandwiched between layers. I lick his fingers, and he growls before he takes the rest of the cake and eats it in one huge gulp. He leans in and captures my mouth with his, our kiss laced with icing and cake, sweet and indulgent.

I'm still licking my lips when he's down between my legs, his mouth on my pussy. My clit throbs, and I stifle a scream as he licks and suckles and bites. My legs are over his shoulders, my knees pressed against the heat of his skin, when he leaves my pussy and goes back to the box.

"Viktor," I whine. "Please."

"Not yet," he growls, reaching into the box for another slice of chocolate, this one layered with peanut butter frosting.

"You're hungry for cake," he says with a smile. "*I'm* hungry for cake. Let them eat cake."

This time, he paints my lips with the icing, like edible lip gloss. I'm grinning, covered in chocolate crumbs, as he places a piece in my mouth and kneels in front of me again. This time, I'm on the cusp of climax when I swallow the last bite of cake, and I nearly cry when he takes his mouth off me.

"Be a good girl," he says, shaking his head at me. "I promise it will be worth it."

He reaches for the pièce de résistance, a quadruple-layered concoction of deep, dark chocolate cake layered between thick layers of ganache. "Here. Eat this," he says, feeding me a piece with his rough fingers. I lick and nibble his fingers as he feeds me. I love the way his eyes flare with arousal. Again, he places the cake in my mouth, this time a large portion that spills onto the tee. The icing tastes like melted truffles, and I am *here for it*. He kneels in front of me, wraps my legs around his head, and growls against my leg, "Come, Lydia. You eat your treat, and I'll eat mine. Come, baby."

My head falls back as he laps my pussy again and again; the tip of his tongue is perfect as I lick the crumbs from my lips, savor the rich taste of chocolate, and soar toward release on his tongue. Waves of pleasure drown me. My hips jerk toward him, milking every drop of pleasure, until I collapse on the counter, spent, my tied hands braced behind me.

My gaze is hazy, my body floating as he gets to his feet and drags a heavy hand across his mouth, his eyes boring into mine.

"Fucking delicious," he says in a low growl of a whisper. "Do you want any more?"

"Oh my God, no," I moan, completely sated. I watch him lazily, half drunk, half mesmerized, while he walks over to the cake, reaches in the box, and finishes every last crumb.

I watch in a daze as he cleans up the mess we made—tosses out the pastry box, puts the top on the whipped cream, and slides it into the fridge.

"How did you know?" I say sleepily. "All my favorites."

He gives me a casual shrug. "I've been watching, baby. That's all you need to know."

CHAPTER TWENTY

Viktor

THE NEXT FEW weeks with Lydia feel like a passing dream. Sometimes, I fear that I'm going to open my eyes and she'll be gone. I don't want it to be that way. I'm not sure I could stop it if I tried. Still, I don't take any of this for granted.

Despite the fact that both Lydia and Aria spend hours trying to anticipate the next attack planned by the *Ledyanoye Bratstvo,* we find no conclusive evidence that they're going to move soon. It might seem like they've shifted their focus.

I know better, though. We can't grow complacent. One of the biggest mistakes we could make is letting our guard down.

So I don't. And Lydia doesn't fucking like it, but I don't care.

It helps that she has a job here with me and my family. My job is of a physical nature—I'm the group heavy. I'm the one everyone comes to when they need a heavy hand or muscle. All of my brothers can hold their own, but no one does it quite like I do. That means Lydia gets to accompany me, for better or for worse.

For better or for fucking worse.

There's no use pretending to be someone other than who I really am. When we marry each other, we'll accept each other for who we are completely, no holds barred. I never understood how anyone would bother doing any less.

I'm going to make it worth her while, though. I swear I am. I'm trying now.

"Alright, so let's go over what you've learned."

I've given her a crash course in basic self-defense that Kolya taught all of us: escape holds and grabs, situational awareness, defense maneuvers, and the use of everyday objects. There's no time to teach her to shoot.

"Okay," she says, standing in front of me in a fighting stance. She's wearing a hot-pink tank top, black leggings, and sneakers. She's lucky I need to teach her, or I'd tear those off and fuck her right up against the side of the house. "Use the flat of my palm or a hard kick against vulnerable areas if I can—eyes, nose, throat, and groin."

I nod. "Go on."

"Don't lose my shit if someone's got me in a hold but focus on escaping. Pay attention to the surroundings and use what I can to my advantage."

I don't want her to have to use the skills I'm teaching her. I want her self-defense moves to be an absolute last fucking resort.

Still, she needs to know.

"Like?" I test, my eyes boring into hers.

"Like if we're near the fire pit. Push them off kilter so their foot hits the drain grate, then shove them into the fire like the wicked witch in *Hansel and Gretel*." Her eyes gleam, and she grins at me.

I grin back. "You've given this some thought."

"Yes, sir," she says in a seductive purr. Good thing she just talked about kicking the groin, or I'd be hard as fuck right now.

"Go on about escape."

"Stay calm. Shout for help as loud as I can. Use my screaming voice." She winks. "Strike if possible, lower my center of gravity, turn, and face my attacker."

"Excellent." Pride swells in my chest. "That's my girl. What else?"

"Use everyday objects if possible. Pens, keys, my handbag weighted down with the latest spree at Sephora."

I nod. "Excellent."

Nikita paws at the back door, jealous of the attention I'm giving to Lydia.

"Take a walk?"

"Mhm."

I get Nikita's leash, and we walk downtown, Nikita obediently heeling by my side. We stop at a stoplight, and Lydia bends down to scratch Nikita's ears.

I thought I loved Lydia before she moved in here. But now that she loves my dog, I'm fucking gone.

"I was thinking of making chicken parm for dinner," she says casually.

"That makes me fucking hard," I tease her.

She grins at me. "I never met a man who was turned on by the food he ate."

"Not turned on by the food I eat. I'm turned on watching you cook it."

"Oh, I get it. Satisfying all the appetites and all that?"

"MHM. That sounds delicious. On Friday night, when we're planning the final details, we'll go out to dinner. Sound good?"

I don't cook. I eat. And if I'm not with someone who can cook, I order in. I had a private chef for a while, but I didn't like it. I don't like anybody in my space except Lydia. It's her space too.

All of a sudden, Nikita's ears go back. Her hair bristles, and she lets out a low, dangerous growl.

Lydia stands up straight. "What did I do? I thought she loved me."

"Behind me," I growl. "It's not you."

Lydia's eyes widen, and for once, she does what I say, thank fuck. I scan our surroundings. At first, I don't notice anything out of place. Just a normal night in the city. But Nikita growls deeper and lets out a loud, vicious bark.

Suddenly, a masked assailant leaps out from a doorway, followed by three more. All of them masked, hooded, and coming straight at us.

Lydia stiffens, a scream caught in her throat, and I bark over my shoulder, "Remember what I fucking taught you."

One attacks us head-on, gun raised. I know in my gut these guys aren't here to murder but to take her. A second reaches for me, a gun glinting in the overhead light. Before he shoots, Nikita is on him. She's got him by the leg with a savage snarl.

I elbow the second attacker in one swift motion, putting all my strength behind it. I hear a satisfying crunch as bone breaks, and he cries out, falling to the ground and clutching his face. The third barely has time to reach before I land a punch squarely between his eyes, sending him backward.

The fourth is one lucky son of a bitch still standing, still defiant. I want to beat the fucking shit out of him with my bare hands, but I need someone to interrogate. There's a dark, primal satisfaction in the idea of feeling his bones break under my fists, his blood staining my knuckles.

The air is thick with the scent of sweat and fear. One reaches for Lydia, and I can't get to him in time, but her eyes blaze with a fury that matches my own. She knees him hard between the legs, and when he crumples to the ground with a pained groan, she stabs at his eyes.

Good girl.

The sharp crack of a gunshot rings in my ears. Nikita cries out. Rage surges through my veins, hot and unrelenting. My vision narrows, and all I see is red.

"Keep one alive," I remind myself. I hang onto the one life-line that keeps me from murdering them all. I'm battling the need to kill, to make them all pay.

I grab the nearest one by the throat, slamming him against the wall. He's the only one conscious, his wide, terrified eyes staring into mine with a plea for mercy. The need to protect, to unleash my fury on him, wars with my need to get information.

"Why did you come after us?" I demand, my face inches from his. "Where the fuck are you coming from, and who do you report to?" He chokes out a weak, garbled response, and I loosen my grip just enough for him to speak.

Over my shoulder, I yell to Lydia, "Get my cell phone. Call Aleks and tell him to get a cleanup crew, now."

I hold him by the neck, but before he can get another word out, his head flings back, hitting the concrete, and a circle of crimson blossoms on the center of his forehead.

Lydia screams. I drop his body to the ground, shove her down, and cover her under my body. Fucking sniper. But no more shots come.

He was the target because I would have made him talk.

Someone killed him. Someone's watching. Someone doesn't want me to know what they're doing. Fuck.

A car pulls up, and I'm immediately alert, but Lydia breathes out, "It's Aleks."

Aleks and a team of our men quickly exit the vehicle. Aleks has been training two of the old Ivanov men, and they're here to help us, and they move in quick succession.

"They got away," I say. "But there's a sniper here, Aleks. He wants us scared but isn't ready to make a move."

"We'll cover every possible area to see where they could be hiding. I want everything swept."

It isn't until the scuffle ends, with our attackers either incapacitated or fled, that I notice the blood on Nikita's fur.

Lydia kneels beside Nikita, her hands trembling as she parts the dog's thick, black fur. "She's bleeding," she says, her voice breaking. There is a small, trickling wound on Nikita's side, but it isn't immediately clear what caused it.

"Is Nikita okay?" Lydia asks, her eyes filling with tears and her face flushed. Is she crying? I can't tell if she's crying. "She'll be okay, right? She's bleeding, Viktor."

"Are *you* alright?" I ask, even as a lump forms in my throat when I kneel beside them.

"I'm fine, I'm fine," Lydia says, though her hand is shaking.

I turn back to Nikita.

Shit. Nikita was hit. *Fuck*. My hands tremble. If someone hurt my dog... If someone fucking hurt my dog...

"Where's the entry point?" I mutter, frustration and fear clawing at me. I examine her closely, expecting to see a bullet wound. But there's nothing obvious, just the slow, persistent oozing of blood from somewhere beneath her dense fur.

Lydia's fingers are gentle but thorough as she probes around the wound. "It looks like the bullet grazed her," she says, sounding relieved. "But the fur is so thick, it's hard to tell exactly where it hit."

It makes sense. The bullet likely skimmed across Nikita's side, slicing through fur and skin without fully penetrating. The impact would have been enough to cause pain and bleeding but not the catastrophic damage I feared. Her fur, matted with blood, hides the exact entry point, making it difficult to see the full extent of the injury.

Lydia does a quick assessment. "She's breathing fine, but she seems like she's in pain." Her hands are steadying now as she gently presses around the area. "We need to get her to the vet to make sure there's no deeper injury. Let's get her to the vet, Viktor."

I have to make a choice—vet for Nikita or safety for Lydia.

"You to safety first, then the vet."

Lydia is crying, swiping at her eyes. "She was defending us."

"She'll be fine," I say, hoping that if I say it enough times, it'll become true.

Lydia looks up, her eyes lighting up. "Harper said Vera got in last night. My sister will know what to do. Even though she deals with human patients, a lot of her knowledge should transfer to pets."

"Where is she?"

"At your mom's."

"Let's get her to come to our place. We shouldn't move Nikita too much. Let's bring her there."

She makes a call. "Please, have Vera come to Viktor's."

We load Nikita into the back of Aleks's car. I sit beside Aleks while Lydia holds Nikita's head in her lap. She strokes her beautiful black fur and wipes her eyes.

As we drive, Lydia keeps Nikita's head in her lap, stroking her fur and whispering reassurances. Every so often, she glances at the wound, trying to see if there is more we can do. But the graze, while bloody, seems to be just that—a surface wound that hasn't penetrated deeply.

I hope.

"I hate him," Lydia whispers. "This is part of his game, isn't it?" she says, her voice trembling. "Any new developments, Aleks? Give me something to decipher, for fuck's sake."

"This is the first one," Aleks says. "Aria will send local blueprints. Might be able to find where the sniper was hiding."

She shakes her head. "Fucking bastard, he's such a coward. I hate him."

"Me too."

By the time we get back to the house, Nikko is on the phone. "We are ten minutes away. Anything else we need to know?"

"Her breathing is shallow," Aleks says. "I can't see where she was injured, but there's blood on the seat. She doesn't look good."

Lydia doesn't let go easily. She's messed up. So am I, but damn it. Was she shot? She had to be.

Back at my house, we get Nikita situated on the couch. Lydia sits with her head in her lap, and Nikko and Vera arrive.

"Vera," Lydia says. When she blinks, fat tears roll down her cheeks. Poor girl. She's traumatized by this. And, of course, she gets one look at her sister and her wild emotions surface. Who can blame her?

Vera walks in, all business. Her hair is tied up in a crazy knot on the top of her head. You can barely tell they're sisters. Lydia is all curves and feminine allure, while Vera has an intelligent grace about her, different from Lydia. But Lydia's eyes are wide and wet, and there's a little dimple on both their chins. The intelligence in their eyes and freckled noses tell me they're sisters. Vera runs to Lydia, wraps her arms around her, and gives her a fierce hug.

"I'm so sorry I couldn't come sooner."

"You were in Alaska," Lydia says, smiling. "I'm just glad you're here now. This is Nikita."

When Vera kneels in front of Nikita, Nikita growls at her. She's afraid, poor thing. I kneel beside her and stroke my thumb over her pretty head. "It'll be okay, girl. She's gonna take care of you. It's gonna be okay." As I gently stroke her head, Lydia begins to cry.

Vera takes her vitals. "Let's take a look. You think she was shot?"

She carefully cleans the wound, searching for any sign of a bullet fragment. "It's tricky," she says, frowning. "The fur is thick, and the skin is tough. It looks like the bullet just grazed her, but I can't find an entry point either."

I watch as she works, my heart still pounding with worry. Nikita lies still, her eyes closing in exhaustion but her breathing steady. The wound, hidden by her thick coat, is minor compared to what it could have been. But the uncertainty, the not knowing, gnaws at me.

"We'll take her to the vet," I say firmly. "Make sure there's nothing we've missed."

Vera frowns. "Agreed. I'm trained in medical science, specifically for trauma response," she tells me. "I don't know much about veterinary care, but I'll do my best to stabilize her. We need to get her to a veterinary hospital immediately."

"Of course."

"I'll call," Lydia says. "Aria will be able to get us an emergency vet sooner than anyone else could." She's reluctant to leave Nikita's side. I suspect she feels somehow responsible for this. She isn't, though. I know she isn't.

A moment later, Lydia looks up. "I've got a vet's name," she says. "It's thirty minutes out."

She looks at me, her eyes wide. "Do you think this is part of the plan, Viktor? Hurt Nikita so we have to take her to the vet, then chase us?"

I nod. "I do. Or put us off guard. Shake us."

She gets to her feet, her eyes alight with fire. "No *fucking way* are we being shaken. No way!"

I can't help myself. I reach for her, wrap my hand around the back of her neck, and kiss her hard. Vera blinks, watching us with wide eyes.

Aleks stands with his hands on his hips. "I'm on it," he says. "We'll go together."

It takes longer than I'd like, but all of my brothers come in force. Three armored cars line up outside. We move as one. Vera sits with Lydia in the backseat of the car I drive, Nikita between them. She lazily licks Vera's hand, and Vera bends and kisses her.

"Elevate her head," Vera says. "Just like that. You're doing great, Lydia."

Lydia sniffles, wiping at her cheeks. In the rearview mirror, I see Vera take her hand and give it a gentle squeeze. "You're doing great," she says again, her voice firm, and it hits me that she's not just talking about this incident.

"Feels like we're VIPs," Lydia says with a sad smile. "Like someone's coming to bring the president to the airport."

"As it should be, of course," Vera says with a smile. "Nikita's invaluable. We need her here with us."

She leans down and kisses the top of Nikita's head. Nikita's eyes close, and my heart thunders in my chest. "Vera," I say, panic in my voice.

"She's okay, Viktor. She's tired."

"I'll get your car cleaned," I tell Aleks.

"I don't fucking care about the car," he says. "I've got that all under control. You worry about her." I don't ask him which *her* he's referring to. They are both my world.

We finally get to the emergency vet. When we enter, there are only two other people in the waiting room: a little girl with a sick kitten on her lap and an older woman with a greyhound that looks like it has a broken leg. The staff runs to greet us.

"This way, Mr. Romanov," one of them says, ushering me, Vera, Lydia, and Nikita into a nearby room. My brothers take over the waiting room.

Vera takes charge. "My name is Vera Romanova. Medical-trained doctor"

"I know who you are," the vet says, extending her hand. "It's an honor to meet you, Dr. Romanova."

There's pride in Lydia's eyes as she smiles.

"We suspect a gunshot but have been unable to find an entry point."

The vet nods as if this were just another day, people bringing in dogs with gunshot wounds. "I see." She takes Nikita's vitals. "Her breathing is shallow. I'm going to put her to sleep, Mr. Romanov," she says.

Panic must show in my eyes because she quickly shakes her head, and Lydia squeezes my hand.

"*Temporarily*. I'm so sorry; I should have clarified. I'll give her something to rest and to alleviate the pain."

I swallow and nod as she slides a needle under Nikita's skin, and Nikita's breathing slows. I stare, unblinking, my heart pounding when Lydia's hand slips into mine with gentle reassurance.

"A graze wound," she says, examining Nikita. "It can be tricky with animals, especially with thick fur like this. It looks worse than it is, but we'll clean it thoroughly and keep her overnight for observation."

"Oh, thank God." Lydia turns to me and buries her head on my chest, her shoulders shaking. I cup the back of her head, and my heart warms. She loves Nikita, just like I do. Vera watches over us, her own eyes shining.

"I think you should keep her here for the night, just for observation. We will call you if anything changes."

"We will stay here." I'm not leaving Nikita, and I suspect Lydia agrees.

Lydia shakes her head, whispering to me. "I don't trust her apart from us, Viktor," she says. "This was intentional. We're playing right into their hands. If we stay here, we're sitting ducks."

The vet's eyes widen, but Vera quickly assures her. "It's not you they don't trust. But Lydia is right. I'll go back with them, and I'll know what to do if there are any changes with Nikita."

The vet prescribes some medication, and slowly, one by one, we leave.

As we leave the vet, I feel a wave of relief. Nikita will be fine. She's been hit but not seriously injured.

We've been lucky this time.

But we need to stay vigilant. Our enemies are out there, watching, waiting for their next move.

CHAPTER TWENTY-ONE

Lydia

"I'LL GO BACK to Mom's. Keep an eye on her and Polina," Lev says. "I'll be there, too."

Nikko nods. "Vera and I can stay with you, too, Viktor, if it's alright with you."

"That would be perfect," I say with a smile. I want to catch up with my sister. "We have a wedding to plan. How long can you stay?"

We're in the parking lot outside the vet's. "I've got a week," Vera says. "I wish I could stay longer. But it's alright, Mom is almost home, and she will come, too. You aren't far from her now, either."

We situate the sleeping Nikita in the back seat between us. Nikko's driving, Viktor in the passenger seat.

"What details do you still need to finalize for the wedding?"

I catch her up to speed. "Polina and Ekaterina are mostly handling all the details. It's not like I really know anyone who's coming."

I'd rather it be like this. Small. Close family, no more, no less.

I'm listening in on Viktor and Nikko's conversation.

"Obviously, security is the main concern," Viktor says, his voice low and intense. He's *pissed*. "I don't trust the *Ledyanoye Bratstvo* to stay quiet for long. We need to ensure everyone's safe. He's doing exactly what we hoped he would do," he admits. "But I'm pissed we haven't gotten him yet."

Nikko nods. "I've already got men scouting the location. We'll set up a perimeter and have checkpoints. We'll make sure security's locked down in all places. No one gets in without clearance."

Viktor glances back at me, then continues, "I want Lydia to feel safe on our wedding day. No surprises. This is her day, and nothing should ruin it."

Vera smiles at me. My heart warms at his words.

"We'll also consider a decoy route so we can keep our movements unpredictable."

Vera chimes in. "What about the guest list? Are we sure everyone invited is trustworthy?"

Viktor answers, "We've vetted everyone, and it's a small guest list."

Nikko looks thoughtful. "And the caterers? Staff? Anyone working the event?"

"Polina and Ekaterina are handling the vendors. They've been given strict instructions to hire only from trusted sources," Vera responds.

I'm thankful they're so on top of things. "And the venue itself?"

"We've chosen a secluded location," Viktor says. "It's easier to control and monitor. Fewer entry points."

Nikko smirks. "Like a fortress. Just how you like it, brother."

Viktor's lips twitch into a rare smile. "Exactly."

I lean into the conversation, feeling a mix of excitement and nervousness. "And what about after the wedding?"

Viktor's eyes soften as he looks at me. "I was thinking somewhere remote. Just the two of us. A place where we can relax and not worry about threats."

Vera squeezes my hand. "You deserve this, Lydia. A fresh start, away from all the chaos." She leans closer to me, her voice lowering. "Someone to watch over you, to make sure you're safe. You deserve that, too."

I squeeze her hand back. "Thank you."

The drive continues in a comfortable silence, each of us lost in our thoughts. As we near Viktor's place, Nikita stirs slightly, her head resting on my lap. I gently stroke her fur, reassured by her steady breathing.

Viktor reaches back, placing his hand over mine. "She'll be okay, Lydia. We'll make sure of it."

I nod. I want her to be alright.

We arrive at Viktor's place—*our* place, and everyone moves with practiced efficiency. Nikita is carefully carried inside, and Vera immediately sets to work checking her vitals again and making sure she's secure.

It feels good to be with my sister, even though we don't really know each other that well. I want to, though. And it's the first time I realize that being around the Romanov family, seeing how their sisters and brothers interact, makes me long for something more.

"Do you want to have a drink?" I ask tentatively. And I have to admit, I am feeling at home here. I like being in Viktor's place... *our* place. I'm hosting Vera.

My sister looks tired, but she smiles at me. "I would love a glass of wine," she says with a smile. "Although I prefer beer if you have that."

"We absolutely have beer," I say, laughing. "We have a lot to catch up on."

I pop open a couple of beers, and Vera and I sit in the large, expansive room next to our bedroom. Nikko and Viktor walk downstairs, planning. "I'm going to sit with Nikita for a while," Viktor says.

"The poor guy," I say softly when they've gone downstairs. "He loves that dog so much."

"Of course. Those two are the closest, you know," she says. "It's almost fitting that sisters are marrying brothers, isn't it?" She takes a thoughtful sip of her beer. "Kind of surprised it doesn't happen more often."

"Right?" I smile. "Viktor told me they like to lift. That's, uh... obvious about both of them."

Vera's eyes perk up, and she wiggles her eyebrows at me. "Indeed."

We giggle into our beer. I bring out a large platter of chocolates and some cookies. "Hungry?"

She nods eagerly. She's always had a sweet tooth, though she's never been as devoted to chocolate as I am.

"Viktor ordered from some kind of bakery earlier," she says. "Something about the Rossi family expanding in New York."

I shake my head. "I don't know who they are, and I didn't know anything about ordering from New York. The only thing I know is that I ordered a bunch of different cakes for the wedding. We're doing cake shooters."

She laughs. "Of course you are. Cake was always your favorite."

"Mhm." I take another sip. "So tell me how you and Nikko met. I barely know the story."

She shakes her head and sighs. "You know these brothers. They don't operate by anybody else's rules. Nikko came with me as my bodyguard to that program I did in Moscow."

I nod. This much I knew.

"Apparently, he was on a mission. I'd rather not get into the details of that mission because you might want to kill him, but his mission was unsuccessful. Instead of enacting the retribution he had planned, he ended up with me."

"Really, whatever he was planning, being with you was definitely a better option," I say with a smile.

Vera nods. "You can say that things worked out."

She continues, "So, um… I sort of lied and said that he was my husband because I didn't want anybody to know that I brought a bodyguard with me to Moscow, especially anybody in the program I was studying. You know."

"Of course not. I wouldn't want that either."

"So we ended up in this room that was supposed to be for a couple. One bed…" She giggles. I laugh out loud.

"Two more beers, and I want all the details, sister."

She winks at me. "He was protective. He really knew me. You know, not just the persona I put on, but the real me. It was… It was hot. And I fell," she says with a sigh. "I fell really fucking hard." She shakes her head. "And then, once the Romanovs found out, they made a deal. Father actually made a deal with them before he passed away that they would have my hand in marriage."

"How did that work into the equation?"

"Our families have done terrible things, Lydia. In our world, bargaining a woman's hand in marriage is the best form of retribution you can make. They didn't want money; they have plenty of that. They wanted stability. Vows. Children."

I think about that. Stability. Children. Is this what I bring to Viktor? I don't know. Part of me hopes so. And another part of me is honestly terrified of being anything more than who I am now—Lydia Ivanova. Snarky, curvy, and mischievous. Who am I as Viktor Romanov's wife?

"It's so disconcerting, being here," I admit, feeling the weight of my emotions starting to surface.

"I know," Vera says, her voice gentle. "But it's not like we grew up in suburbia with a regular old white picket fence and all that." She sighs, a hint of sadness in her eyes. "Especially you, Lydia. You dealt with so much shit from Father. I'm sorry."

A lump forms in my throat, and I feel a strange wave of emotion I hadn't expected. My throat tightens, and my nose starts to tingle. I don't want to break down in front of her, but I know the only way forward is through this.

"It wasn't your fault," I continue, my voice wavering. "You are not to blame."

I look away, sitting on a little step stool in our bedroom. For the first time, I notice a small door barely visible behind the open closet door. It's a strange place to have a door. I just shake my head and look away. I want to have this conversation.

"It's not like I grew up with a parent who actually liked me. But I tried." I sigh deeply. "You can only blame your shitty parents for so much, you know? And you just have to decide, this is my life now. And I can take it and make it my own."

It feels like an odd thing to say, considering I'm being forced into marriage.

Vera bites her lip, lost in thought or perhaps trying to find the right words. "You know, parents can be so complicated," she says softly. "They expect so much from us."

I nod. "Yeah, it's like they're always pushing and pulling, never really seeing us for who we are."

She smiles hesitantly. "Let's just say, you're definitely better off here. I don't know what it would take to convince you, but I can show you that Viktor... he's a good man. Out of all these guys, he's the best one. He doesn't have an agenda. He just wants you."

I sit back, mulling over her words. "Listen," Vera says, leaning in to capture my gaze. "Being married to Viktor is not going to be easy. Being married to any of these men isn't. It takes someone who is strong to do it. Have you met Harper and Aria yet?"

I nod. "Yup."

"So the Romanov brothers have chosen women who have something to offer their family. Have you considered that?"

"What? No. What are you talking about?"

Vera stands and walks the length of the room, tapping her chin as if trying to come up with the right words. "It's like this. Aria, she was a hacker. She *is* a hacker. Mikhail loves her, but she became head of cybersecurity here alongside Aleksander. Harper," she shakes her head, "she's the best marksman you could imagine. She outshoots any of those guys. Literally any of them, Lydia. Aleksander didn't necessarily know that when he married her, but she has become a powerful member of this group."

Ahh. "Your knowledge of emergency medical response, I could imagine that comes in handy here."

I shake my head, feeling uncertain. "What do *I* have to offer?"

"What do *you* have to offer? You're brilliant. Nikko told me that you were the one who figured out that your fiancé was a fraud. Nobody else knew that. You did, though." She sighs. "My point is this. You won't just be a pretty little thing meant to be set on a pedestal and have babies. You'll be a very active member of this family. They will lean on you... hard."

I nod slowly, reassured. "That helps," I say, feeling a bit of relief.

Vera smiles. "Nikko has been texting me for an hour. If you're ready for bed, let's look at the wedding details tomorrow?"

"It's hard to believe it's coming so soon. We put it off, and we were planning a month, but everyone's in agreement we need to move this up. But yeah, I'm good."

Vera stands up.

"Go to your husband. I'm sure Viktor and Nikko are done soon. I need to find my future husband too," I say with a laugh.

Vera leans over and gives me a hug. "I love you, Lydia," she says softly.

I hug her back, warmth spreading across my chest. "And I love you." Maybe one of the best parts of all this is that I might get to know my sister a little better.

Vera leaves, and I start my hunt for Viktor.

It's dark in the hallway as I look around for Viktor. The distant roll of thunder catches my attention.

Wandering the halls of his home—our home?—I feel a sense of foreboding. Everything is dark, moody, and the thunderstorm outside these windows doesn't help. I pause on the landing of the stairs, staring out an oval-shaped window into the night.

Lightning strikes overhead, lighting up the yard below. I pause, my heart skipping a beat. What is that down there? What is that?

I strain my eyes, thinking it must be Viktor, for some weird reason, taking a walk in the rain. But then, when the clouds shift, allowing more light to illuminate below, I realize it isn't Viktor or even one person but several. I stand up straighter, my heart beating faster.

There are half a dozen men with weapons outside this window, surrounding our grounds. Oh my God.

"Viktor! Viktor!" I can't stop my voice from shaking. I need to see him; I need to see him right now. "Viktor, where are you?"

My voice is shaky despite my best efforts to keep it steady. When I get to the landing, he pokes his head out from the den where Nikita lies. Of course, he's with Nikita. That makes perfect sense. I blame the stress for not figuring it out sooner. I'm so foolish.

He's immediately at attention, ready to kill.

I run to him, and he quickly gathers me in his arms. The immediate feel of his hand on the back of my head and his other hand around my waist makes me breathe easier, if only for a moment. "What is it? What happened?"

"People outside with weapons. Lots of them! Are they going to attack?"

"Where?" he snaps, running to the window to look. "Oh. Damn. I'm sorry, Lydia. Baby, I should've told you. Those are the men I called in as backup. Our guards."

I swallow. "Of course. The guards. God, I'm so dumb."

"Don't call yourself dumb. I don't want to hear that again," he says gently, though there's an element of steel in his voice that reminds me exactly what it feels like to be under his command.

"They are here overnight, even in the rain?"

"Of course. They'd stay there through a snowstorm or a blizzard. They're here to protect you."

Not us, I think to myself.

"Okay, that makes sense."

He kisses my cheek. "I'll tell you next time. Are you going to bed? We've had a long day. I'll join you in a few minutes. Did you have a nice visit with your sister?"

"I did, but we need a lot more time to catch up. I hope we can get that."

"I'll do whatever it takes. If she has another job to go to, I'm happy to travel so that you can visit her nearby, if it's feasible. Same with your mother."

"But they need you here—"

He smiles. "And you're needed too, but most of the time, what you'll be doing for us can be done remotely." He bends over and kisses a little curlicue on the corner of my temple. I love it when he does that. I think over what Vera has said, what she's revealed.

He's known me and wanted me for a very long time. And maybe that should freak me out. Maybe it's just a part of who he is, who *we* are as two unconventional people.

"You'd do that for me? Travel so I can be with my sister?"

"Of course," he says warmly.

"I would love that, thank you."

His lips meet mine, and I'm instantly aroused, instantly malleable and molded to him. I lick his tongue, savoring the thrill of his moan. It feels like lighting a match when I kiss him back. I run my hand down the length of his front, relishing the feel of his muscles, his hard abs, his bridled, unfathomable strength.

He kisses me again. "I have one more dose of medicine I'm going to give Nikita, then I'll join you. Why don't you get some rest. It's been a long day."

He's not wrong. Part of me wants the assurance of him next to me in bed more than anything now. I follow him back to the room beside Nikita. I bend over the top of her head. "You're such a good girl, and I am so proud of you," I whisper to her. "Get some rest now."

His eyes meet mine when I rise. I love her.

I try to puzzle out how I feel about being a member of this family. It isn't just my husband's family anymore, but my sister's, too. Joining with the Romanovs is an excellent decision for all of us. Even my mother will be better off.

Not that you have a choice, a little voice in the back of my head says, but that voice is getting quieter.

I walk softly over to the dresser, my hands roaming over the folded clothing. It's all so beautiful, and it fits me so well. The smallest of luxuries, but I cannot take it for granted.

I open his drawer beneath mine and bury my head in the clean, folded white tees. I inhale deeply. They smell like him, invigorating and manly.

It's a little chilly tonight with the thunderstorm rolling in, but I'll be warm in his tee. I steal one from the drawer.

A little golden key beneath his tees catches my attention. Huh. I eye it thoughtfully before I put it back. It looks like a small key you might use to open a desk drawer.

I strip off my clothes, feeling the cool air on my skin, and toss them toward the laundry basket. They fall to the floor.

"Good one, Lydia." I shake my head and walk over to pick them up. I'm about to put them in the hamper when I look at the door again. I step over to it, curious. I feel like Alice in Wonderland. Something tells me I'm going to turn this handle and find myself upside down.

I take a deep breath and slowly turn the handle, curiosity and a touch of dread swirling within me.

The door is locked. Huh.

Strange.

I try the handle again, but it doesn't open. Not sure why I do because if it didn't open the first time, it definitely won't the second time.

The key... there was a key among his T-shirts. What if I... I walk over to his drawer and remove the key; my movements are hurried because I know I shouldn't be doing this. It's what he calls snooping.

He's against it, but dammit, I'm going to be his wife. He shouldn't have locked doors from me.

I walk back to the door and slide the key into the lock.

My heart races when it fits. I push the door open and stare for a moment before I realize what I'm seeing.

My hand covers my mouth in disbelief.

CHAPTER TWENTY-TWO

Five years ago

Viktor

KOLYA and I sat at a local diner we frequented. It was hard to blend in for a guy my size, so I had to find a place where people might notice but not care. This diner was one of them.

"They say there's a virus at Liberty Ridge Academy," Kolya said with a smile. "You wouldn't know anything about that, would you?"

I shrugged my shoulders and didn't meet his eyes.

"A virus? That's bullshit. There were a few incidents, yeah, but maybe they're exaggerated."

I stared at the wall and took a long drink from my bottle. I thought about what I had done to reward her for being kind to Lydia. Another teacher had received similar treatment for showing her kindness.

The boy who called her fat got a merciless beating. Retribution can be both sweet and painful.

The girl who mocked her? I made sure her name was smeared on social media, branded as a blackmailing bitch.

And the others who tormented her? One by one, every teacher and bully classmate who hurt her faced brutal consequences. It's no fun being stranded in the middle of nowhere with slashed tires or finding your bank account drained. It took strategic planning, but it was done.

Now, there's an exposé about the strange and mysterious events that happened at Liberty Ridge. I tried to stagger them initially, but I got impatient. If I had my way, they'd all be gone. Every last one of them.

"They're lucky they're alive," I muttered.

Kolya leaned forward and tapped my beer bottle with his. "Another?"

He allowed me to drink once a month. No more, no less. I didn't like to indulge because I wanted to stay in control, but I enjoyed a beer with him. Fortunately for me, I could handle quite a bit.

"I want you to keep something in mind, Viktor," Kolya said.

I nodded. "Yes?"

"Revenge can be a powerful motivator. But it can also eat you alive. Consume your every waking thought and your dreams as well. I ought to know. I've been there."

I nodded and polished off my drink just as the waitress brought over a second. With her full bust and curvy ass, she leaned closer to me, trying to get my attention, but I turned away.

I only have eyes for one woman.

"You've done what needed to be done to protect her. I get it. But don't let it destroy *you* in the process."

I grunted and turned away, taking another long pull from the beer. "I won't let them get away with what they did."

"And you shouldn't," he said. "But there's a line between justice and obsession you don't want to cross."

I took a deep breath and sipped my beer—my taste soured with bitterness. "I get it," I said, though part of me wondered if I really did.

Kolya nodded, seemingly satisfied. "Good. Now tell me what you plan next."

CHAPTER TWENTY-THREE

Lydia

I STARE in front of me, hardly believing what I see. This is beyond what I ever imagined I'd find in Viktor's possession.

An old bottle with the golden letters reading *Opulence*, a perfume I used when I was younger.

Where did that come from?

A napkin with a smear of lipstick and a torn page from a notebook that looks eerily familiar. I don't recognize the napkin, of course, but when paired together with the other things...

When I pick it up, my skin prickles as if someone's standing behind me right this very minute.

I look over my shoulder and see no one.

There's an empty coffee cup with my name scribbled on it from a coffee shop.

Lydia

The letters are smeared now as if someone… rubbed their finger over the thick black lettering over and over again. A ring of coffee still stains the bottom.

An old grocery list in my handwriting.

And the one thing that makes me clutch my chest while I rifle through the pages: an old, tattered copy of *Wuthering Heights*. When I open the cover, "Liberty Academy" is stamped in faded purple ink.

He took this. I was a *child* the last time I held this. And if there was any doubt about these items—why they are here and where he got them—my high school photo, curled around the edges and in the center of this small collection, removes all possible uncertainty.

"You found the shrine." Viktor's deep voice booms behind me.

I spin around on my heel, still clutching the worn book in my hand. His gaze skates down the length of my body. He loves it when I wear nothing but his tee.

Oh no, buddy. We are not getting sidetracked.

"What is this?" I ask, my voice high-pitched. The hand holding the book trembles slightly.

Viktor shrugs a massive shoulder with not a trace of guilt. "What do you think it is?"

I take a step back and shake my head when he moves toward me. "No, don't touch me. Don't come near me, Viktor." When he ignores me and takes another step forward, I rear back and whip the book at his head as hard as I can throw. He ducks just in time. The old book falls to the floor, loose pages fluttering down like dead leaves from the maples outside.

He advances on me, and before I can stop him, he captures me, his hands on my wrists, and lifts me straight into the air.

"Not now!" I scream at him, clawing at him. "Put me down!" I pound on his back with my fists, but they're little fluffy snowballs against a glacier. He doesn't even flinch.

"Viktor!" I scream. "Let me *go!*"

Despite my best efforts, my heart is pounding, and I'm so fucking wet. I can scream and rail against him, but he's immovable.

This is him. This is us. My protests only ignite my own need for him. Still, rage courses through my veins, even though I know exactly where this will end up. He'll either spank me or fuck me or both.

"Fuck *you!*"

With a growl, he lets me down and spreads me belly-down over the table. The bottle of perfume falls and shatters, and the napkin flutters to the floor like the falling petals of a flower. The faintest scent of perfume fills the room.

Without a word, his heavy palm slams across my ass once, twice, three times. I can't breathe, gasping over the table. I clutch the edge, and he lowers his mouth to my ear.

"I've wanted you for as long as I can remember," he growls. "You know that. I haven't hidden it."

"This is creepy!" I scream as he shoves his tee up so it's around my breasts, the rest of me nearly naked for him.

Another slap of his palm makes me go up on my toes as his hand falls hot and heavy. I scream myself hoarse until it hurts, but it does no good.

"Stop shrieking at me. I told you if you didn't watch that mouth, I'd give you a use for it."

"Fuck *off*!" I yell. I feel wildly out of control like I'm spiraling into an abyss, and there's no way for me to stop myself. He spanks me again so hard I can't breathe.

"Fine, then," he snaps. "We'll do this another way."

He spins me around and shoves me to my knees.

"You should apologize!" I glare up at him, but I'm sopping wet and so needy; if he swiped one finger across my clit I'd probably explode right now. I'm still angry with him... but this is how we do things. I'm the puppet, and he's pulling my strings. This is our dance, and I was the one who stepped onto the dance floor.

He holds me down with his left hand. I swivel my head and snap at his fingers seconds before he pulls them away from me and unbuckles his belt with his right hand.

"Lydia," he growls. "If you'd only fucking *listen*."

"Listen to your fucking justification about why you're obsessed with me? Fuck off! Ow!"

His belt slaps against my ass so hard I can't breathe, the searing leather instantly welts my backside. He reaches down and fists my hair with his other hand. I scream as he yanks out his cock.

"Don't you even—"

Another yank of my hair, and my mouth falls open in a scream seconds before he shoves his cock down my throat. Arousal washes through me in a tidal wave at the feel of his hardened, throbbing cock, satin-covered steel, filling my mouth. He fucks my mouth with a savage thrust. My eyes water.

"You talk to me before you lose your fucking mind," he grates, lifts his hand and snaps the belt across my ass again. Tears blur my vision. "You had your chance. Now, you'll suck while *I* talk, and you listen to me."

I whimper and suck, closing my eyes as I drown in sensation and warmth. I want this so badly; my protests and anger ebb away with every vicious thrust of his cock. Again, he thrusts, and I gag, my eyes watering.

"Yes, I was fucking obsessed with you," he growls, his hand on my cheek painful as he holds me in position. "Not was. Am. When I go to bed at night, all I think about is you. When I wake up in the morning, where you are and if you're safe are my first thoughts. Even now, I fucking pat the bed the second my eyes open to check for you."

He thrusts, and I lick and suck, taking this all in as he throbs in my mouth, and my clit aches to be touched.

"Yes, I stalked you. Yes, I fucking tracked you. Yes, I spent *years* seeking revenge on the bullies who fucking tormented you. Where do you think I got this scar? One of the assholes cut me, but I wear it with pride because it's a battle scar. The memory of what I did for the woman I love."

My eyes go wide, and still, I suck—licking the tip just to gain some control, but he's impermeable, immovable, his gaze locked on mine as he lifts the belt and snaps it across my ass. "And maybe I thought of this, Lydia. You, here, on your knees with your mouth wrapped around my cock." When he whips me again, I feel a trickle of arousal slide down my leg. I stifle a whimper.

"Maybe I imagined what it would be like to fuck you. To be near you. To fucking own you. But most of all? Most of all, I thought about what I would do if you were mine. How I'd never let anyone harm a hair on your head."

He slaps my ass with the belt again while I obediently suck his cock, before he drops it to the floor, grabs my head with both huge, rough hands, and forces me to suck him deeper. I gag, but he keeps fucking my mouth. "I told you. All I've ever wanted was you. All I'll ever want is you. All I'll ever need is *you*."

His hips jerk, and I can tell he's just on the verge of coming when he grasps my head and yanks me off of him. "Bend over that fucking table before I jerk off all over you, tie you to my bedpost, and set this fucking house on fire."

Oh dear God.

I'm reeling from what he's saying, what he's doing, my mind a blank slate and my body deliciously pliable. I bend over the table and spread my legs, unable to stop myself if I wanted to. His hot, thick cock lines up at my entrance while he fingers my ass, and my mouth falls open in a silent scream.

He bends his mouth to my ear. "I love you, Lydia. And yes, I'm obsessed with you. I have no regrets. *None.*"

He thrusts in me so hard I scream, bracing myself on the table. I'm so full, so perfectly filled with him, that I can't think beyond the need to feel him thrust again, and again, and again. I need him. I want him. I'm fucking dying to have him come in me.

"You are mine, Lydia," he growls as the first wave of ecstasy consumes me. "Mine," he says with another savage thrust. "And don't you ever fucking forget that." As his hot seed lashes into me, he fists my hair and yanks my head back. "Tell me. Tell me you're mine," he demands before he sinks his mouth to my neck and bites.

I scream, hot pain melding with pleasure as he thrusts into me again and again. Bliss explodes in my body, my pulse racing as it washes through me. I grip the table and give myself over to the kind of pleasure only Viktor could ever give me.

This. This is what I want, what I need. I can't be with a man who doesn't love me like this. I can't be with a man who doesn't make me fucking burn for him.

I scream his name while I come. I take every drop of his seed until I collapse to the table. The torn bit of paper clings to my damp skin as the cup rolls off and bounces off the floor.

"I'm yours," I say with abandon, breathing into him. "*Yours,* Viktor."

As always, when we're spent, hot, and sweaty, and he's come back to his senses, he lifts me to his chest and carries me to the bedroom. This time, though, he takes off all my clothes so he can inspect me.

He kisses the red lines of welts on my ass and thighs.

I hiss in a breath when he frowns and shakes his head. "I like those," I tell him. I do. I love looking at them in the mirror and remembering how I got them. I love the pain they bring. I smile wickedly to myself at the sting the day after he welts me.

"Stay there," he says. "I'm cleaning you up."

He comes out with the warm washcloth and washes me all over before he kisses my temple again. "I love you so much, Lydia. So much."

My eyes feel heavy as I lie next to him.

I haven't told him I loved him yet.

It seems so fast as if I'm in a race car that's gone out of control, and at any minute, I'm going to careen into something that destroys me.

I fall to sleep with his arm slung around me and wonder what is so wrong with a girl like me that I can only come when it hurts and only love when it's wrong.

CHAPTER TWENTY-FOUR

Viktor

"I THINK it's probably best if we go to my mom's," Vera says over coffee the next day. "She's supposed to be getting back from her trip today and will be able to go over the final guest list."

"I think that's a good idea. Have you asked Lydia?"

"No," Vera says, frowning. "I thought she was with you." I look around the room as if she might suddenly materialize out of thin air. Of course she isn't here.

I would know.

Where the hell is she?

"Supposed to?" Nikko says with a frown from the couch.

"Vera, I thought she was with you," I snap. "Where is she?" The next thing I know, Nikko is in my face. "Talk to my wife that way again," he snarls.

I shove him back. "Step down, brother."

"Boys, boys, settle down," Lydia says, coming around the corner. "What the hell is going on?"

"Prince Charming was losing his loving mind because he couldn't find you," Nikko retorts.

After what happened last night, I half expected her to try to escape. Not that she'd have an easy time of it, with the guards at every exit, the surveillance on her, and the tracker she doesn't know about yet.

I told her last night, when I had her bent over the table, fucking her senseless, that I was tracking her. But she probably assumes it's just the tracker on her phone.

"I was checking on Nikita," she says. "So sue me."

I catch her eyes, blazing with anger. "Don't even think about it," she warns.

"Think about what?" I challenge, rising and walking over to her.

She only narrows her eyes at me. "I'm not gonna leave without telling you, okay? I was just checking on Nikita, so relax."

"I was saying we should go to Mom's," Vera says. "That way, we can talk to her about the final details and solidify everything for this wedding. Have you seen her since you and Viktor got engaged?"

"No, we've texted a few times and talked on the phone, but I haven't seen her in person."

"We fully expect an attack from the *Ledyanoye Bratstvo*," Nikko says. "Are you girls prepared for that?"

"Yes, of course," Vera says. "Lydia?"

"Of course," she snaps, pounding her fist in her hand. "I hope he *brings* it."

In our recent self-defense class, I showed her how to use a knife. It's not too hard if you know what you're doing and you're not afraid to slice through muscle and veins.

"I want more practice with my knife," she says. "Is there any way to do that?"

"Got a place near our headquarters called The Hidden Mark. It's a private place with dummies we use for knife work. It's secluded and on the way."

"Yes, perfect. Can we go there before we head to Mom's?"

"She texted me this morning and said she was there," Vera says. "It was a strange message, though. Have you talked to her?"

I give her a sharp look. "Maybe she's just distracted about the wedding. She's been planning a wedding for Lydia with such detail—" Vera stops mid-sentence, her cheeks coloring. She was going to say more, but we do not need to discuss Lydia's previous engagement.

"I'm going to send a car out there to check on her," I decide.

Nikko is still glaring at me, probably because I raised my voice to Vera. Jesus, it's not Vera I have a problem with; it's anything that threatens the safety of Lydia. I'd think he'd get that.

"You get your fucking boxers out of your ass and chill," I tell Nikko. He takes a step toward me, and Lydia shakes her head.

"Stop," she says warningly. Nikko still advances on me. I grab him by the front of the shirt, lift him up, and casually place him back in the living room. "I said sit down, Nikko."

"Call Lev," he snaps.

"Are you guys always like this? These pissing matches. Honest to God!" Lydia throws her hands up in the air.

Vera pipes up. "I've heard they even fight about who has more kids than the other ones."

"Well, that's easy. Knock me up with triplets, and we'll blow everybody out of the water," Lydia says to me.

Not a bad idea.

I punch the button on my phone, and Lev answers. "We're heading over to The Hidden Mark. I want you to check in on Zofia. You'll get there before we do because we have a quick stop first. Can you do that for me?"

"I'm not there, brother. Mikhail sent me to Manhattan for the day."

"Shit. Aleks. He probably can."

"Maybe we should skip the range and just go straight to Mom's," Lydia suggests.

"She hasn't answered the phone?" I ask.

"No," Lydia says. "She never answers her phone or texts. She's kind of a... what do you call it? Someone who hates technology."

"Luddite," Vera supplies. "Oh wait, I just got a text from her," Vera says. "She says everything's fine, don't worry about me. I'll be out here all day. When are you coming? Love, Mom."

She shrugs. "Sounds like Mom."

We head down to the range where we train and have large stuffed dummies suitable for knife practice. We go over everything again and again until she's panting, her face red with the exertion. "How did I do?" she asks, her eyes fierce.

"I'm proud of you. If anyone comes to attack you and you have your knife on you, they don't stand a chance."

"On me? How do we do that, by the way?"

"I can get a little harness strapped to your leg, a sheath that goes in the small of your back, or you... there are lots of options, and we can use more than one if you'd like."

"Yeah, I would like that."

As we head out, an alarm sounds.

"What?" she asks, giving me a wary look. She doesn't trust me at all after last night. Not at all.

"Metal detector."

"Everybody has to have their weapons checked. But it doesn't make sense that it's going off," Lydia says. "You're holding the knives, not me. I don't have any on me."

Fuck. It's her tracker.

She looks at the display that shows what's causing the alarm to go off.

I note the second she realizes. The second she *knows*.

"It's pointing to my *neck*. It's that thing at my neck that I thought was a bug bite, isn't it? Isn't it!" she demands.

"Look, hate me later. Scream at me, whatever. We have to go to your mom's, and I want to be sure that you're safe. Don't do anything fucking stupid."

"Nice double standard, Mr. Romanov," she snarls. "'Don't do anything stupid,' but it's totally fine for you to install something in my neck like I'm a dog? When did you do this?"

"When I first got you," I say between clenched teeth.

"When you... *got* me? It's really like I'm a dog. Viktor!"

"No, it isn't, Lydia," I say, losing patience.

"This isn't normal! This isn't okay."

"I'll take it out once we have the ex in custody."

"No!" She claws at her neck, her fingernails digging into her skin. Blood bubbles to the surface. "Do you know what it feels like having some kind of foreign object in your body? Are you crazy?"

I move closer to her, her smaller body cast in shadow next to mine. "Calm down, Lydia," I say, trying to keep my voice calm and steady. "You're safe with me."

She looks up at me, her mouth open. "Safe? How can I be safe when you put this... this thing inside me?" Her eyes blaze with anger, her hands clenched into fists, trembling as she reaches for her neck and tries to claw at it again.

I reach out, but she flinches and turns away from me. "You say everything is about my protection, but maybe this is your control. Have you thought of that, Viktor?" Her voice drips with sarcasm and fury. She backs away from me, her eyes darting toward the door, clearly weighing her chances of escaping.

"Both," I admit, my voice low and rough. "You don't understand the danger you're in. You're a smart girl, but your former fiancé is a lot more than a narcissistic bastard. He's deadly. We don't know what his plans are for you, and I don't want to take a single risk of anyone, especially him, hurting you. At this point, he wants you out of sheer vengeance."

Her breath comes in short bursts. "You mean you won't let anybody but *you* control me." She shakes her head, laughing bitterly.

I clench my jaw. "I'm the only one who cares about keeping you alive."

She grits her teeth, her cheeks flaming as hot as the fires she's obsessed with. "This isn't about you caring about me. You're obsessed. Who keeps a napkin, Viktor?"

I take another step forward. "Call it what you like. You know where we stand. You know I know you better than anybody."

Her eyes narrow. "You think you know me. But do you really?"

"I would if you let me in."

She crosses her arms over her chest, her body taut with defiance. "I would rather burn, Viktor."

I give one sharp shake of my head, my patience waning. The room is thick with tension, our battle of wills evident. This is how it will always be with us—thunderstorms and fire, volcanoes and eruptions. But that's who we are.

"Viktor," she says, her voice softening. "I know you need to protect me. I know what happened to your sister."

I look away, not meeting her eyes. I don't know who told her, but I wouldn't have withheld it from her. I just wasn't ready. "I can't be controlled like this. I feel like I'm caged."

I give her a dark look. "That can be arranged."

Despite her anger, I know by the way her pupils dilate and she clutches at her collarbone, pink rising on her cheeks, that she likes this. She might fight me, but she needs this.

So do I.

"It feels like you're suffocating me," she says in a soft voice.

I take a step closer to her, wrapping my hand around the front of her throat and tightening it. "Like this?" I say, my voice a growl. Beneath her fear and anger, a small part of her is drawn to this intensity, the raw, primal need I have for her. It's dark, dangerous, and twisted, and it scares her, but she craves us.

"Don't distract me," she says, but it's a last-ditch effort. She wants this. I know she does.

My mouth slams on hers with a punishing kiss. I tighten my hand on her throat until she is gasping for breath and only release it when her mouth opens. She moans into my mouth, trying to push me away, but I tighten my grip, grab her ass, and squeeze her while I pull her into me. When we pull away, we are both panting.

I reach down and gently brush my thumb over her hardened nipple. "This isn't over, Viktor. You can't distract me with sex."

"I'm not trying to distract you with sex, but I'm also not going to pretend that I don't want this as much as you do."

"I'm not marrying you until you take this out of me."

"I'm not taking it out of you until he is dead in the fucking grave." We stare at each other in a battle of wills.

"You *don't* own me," she snaps.

I shake my head in grim determination. "We'll see about that."

"God, you seem to think the best thing is to find him and fuck him up," I tell her. "Then we can both sleep in peace."

She throws her hands up in the air. "Will we, though? What about the next threat? What about the next person who wants to hurt me? What are you gonna do then, bubble wrap me? Chain me to the floor?"

She glares at me, and I glare right back. "I will chain you to the fucking floor if that's what it takes."

"Hot, Viktor," she says through gritted teeth. "That's not toxic at all."

"Woman..."

I bend her head back and kiss her, silently pleading for her to give in. To understand. To accept.

But when I pull away, she doesn't meet my eyes.

Have I gone too far?

We meet Nikko and Vera outside the range, Nikko giving me a wary look. He hasn't forgiven me for not talking to his wife the way he thinks I should. He can kiss my ass.

I am in a fucking mood, and so is Lydia. I reach for her hand, and she yanks it away. Vera's eyebrows rise in mild surprise, but I only open the door to the car, and as Lydia starts to climb in, I slap her ass, hard. .

"Hey!" she exclaims. I lean in and kiss her cheek.

"Behave yourself. You're not letting this come between us."

She gets into the car and shuts the door. Vera chatters on about plans for the wedding, and Lydia participates, but I can tell she is reserved.

I don't know how to explain to her what it means to me to have her with me. I don't know how to explain to her how important it is that I keep her safe. I don't know if her objections hold a candle to what I certainly know to be true.

"Your mother wants to know if you want any candles at the reception," Vera says, meeting my eyes in the rearview mirror.

"Yes," Lydia and I say in unison. Vera smirks. Lydia turns away, looking out the window.

"Do you want a photographer?"

"No," we both snap in unison. Lydia blows out a breath and sulks, but I crack a smile as Vera jots it down on her phone.

"Music? Do you want music?"

"Music would be nice," Lydia says. "And Viktor would probably say—"

"I don't care. Do what you want."

"That's what I was going to say you'd say," she mutters.

"Music it is," Vera says, jotting it down.

She turns away from me, looking out the window. The drive to her family home is mostly quiet until we get a few miles away.

"Do you remember how we used to throw rocks at that little pond behind the house?" she asks Vera as she traces the edge of the door lock with her fingernail. "And how Mom would get so mad because our clothes would get all mud-streaked and stained."

"Hard to forget," Vera says with a smile. She turns her head to speak to Lydia over her shoulder. "Mom didn't care so much; it was Father who'd lose his mind."

"Mmm." Lydia nods. "And we didn't want him to yell at *her*, so we started wearing those smocks when we went down to the river. Remember?"

Vera laughs out loud. "Oh my God, I *do* remember. How could I forget? You told Mom it was for an art project."

I shake my head. "Causing trouble even then." I squeeze her knee, but she still doesn't look at me.

If we were alone right now, I wonder what she'd say.

Curious, I pull out my phone.

You still pissy with me?

You make it sound like it's my fault.

Now you're assigning motives. For real?
Okay, are you still angry?

Yes, Viktor. I am still angry. You have
tagged me like I'm an animal, and you
aren't the least bit repentant. It hurts badly.
It makes me think you're no better than the
vindictive asshole I ran from.

I grip my phone so hard my knuckles whiten.

I am nothing like him!

She sighs.

So you say.

I love you! He only wanted to use you

And you don't want to use me?

of course not

You make me feel betrayed and
claustrophobic

I glare at the phone, unsure of how I'm going to respond when she shoves her phone in her pocket.

Guess that conversation's over. I'm trying to keep my head on straight, trying to see things from her perspective.

How do I make her feel free… while keeping her safe? It's a conundrum I can't quite get my head around.

I shake my head and don't meet her eyes for long moments as we drive toward her family home. I'm checking in our rearview mirrors, checking my phone.

I can't shake the feeling we're being followed, but that's afflicted me for so long it's almost become routine.

"We're almost there," Vera says with a smile. "I'm glad you're coming back with me, Lydia. We've missed you." Nikko reaches over and tweaks an errant lock of hair. "And I suppose it isn't that bad coming back home with my husband in tow." She giggles to herself. "The first time I met him—which was the last time we were here together, I thought he was Jason Bourne plucked straight out of the novels, turned Russian. I didn't know he spoke English."

"That was intentional," Nikko says with a smirk.

Lydia shakes her head, clearly judging Nikko. She doesn't know the half of it.

And look how they turned out.

At least by now, she hasn't demanded she have distance and stormed out on me, but it seems like she's one step away from doing exactly that.

We pull up outside her home. I know it well, as our family didn't move away from this city until my father began planting roots in The Cove. This was where her family grew up, though. What's familiar to her.

I know the front yard is where she'd sit when her father was on her case and she needed some space. There's a bench made of stone a good distance from the front of the house, so she could come out and be left alone for a while. Her mother's made some nice homey adjustments since her father left because when he was home, he didn't care for what he'd call "frivolity."

Quite something coming from a man who had a different mistress in every major city in both America and Russia.

But I do know her little haunts in this home. She had a small area in the unfinished basement, complete with concrete floors, where she'd strike one match after another after another until her father came home or her mother caught her. They'd both stop her, but with different responses. Her mother would beg to know why, and her father would rage, throwing and breaking things, occasionally striking her.

He didn't need to ask why. He largely *was* the reason why.

And way down by the creek, there was a small access point to a local state park with camping and picnic areas. She would sometimes sneak down there and make good use of the grilling stations. She never cooked food, of course.

Lydia opens the door to the car and slams it shut behind her.

"Lydia." I don't want her storming ahead of me or doing something rash. She looks over her shoulder at me, her lips pursed.

"What?"

"Wait for me."

"Why don't you follow me?" she tosses back defiantly. A brisk wind kicks up, reminding me of the lonely, stark moors we've both read about in *Wuthering Heights*. I realize our relationship—tumultuous, marked by passion and intensity—is not unlike theirs. Like Catherine, my Lydia almost married the wrong man.

I'm the one who knows her.

I'm the one who loves her.

I'm the one who would lay down his life for her.

Then why don't I love her enough to trust her? To give her the smallest measure of freedom? I tell myself it isn't Lydia I don't trust, but our enemies...

"Leave me alone, Viktor. I need some time," she says when I reach her. "I want to talk to my mother and my sister. Can I do that in privacy? You'll be right here. No one's going to swoop in and kidnap me *here,* right?"

I shrug. "I have no fucking idea. All I know is that you have a target on your back, and there isn't any place too low for that asshole to stoop."

Vera rings the bell at the front door. There's no answer.

"That's strange," she says thoughtfully, biting her lip before knocking. "I had a key, but it isn't working. Mom must've changed the locks."

"A good idea with Yudin on the loose," Nikko says.

"Yeah, but wouldn't she tell me?"

Nikko and I meet each other's eyes. He draws his gun. I

prefer my fists in situations like this. Together, we make a good team, though.

I put Lydia behind me. She frowns, her jaw clenched, but even she can't hide the fear in her eyes. She texts her mom.

A few minutes later, there's the light sound of footsteps. We can't see anything as the windows are too high up, even for me and Nikko, but a moment later, we hear a series of locks being undone. We're tense, but a moment later, Zofia Ivanova opens the door and stands, smiling at us.

"Mom, you scared us," Vera says, shaking her head.

"Why?" Zofia asks, opening the door wider. "Come in, come in. I'm sorry if I haven't been in touch. I've not been feeling well." She looks over her shoulder. "Nikko, why are you holding a gun? Are you expecting someone to ambush you?"

Well... yes.

Lydia frowns at me. I only shrug as she leads us into the house. She embraces both girls, one at a time, holding them tight before she lets them go. .

"Nice to see you again, Nikko." She gives him a big hug before she turns to me. "And you must be Viktor?"

She's completely lost in my arms, she's so little. I hug her back and wonder why she's trembling. When I let her go, she turns her head and coughs into her arm.

"Oh, we have so much to chat about," she says. "Please, let's go to the living room."

Vera makes herself at home in the large living room, heading to a sideboard.

"You guys want drinks for this planning sesh?" she asks.

"I'll take the wine," Lydia says. "Mom doesn't have beer."

I shake my head. I want to be on full alert. Nikko declines as well.

Kolya got into our heads hard.

Lydia sits beside me, sipping a glass of sparkling prosecco.

"Mom, why aren't you feeling well?" Vera asks, sitting down beside Lydia.

"Oh, I don't know," she says. "I've had this cough I can't get rid of, but I'll get better soon." Her smile fades. She takes the drink Vera gives her and takes a small sip as if to steady her nerves. "Though honestly, Vera, I think it's stress. We have a lot to talk about."

Vera looks sharply at her mother. "What do you mean, stress? What other symptoms do you have?" She's in full-on Dr. Ivanova mode.

Her mother tells her her symptoms, waving her hand as if to pass her off. "I'm fine, Vera."

"Maybe you're not, though," Vera says with a frown. "And why are you stressed?"

Zofia opens her mouth to speak, then shuts it. She swallows. I'm struck with how alike Vera and Lydia's eyes are to hers. While Vera is slender and has a touch of the "mad scientist" vibe to her with her wild hair and the occasional times she wears glasses, and Lydia is all curves and feminine allure with a heavy side of snark, all three of the women have a strong resemblance.

She stands, pacing the expansive living room. It's a calm atmosphere with neutral-toned, modern furniture, clean lines, and wide windows that let in bright light, but it feels anything but calm in here right now.

She turns and looks at Lydia. "I wasn't entirely honest with you."

CHAPTER TWENTY-FIVE

Lydia

I STARE AT MY MOTHER, unsure of what she's going to tell me. For all I know, she could divulge that I'm not her real daughter, that my father had an affair, and the reason why she spent more time and focused attention on Vera than me was because my father forbade it.

It could be anything, but I'm distracted by my need to claw at my skin. I want this fucking tracker *out of me*.

I want to build a fire so big, so hot, so powerful that it melts everything around me to dust. I want to sit and watch the flames consume my past so I can walk scot-free into my future.

First, this fucking tracker.

But I'll have to wait. Bide my time.

Viktor looks at me, concern etched on his face. I turn away, and Vera's eyes meet mine. We're both concerned about Mom.

"What is it?" I ask my mother. "Can you tell us the truth now?"

She opens her mouth to speak, her hands clasped in front of her, when she's seized with a coughing fit. She tries to be delicate about it, but her entire body is wracked with the fit. After a full minute of this, Vera is on her feet.

"Mom, I think you need to see someone," she says, shaking her head. "This isn't alright. You're not well." Her face is lined with worry as she holds Mom and helps her sit down.

"I'll be fine, Vera," Mom says weakly. "All that travel did a number on me." She gives me a wan smile. "I'm not as young as you two anymore." Waving her hand, she shakes her head. "But that's of no importance. It's vital that we have this discussion." She sits up straighter and clears her throat. "It is time. Lydia... you were our firstborn. And you are due the inheritance upon your marriage. Because of the nature of your inheritance, the rules stipulated that you were to marry Bratva. At the time, we were not on friendly terms with the Romanov family. The only possibility was your marriage to the *Ledyanoye Bratstvo*. However, when I agreed to your marriage to the *Ledyanoye Bratstvo,* I thought you'd be marrying the oldest brother, a man I'd met on many occasions and deemed appropriate. I had no idea who you'd be marrying."

She folds her hand on her knee.

"Enter the Romanov family. Through Vera and Nikko's marriage, we became friendly. I shared my concerns with Viktor and Nikko's mother, and Ekaterina and I decided it would behoove both of our families if you were to marry into the Romanov family. We perhaps thought you could marry Lev or Ollie, as…" She gives Viktor an apologetic look. "Forgive me, Viktor, but you terrified me."

"You're not the only one," I mutter. Vera giggles, and Nikko coughs into his hand. Viktor remains stoic, listening to my mother.

"No harm, no foul," he says calmly. "Go on, Zofia."

"Timur Yudin didn't take kindly to this news. I didn't realize at the time that his lawyer was privy to the inheritance due to you, Lydia. When I told him the marriage was dissolved, he had a fit. My guards had to escort him off our property." She leans forward and holds my gaze. "That evening, he met you for dinner. He already knew you wouldn't marry him. His intent was to hurt you. If he couldn't have you, no one could."

She looks over at Viktor. "You must find him."

Viktor nods. "I know, Zofia."

"You might even orchestrate a public break-up. Something bad. If he thinks he can take advantage, he will." She shakes her head. "I'm sorry you even have to think about this."

My mother releases a shuddering breath. "He is going to make his move. He's likely planning it already. Do not let your guard down for a moment. He will attack, and soon."

She coughs again, her entire body shaking. Vera gets on her feet and walks over to her, frowning. She waits until Mom stops coughing. "Who are you seeing? What do they say about this?"

"I saw a doctor at the local clinic. You know I don't like to go to the doctor for these silly things."

Vera frowns. "Did they give you any medication?"

"They did. It's in the kitchen. But I swear, Vera, when I take it, the coughing only gets worse, and I feel terrible. It doesn't help at all."

"I'll be right back," she says, heading toward the kitchen.

"I'll go with you."

Viktor's shadow looms behind me.

"I'm fine, Viktor."

"I know you are."

I turn and glare at him. "I want a moment of privacy with my sister, dammit."

"This isn't about limiting your privacy. You know that," he scoffs. "I'll stand behind to make sure you're safe."

We make it to the kitchen. I remember what it was like as a child. We had staff when my father was home, but when he traveled, my mother paid them all and gave them leave while the three of us took care of ourselves. We baked cookies and cakes. My mother's *Wuzetka,* a layered chocolate cake with whipped cream and a chocolate glaze, was my absolute favorite, one of the few links to her Polish upbringing that remained.

"This is not normal, Lydia," Vera says in a low voice. "This is not medication you give to someone with a cold or even bronchitis. It's a drug you give someone with cancer."

My blood runs cold. "What?" I whisper. "Are you sure?"

But this is her strength, her talent. Vera knows medical science front and back.

"I'm positive," she says, shaking her head. "Lydia…"

"Why would she lie to us, though?"

"She doesn't want us to know, I would guess. Maybe she wants to get you through the wedding." She leans in and hugs me. I don't even know what to say or what to do. Viktor stands nearby, but I don't think he can hear what we're saying. He's staring out the window at our backyard, seemingly lost in thought.

"Alright, listen, we can't make this right, not today. For now, we're heading back in there, and we're going to plan this wedding."

But I don't feel right about this anymore. I don't feel right about anything.

I shake my head and raise my voice.

"No. I don't want to talk about the wedding. I want to find Timur and be rid of him. I don't want this hanging over my head any longer. I want this behind us." I shake my head. "I'm sorry, Vera. I need a minute. Stay with Mom, and I'll be back in soon."

I shove open the back door and march into the yard. I can see Viktor behind me, following me.

I couldn't stop him if I tried, so I let him. But I don't make it easy on him.

We need to stage a public break-up.

Done.

How public do we need? If Timur is nearby or watching my mother's home in any way, this should do just *fine.*

I walk with purpose back to the place I went as a child. If I close my eyes and remember, I can still see where I snuck between the pickets of the fence and got into the campground. I can still smell the campfires, the roasted marshmallows, sizzling hot dogs, and burgers.

I stare at the fence. It's still dilapidated like it always was, only now it doesn't seem I could fit through them. I walk up to one of the fence posts.

"Don't even think about it, Lydia."

Orchestrate a break-up. *Orchestrate a break-up.* I pour all my anger, my frustration, and my fear into my voice.

"Fuck off, Viktor. You can't stop me. I want to be alone for a little while." I turn around and face him, my fueled emotions real. "I know that's a foreign concept to you, but I want you to fucking leave me *alone.*"

"Lydia," he growls, but I can tell he's wondering if I'm faking or if I'm serious. His brows snap together in concern, and he takes another step toward me. "I know we have to hash shit out, but this isn't the time or place."

I scoff. "So my mother's place is? Yeah, let's have a fight in front of her. Great idea." I turn away and take another step toward the hole in the fence. Just beyond it, there's a shadow of pine trees. It doesn't look like there are many people there.

"I'm sick of you following me," I say, loud enough for anyone who's listening to hear. "I'm sick of you controlling me."

A part of me believes this, and a part of me knows... I crave this. I do. It's sick and twisted and fucked up beyond recognition, so far from anything healthy that I wouldn't even know where normal began at this point, but... but it's a part of *us*. It's a part of who we are.

"Lydia," he growls again. He's only a step away from me when I turn and shove myself through the hole in the fence. He reaches for me, grasping at me, but he can't reach me.

"Give me space," I say, my voice wobbling. Why is my voice wobbling? "I just need a little time."

"I can't fit through here," he growls. "You did this on purpose."

Of course I did. I can't remind him now that we needed to fake a fight. Someone could be listening.

"I need time," I repeat.

He reaches toward me, his eyes flooded with panic. "Lydia!" he shouts, shaking his head. "For fuck's sake, listen to me. You're not safe. Hey!" he screams.

I swear it's a part of the entire game. He's playing it this way so that I can come back to him.

I will, just not yet.

I hear the snap of a tree branch behind me—the skin on the back of my neck prickles in awareness. I turn to see if there's anyone behind me, but it's just me. Just me in the forest and no one there. I shake my head and take a look around.

I remember lighting a fire by those fire pits. I wish I had something with me now to do it again, just for old times' sake.

"Lydia!" Viktor screams, but his voice is getting fainter as I'm walking away from him. Did he completely forget we were supposed to be mimicking this? That we're *supposed* to break up?

We need to bring the *Ledyanoye Bratstvo* out of hiding.

I walk over to a fire pit and lift a stick from the ground. I draw in the ashes, and it feels weirdly symbolic.

I shouldn't be here alone; I know that. It isn't safe. I tell myself I'll just stay here a few minutes and reminisce.. I remember what it was like being away from everyone else. Untouchable. How the whole world outside these fences seemed high paced and loud, but here, I stepped back in time and reconnected with a part of me that was waiting.

I take in a deep breath and let it out slowly.

I turn to pick up another branch when black covers my face, and my world is plunged into darkness. I scream, but it's muffled. I try to remember everything I learned about self-defense, but my brain won't cooperate. It feels sluggish and confused as I try my best to muddle through. Without oxygen, I feel half drugged.

I try to remember what Viktor taught me, but I can hardly think.

Always stay calm. If you lose your shit, you can't fix a damn thing.

Do I have my knife? Do I have the strength to hold it?

What the hell is going on?

I've got this. I can do this.

I elbow whoever's holding me, but my eyes are growing hazy. I scream and try to thrash, but someone's got their arms around me, holding me in place. I need to escape.

I can't breathe!

"Let me go!" I try to scream, but my voice is muffled, and I'm losing consciousness. "Let me go!" I say, softer this time, my voice barely audible. *"Let me go,"* I whisper.

CHAPTER TWENTY-SIX

Viktor

I CAN'T GET through this fucking fence. I try to break it with my fists, but it's going to take too long to do it this way. I need to get in there, and I need to find her.

I wish I had my phone with me. I run back to the house at top speed, my feet pounding on the pavement. "Nikko!" I scream. "Nikko!"

Vera leaps out onto the front step, her eyes wide.

"They're in the campground. They've got her. I need to get in. Tell Nikko I need him. Now! How do you get in there? Where is the entrance?"

Shit. I can't take Nikko with me. What if he has someone here, just lying in wait, ready to attack Vera and her mother?

Nikko stands in the doorway. "What happened?"

"We got into our fight like we planned. She went into the campground. It's an old haunt of hers. I swear to God I heard someone there. They've got her."

Nikko nods. "We'll come with you."

"Shit," I shake my head. "I have to go in alone. You stay here with Zofia and Vera, you have to. Toss me my phone!"

He looks behind him at Zofia, too weak to run with them. He can't take Vera with him either and put her in a vulnerable position. With a growl, he goes in to grab my phone.

I'll have to go in alone. Just me and Lydia against our enemies. Maybe it's only ever been me and Lydia against the world.

"I'm calling in backup," Nikko snaps, tossing me my phone.

Zofia stands in the doorway. "Go, *go!* Leave me. I'm an old woman. Leave me and go get her."

"You're safer here."

"We'll all go," Vera says. "Nikko, we *have* to."

Nikko's jaw clenches and hope soars in me. We'll get her so much more easily if it's not just me alone in a vast, vacant campground.

"Zofia, get on my back. I'll carry you in."

"Give me a weapon, Nikko." Vera's eyes widen, and Zofia shakes her head. "Do you think I spent the better part of five decades in this life, and I don't know how to use a weapon?"

Nikko hands Zofia a gun, and I turn and bend so she can leap onto my back.

"This way," Vera says. "Follow me!"

We go all the way down to the driveway and take a right. About a mile down, I finally see the entrance.

"Listen," Vera says. "They'll be looking for you at the main entrance and by the gate. But there was another entrance for deliveries or something that Lydia and I knew about. This way." She leads us off the main path and shows me a break in the fence covered by a worn wooden sign.

Due to current dry conditions, open fires are strictly prohibited. Help us protect our forests and keep everyone safe!

Vera pushes the sign. It wobbles. "Lift it, and I can get in and open the gate for you."

I yank it off its hinges, and it splinters in my hands. Behind the sign is a small space, just big enough for her to squeeze into.

"Well, that will do the job, too," she mutters to herself.

"Careful," Nikko growls. He reaches for Zofia and gently takes her off my back. "Once Vera opens it, you come in," he says gently. Zofia stifles a cough and nods. Her hand on the gun trembles slightly.

The gate creaks open, and we enter. I pull up my phone and remind myself of what I tell Lydia.

Staying calm is most important and gives you an advantage.

The tracker I have embedded in Lydia's a high-end deal Aleksandr helped me secure and will track her to within one centimeter. I flip open the app. Immediately, a map of the campground comes into view. There's a tiny red dot behind several cottages further down the road.

"He's got her in one of the cottages."

We walk through the nearly vacant campground. I swivel my gun toward the sound of a twig snapping, only to find a doe staring at us with wide, sad eyes.

"A sign of good luck," Zofia says softly. "The Native Americans believed seeing a deer in the wild like this was a sign of good luck or good fortune." She sighs. "Let's find her."

We can do this.

I didn't even tell Lydia before she lost her shit that everybody in my family has these, including Vera. Me, all my brothers, my mother and my sister. It doesn't just track our locations but our biometrics.

I scan her reading. Her heart rate is elevated, but it's still beating. She's alive but terrified.

Clouds move in, covering the sun, and a brisk wind kicks up. Distant thunder rolls overhead just before fat raindrops begin to fall.

"You have her?" Nikko asks, standing behind me, Zofia and Vera between us.

I nod. "Yeah. It says she's about half a mile up ahead."

"It's one of the cabins," Vera says, swallowing hard. "It's apart from the rest on a little island... there's no possible way to get there without them seeing us. It's a trap, you guys."

"I don't fucking care," I say, shaking my head. "If I had time, I'd get a helicopter and a bomb squad, but I don't trust them."

"You'll go after her," Nikko says. "I'll stand on the shore and shoot anyone who fucking moves." I nod. It helps to have a trained assassin on your side.

"You'll save some for me," Zofia says softly, her eyes gleaming. Nikko gives her a look of surprise. Her eyes narrow. "That's my *daughter,* Nikko. You know how I feel about my daughters."

"I do," he says. "And I'll give you whoever you shoot first. Deal?"

The skies open, and rain pours down in torrents. I'm glad Vera is with me because she knows the layout of the campground better than anyone else.

"This way," she says, speaking above the sound of the pouring rain. Mud splatters onto us, our footsteps slippery. Zofia slips, but Nikko grabs her arm and rights her. We move forward as one.

Lightning strikes, the campground temporarily illuminated in vivid white before we're cast back into a cloudless darkness. I look back at the monitor and see Lydia's pulse has slowed, only a little. She's remembering to stay calm.

Good girl.

"Here, Viktor." Vera comes to a stop. "Do you see past that huge tree, there's the water—"

I'm already past the clearing of trees, trying my best to see the small cabin in the middle of the water.

Suddenly, a gunshot rings out. Two. Three. Zofia screams, and the heavy sound I know too well to be a body thuds to the ground. Lightning strikes again, lighting up Nikko's face. "Sniper," he says, jerking his chin in front of us to where a man lies on the ground, blood pooling from his head onto the earth.

"Good catch, babe," Vera says, her voice wobbling.

Nikko nods. "But we just rang the doorbell," he says as the cabin door flies open. "They know we're here."

His gun is poised next to Zofia's. "Viktor!" she screams. "Behind you." She pulls the trigger just as the cold blade of a knife hits my neck. I turn on instinct and grab the fucker who tried to hit me by the throat as Zofia's shot goes wide.

I squeeze hard, feeling the cartilage crunch beneath my fingers. He gurgles, clawing at my hand, but I don't let up. Time slows. The woman I love is in danger, and I'm going to fucking murder anyone who gets in my way. I don't let up until I feel him go limp. I release the man in my grip, his body crumpling to the ground. Nikko doesn't hesitate and with one quick shot, he finishes what I started.

"Dammit," Zofia says, shaking her head. "I promise you, I won't miss a second time. There!" She screams and pulls the trigger again. A body falls to the ground, and Nikko swivels to get another and another.

"It's an ambush," he yells at me. "*Go!* We've got you covered here. We'll use them as a diversion, and I'll cover you when you surface."

Two more come out of the forest, barely visible through the downpour. Thunder roars overhead as I yank off my shoes and shirt and toss my phone beside both of them. I step toward a roughly hewn pier and dive into the water.

The icy cold drags me under. I hold my breath and go as far as I can until my palms hit the soft mud of earth. I swim hard and fast underwater toward the cabin, as close to the surface of the ground as I can so no one sees me. The muted sounds of gunshots ring overhead. Someone knows I'm coming, and they're trying to shoot me, but I'm a moving target and too far, too unpredictable.

I can estimate I'm almost there. In front of me, the water begins to shallow as I near the cabin on the island. Through the murky haze of the water, I can see the thick chains where Yudin anchored his boat.

I grab onto the chain to keep myself in place and slowly rise to the surface. Another gunshot rings out, then another and another. I have to have hope that my brother's hit his target. No one outshoots Nikko. And no one outfights me.

I need to breathe. My vision is beginning to swim.

I can go on.

I'm going to strangle Yudin's fucking neck and feel the life drain out of him until I feel his pulse stop beneath my fingers, and I know my woman is safe.

The pressure engulfs me, muffling all sound but the frantic beating of my heartbeat. My chest tightens as my lungs scream for air, each second stretching into eternity. My vision begins to blur, and I'm engulfed in a sense of urgency to breathe, my body begging for oxygen. The need for air becomes a relentless force, my primal needs demanding to be met. My muscles tense as I head for the surface, my hand gliding along the heavy chain as I push toward the surface. I'm almost there.

I break through the surface, gasping for breath. Gunshots ring out, splashing the water beside me. I take another breath and plunge below the surface one more time, my murky gaze riveted on the boat. I anchor my feet on the rocky foundation of the cabin and push the paddle boat to break the surface of the water. Gunshots sound all around me. I can feel them embed into the wood of the boat I'm using like a shield. In front of me, I can see the door to the cabin.

"Go, Viktor!" Nikko shouts from shore. "I've got you covered. *Go!*"

I throw the boat into the water, turn, and leap onto the island, my bare feet clinging to the rocky surface. The door's locked, but I could knock down the Empire State Building now with the fury and adrenaline I've got coursing through my veins. I rear back and throw my entire body weight into it. It splinters and groans. I do it again as someone comes around the corner. A gunshot sounds from the shore. He trips, hits, and falls into the water. Nikko's got me.

I throw my weight into the door again, and it splinters, falling to the ground.

Lydia's in the middle of the room, gagged and tied to the chair, naked. I see red momentarily and take a deep breath to clear my vision. Lightning strikes overhead. She's shaking her head as if to warn me, her eyes wide with terror. I feel someone behind me and immediately snap into action the way Kolya taught me.

I pivot swiftly on my heel, blindly grab for the arm reaching for me, twisting it sharply and forcing my assailant to his knees with a pained grunt. Lightning strikes again, illuminating the face I fully expected to see—Timur Yudin, his face twisted in shock and pain. I stare into the face of my enemy for only a second before I drive my knee into his ribcage, winding him. He collapses to the ground.

"Stay down," I growl, my voice low and menacing as I pin him beneath me. "*Down.*"

The room is a mix of shadows and flashes of light from the storm outside. I turn my attention back to her, tied to the chair, vulnerable and scared.

"Are you alright?"

She nods and blinks, fat tears rolling down her cheeks.

"Did he hurt you?" I'm barely breathing, holding out for her answer.

Swallowing, she nods. I turn back to him and lift him by the back of the head, slamming his face into the wooden floor. He lies limp beneath me. I look up at her, and she shakes her head, her eyes widening as Yudin comes to life beneath me and slashes at me with a blade. It slices into my bare chest, and pain radiates through me. I hit him again and again, but he fights hard.

With a roar, I grab him and slam him into the floor. The force of the impact knocks the knife from his hand. I lift him and slam him against the wall. His head cracks against it. A lamp crashes to the floor as thunder rolls overhead, lightning coming closer. I unleash a flurry of hard, deadly punches, each one driven by years of pent-up fury and the need to punish him for hurting my Lydia. Blood splatters with every hit, his face a broken, unrecognizable mess.

He crumples to the ground, and I kick him away. He doesn't move.

I lift him with one arm and drag him behind me, holding onto him with my left arm as I bend and take the blade he used against me. I slash at the knot where the rope tied her up. I can't cut it into shreds like I want to.

I need that rope.

Lydia rushes to my side, her eyes wide with a mix of fear and relief. I pull her into my arms, holding her tight against me.

I slam Yudin into the same chair he used for her. He slumps forward, one eye swollen shut and the other focused with hatred on me.

"I'd slit your throat," I growl at him, shaking my head. "But I won't take this from her. You don't get to see her naked, you fucking asshole." I lift the knife. "Turn away, Lydia."

She buries her head in my shoulder while I advance on him. He screams in terror while I slice at his face and blind him. Blood drips down his face in torrents. I throw the blade to the floor.

"I want you to know what you lost. You wanted her money. You wanted the power. You hurt her mother and tried to hurt the woman I love. You worthless piece of shit." I turn to her, my hands covered in blood. My thumb slips along her cheek as I raise her face to look into mine.

"It's over," I murmur into her hair. "He'll never hurt you again."

Lydia pulls back slightly, looking up at me with tears in her eyes. "Thank you," she whispers, her voice trembling. "Oh God, I was scared. I still am."

"We're going to end that now. You're safe, baby." I cup her face in my hands, my thumb brushing away a tear. A streak of red smears across her cheek, and I kiss her temple. "I'll always protect you, Lydia. No one will ever harm you as long as I draw breath."

"I love you," I say to her as the sound of rain overhead begins to slow. "He will never, ever hurt you again," I repeat. I want her to know this down in her bones.

She nods, blinking tears away. "And I love you, Viktor. Let's end this. Let's end this once and for all."

I look around the cabin and find a fireplace with firewood and lighter fluid.

Perfect.

I lift a blanket from the bed and cover her with it.

Hand her the matches.

Lift the lighter fluid and douse the cabin with it. The liquid sloshes onto the floor. I make sure Yudin's fucking drenched.

"This place is going up in flames, Lydia. But I've got you. Do you trust me?"

She licks her lips and nods. "I trust you with my life."

"Here, baby. Light it up."

CHAPTER TWENTY-SEVEN

Lydia

I'VE NEVER FELT MORE powerful in my life. I tell myself that he is almost dead, that he'll bleed out in minutes anyway. I tell myself that ending him means my mom will be safe. Vera, Nikko, and sweet little Ivy. All of them. Everyone. And Viktor.

Especially Viktor.

I stand with Viktor at my back, his presence reassuring, my enemy in front of me. He's bleeding and gasping his last breaths.

I take a deep breath, and I light the match. The familiar, sweet scent of sulfur fills the cabin. The tiny flame dances, casting flickering shadows on walls. I watch the flame lick down the matchstick until it nearly burns my fingers. A part of me wants to feel the pain.

I release it, and it falls to the fluid-soaked floor. Flames instantly erupt, hungry and fierce, devouring everything in their path. I light a second match and then a third, dropping them around the first. The fire grows around us. Flames bite at my skin, a sharp reminder of the danger, until Viktor's arm wraps around my waist, pulling me back.

"It's enough, baby. You did it. Let's get to safety."

His voice is a low, gravelly rumble. I toss the rest of the matches into the fire, watching as they are quickly swallowed by the inferno. Viktor bends and effortlessly lifts me in his arms. The flames lick at my back.

We burst through the door of the cabin, the heat and smoke following behind us, greedy and hungry.

Viktor marches to the boat Timur used to get us here, anchored to shore. He reaches for the chain with one hand and yanks it closer, places me on my feet, and leaps into the boat. It wobbles under his weight, but he quickly rights himself, his movements swift and assured. He reaches for my hand, his grip strong.

He nestles me into the boat beside him as flames roar behind us.

"Are you alright?" Vera screams from shore.

"Yes!" Viktor shouts back.

We take a moment to watch in silence, secure on shore, as the cabin erupts in flames. I stare, mesmerized by the destruction, the finality of it. Purging.

Viktor's hand rests on my knee, a grounding touch amidst the chaos. I turn to him, seeing the reflection of the fire in his dark, intense eyes. He is my protector. His obsession with me, his unwavering determination to keep me safe, it all makes sense at this moment.

"Are you okay?" he asks, his voice a soft growl filled with concern.

I nod, unable to find the words. My throat is tight, my emotions a tangled mess. But in his arms, I feel safe. For the first time in a long time, I feel like I have control over my life, my destiny.

As the cabin collapses in on itself, the flames roaring in triumph, I lean into Viktor. He holds me close, his warmth a stark contrast to the inferno behind us. We are survivors. Forged in a crucible. His world is brutal and chaotic, only interspersed with quiet like this... but now I know.

It's my world, too.

CHAPTER TWENTY-EIGHT

"I'M FINE," I tell Vera, but she insists on inspecting every wound.

"You're not fine," she snaps. "Lydia, for the love of God, tell him to let me do this."

"Viktor, please," Lydia says. "Let her take care of you."

"As long as I know you're fine."

I'm a mess, but it's nothing I can't handle. I'll be fine. I made sure she saw Lydia first, but now that Lydia's few injuries are doctored up, she's showered and changed and is sitting by the fire beside her mother.

"How are you feeling?" she asks Zofia, her brows knit in concern.

"My God, don't worry about *me,*" her mother says. "All that I care about is that you're okay." She shakes her head. "You two did a thorough job of it, didn't you?"

Lydia meets my eyes. I wink at her. "We did."

Nikko and my brothers are in the campground. Thanks to Aleks and our connections, no one called the fire department until hours after we were done. I'm thankful Yudin had the foresight to see that his crematorium was apart from everything else, so we didn't have to burn the whole campground to the ground.

Not that I wouldn't have done it.

They've taken the bodies of Yudin's accomplices, all now safely in the ash of the cabin. We'll come up with a story for the press. Mikhail's already dealing with the blowback from the *Ledyanoye Bratstvo*, but he'll have that under control. With the combined forces of the Ivanovs, we've got this handled.

"You cut your feet on the rocks," Vera says, shaking her head. "And you've got knife wounds. But I think this time you're going to be fine." She puts one final bandage on me and stands.

"Thank God, Viktor. What did Aria find?"

"Aria sees no further evidence of any of his men nearby. Apparently, some of his men staged a coup, and he only took the last of them with him."

His men likely knew it was not a smart idea to take us on because being enemies to us makes them instant enemies to the Ivanovs as well.

"You can breathe easy again," Vera says softly, resting her hand on my shoulder but looking at Lydia. "Can't you?"

Lydia nods. "I'm so relieved."

"And now," her mother says. "We move on to the wedding." She holds Lydia's hand tightly. "It means so much to me to see my daughters married well. Let's make this happen, girls." She smiles sadly. "No more travel for me for a good long while."

We spend the night in her family home. Lying beside her in the guest room bed, she sidles up to me and lays her head on my chest.

"I'm sorry I gave you so much shit about everything. Vera explained it to me, you know."

"Explained what?"

She sighs. "That all the Romanovs have biometric trackers on them. I mean, don't get me wrong—it's extreme, but at least I know it isn't just you and your insanity."

I bend and give her a chaste kiss. We're exhausted, both of us, and in need of rest.

"But make me a promise, Viktor, will you?"

"Mmm?" I hold her to me. I can hardly believe she's here. Safe. In my arms. I don't want to fall asleep for a while. I want to assure myself that she isn't going anywhere, not for a long, long time.

"When we get back to our place, you'll get rid of those creepy things of mine you kept."

I laugh out loud. It feels so damn good to laugh.

"Promise. You can even throw it all in the firepit and have a nice bonfire, alright?"

"Well," she says thoughtfully. "Maybe we keep *Wuthering Heights*. I do love that book."

"Deal."

I kiss her cheek. "Now get some sleep, baby. We had a long, long day."

She closes her eyes. "I know. You too. Put it all down for a while, alright, Viktor? Your brothers are here, just downstairs." She kisses my chest and lies back down. "You don't have to be Superman for a little while, okay? Just be..." She yawns widely. "Viktor. My almost-husband. Oh, and tomorrow?"

I open one eye, still thinking over the Superman comment. "Mmm?"

"Let's plan the most epic of all epic honeymoons known to man with that inheritance I'm getting. Deal?"

I grin against her hair, still damp from the shower she took. "Deal, baby. Someplace with the best cake you've ever put in your mouth."

She grins. "You do know me so damn well."

CHAPTER TWENTY-NINE

Lydia

THE DAYS LEADING up to our wedding are filled with memories I don't ever, ever want to forget.

Another cake sampling Viktor made me go to just because he wanted to. A bachelorette party with Aria, Harper, Polina, and Vera. Vera's only here until her next travel date, but I get to keep her for a few more weeks.

I get to pick out stuff for our bridal shower and have a lot of fun, especially with the kitchen things.

The dress fitting was with Vera and Mom. I settled on a gorgeous wrap dress made of satin and trimmed with hand-knit lace. It dips low in the front, accentuating my full breasts and flowing over my curves. I feel like I'm a Disney princess who stepped right out of a movie set in it. My eyes sparkle in the mirror, and I grin.

"I love it. Oh my God, it's perfect."

I make Viktor practice dancing and take an engagement photo shoot. We don't have a lot of time, but we have literally nothing on our agenda except the next big step: tie the knot.

We have personal, quiet moments together. Walking around our property, hand in hand, talking about where we're going to honeymoon. Roasting marshmallows by our firepit, where I run our future children's names by him until we have a suitable list.

It's days before our wedding when I run something by him that I've been thinking about for a while.

Viktor leans back in his chair, nursing a beer. I've got one of the craft brews next to me on a little table near the fire pit. The ashes of the memory he took down from "the shrine," as he called it, rise with the heat of the fire.

"So, I've been thinking…"

"Mmm?" he says. "What's that?"

"Well. You know I want children. I know you do, too. But I've been thinking about your childhood and your sister, and… this money that I'm getting, and God knows your family has more money than God." The wedding dress, the diamond ring he gave me, and a quick glance into the accounts we now own together made that abundantly clear. "You're so protective. So good with the kids, Viktor. And your family is amazing."

He looks at me curiously. "And?"

I swallow. For some reason, my heart is beating really fast right now. "What if we… you know… adopt? What if we adopt some kids that are in need of a good home?"

"Lydia," he says seriously. "We're *Bratva*."

"Viktor," I respond. "I mean, don't show them your weapons."

He grins at that. I love when he grins. My heart turns in my chest.

"We'll be good parents. Just like Mikhail and Aria are. Harper and Aleks. And Vera and Nikko will be someday."

"We will. Because we love each other, and we know what it's like not to have that love." I nod. We'll lavish love and attention on whatever children we bring into our home. "And," I say with a serious nod. "You'll *immediately* beat your brothers in that race to see who has the most kids. Like you'll advance right to the finish line."

He snorts into his beer bottle, upends it, and polishes it off. "Now you're talking. Perfect. Let's look into it, baby."

I nestle against his arm. "I have this feeling I could tell you I wanted to run a marathon, adopt an entire litter of puppies, sell this house and move into one of those RVs, or open up a mobile food truck bakery, and you'd smile at me and say yes."

He holds me close to him and kisses the top of my head. "Of course I would. Though I don't know if the entire litter of puppies *and* a mobile home at the same time is wise."

I laugh along with him.

"I told you, Lydia," he says quietly, his eyes growing soft, the flicker of flames reflected in his gaze. "I've only ever wanted you. And now you're mine." I bend and brush my lips against his. My heart swells, and I think, for the first time, I actually, truly, *really* believe him. I lie in his arms as he assures me one more time.

"You're all I've ever wanted and all I ever will."

I lie in his arms, blissfully content. I don't feel the need to run anymore. I don't feel like I have to constantly look over my shoulder, waiting for the next wave of doubt or uncertainty to haunt me. His words mend my years of insecurity and heartache. My past no longer holds me in its grip.

As I nestle closer, I can feel the steady rhythm of his heartbeat along with mine. "I've spent so much time running," I whisper, "but now I feel like I can finally... stop. Like I'm finally home."

His arms tighten around me. "We all have scars, Lydia," he says. "But they don't define us. They remind us of what we've fought and how we became who we are today."

"I love you," I whisper.

"And I love you." He holds me.

We lie there before the fire, our pasts behind us and untold years ahead of us. I feel like, for the first time in my life... I'm happy. For the first time in my life, *I'm free.*

EPILOGUE

Six months later

Lydia

IT'S LATE AT NIGHT, but Viktor and I have lost track of the time. We do that sometimes when we're with each other. The minutes tick by into hours, and before we know what's happening, the sun is rising, and it's a new day. We have flexible work schedules, though, so it's all good. He does what Mikhail demands when he calls him, and I've recently gone back to online grad school.

But tonight, I'm restless. The air is pregnant with the threat of coming rain, held at bay and only momentarily forgotten when I light a fire.

I love it here. It may be my very favorite place to be, the fire pit in front of me and flickering candles on various surfaces. I especially like it when there's a chill in the air like tonight, the cold at our backs, and the warmth of the fire in front of us.

It's early autumn in The Cove, the maples bordering the fire pit tinged with hues of gold and rust still mingled with hunter green. I stand before the flames, warming my hands. We roasted marshmallows after dinner, burnt the ends of our roasting sticks so they weren't sticky with residue, and laid them where we like to keep them behind the pit. Viktor sits silently behind me, wearing a contemplative expression.

"What's on your mind?" I ask him, reaching for one of the sticks to stoke the fire. It kindles as sparks fly, the crackling sound of fire rising. Viktor rises and approaches from behind, his hulking frame softened by the flickering light.

"Lots of things," he says, his deep voice a low rumble in the fire-lit quiet. "I got you something." Though he isn't a gift-giver by nature, frequently forgetting his siblings' birthdays and needing to be reminded it's occasionally a good idea to toss a few gifts or cards at loved ones, he never seems to neglect giving anything to me.

"Mmm?" I ask, my heart beating a little faster. I never had anyone who was interested in buying things for me before, and I'm always touched by the gesture. "Let me guess. You bought me one of those Caribbean islands I was ogling the other day online."

He snorts and shakes his head. "Caribbean? Definitely not. Though I might be persuaded by Hawaii."

"Oh? Are you prejudiced, sir?"

"I am. I'm not really fond of hurricanes," he says, weaving his fingers through my mass of curls. "Unless they're in the form of a woman, of course, who happens to wear my ring and bear my name."

I stifle a giggle. "Of course."

"Hawaii's easier to travel to. Communication's easier. We can use the same currency."

"Fair, fair. Are you telling me you want to go to Hawaii?"

"Some day, yeah. You?"

I nod. "Absolutely. Have you seen that macadamia nut cake that went viral?"

He grins. "No, but I'll take your word for it. I love how you prioritize travel based on cake options."

I nod decidedly. "I do have my priorities."

He holds a box out to me. "No tickets to Hawaii here and sadly no cake, but maybe you'll like this just the same."

I open the box to find a set of ornate matches and a small bottle of the perfume I used when I was younger. "You remembered," I whisper, my voice thick. I swallow hard.

He brushes a tendril of hair off my cheek. "I remember everything about you."

I laugh. "Sometimes I wish you'd forget the darker parts."

Bending down to me, he kisses the top of my head, where my hair's gone all frizzy with the heat of the fire. "Never. Those are my favorite parts."

I place the little gifts down by our chairs. We stand together watching the fire when Nikita starts barking with a vengeance. Viktor and I exchange a look. She only ever barks like that when we have visitors, and none of our typical security alarms have triggered.

He pushes me behind him, closer to the fire, on instinct, while he scowls into the darkness. At first, we see nothing.

"Show yourself," Viktor barks out. "Immediately, or I'll give the command to my dog to attack." He snaps his fingers at Nikita who sits obediently, still growling.

It's no idle threat. I peek to the right of Viktor's enormous bicep and draw in a quick breath when a woman emerges from the shadows, her small hands in front of her in a gesture of surrender. As she draws closer, the flickering fire illuminates her features. Striking green eyes radiate determination and intelligence, and something else I can't quite put my finger on, but it makes a shiver snake down my spine. There's an air of fearlessness about her that borders insanity—it's downright terrifying.

Long, chestnut-brown hair hangs in a thick ponytail, and her petite but athletic build exudes strength and agility. I have a strange feeling she could leap over the fire unscathed and disappear into the night like a leopard. Dressed in sleek all-black clothing, she looks ready to rob a bank or overthrow a tyrannical regime, depending on whatever tickles her fancy first.

She shouldn't be here, and yet I'm somehow completely entranced and want her to stay. I'm madly in love with my husband, but in the few seconds I've observed this woman, I think I've already developed a girl crush.

Still, I don't trust her. She got here by some sort of witchcraft. No one enters our estate unnoticed. Nikita's barking is the last warning, not the first.

"You." Viktor's voice holds a world of accusation, but the woman only grins as if flattered by the recognition.

Bowing, she gives him a grin, flashing perfectly straight white teeth and full lips with a glimmer of pale pink gloss. "Isabella Morales, at your service. Really, Viktor, you need better surveillance."

He narrows his eyes. "Why the hell are you here?"

She pokes her head around his arm but doesn't come any nearer. "I'd like a formal introduction to your wife, of course."

He growls, but I tug on the hem of his tee. "I don't know her, Viktor, so maybe you can indulge her." I want to know who she is.

"Lydia, this is Isabella Morales, the sister of Javier Morales of the Los Sangre Dorada Cartel."

Oh God. I stare, my mouth unhinged. The Los Sangre Dorada—or LSD, for short—is the most cutthroat cartel south of the border. Aria's told me at length what they've done and why they are to be feared.

"Isabella, this is my wife, Lydia," he says through clenched teeth.

"I know," she says with a slow, menacing smile. I take an involuntary step closer to Viktor. "You looked stunning in that wedding dress, Lydia. It would be such a shame if anything were to happen to such a beauty. Pleased to see someone's managed to hook this guy. I thought he'd be single forever." She winks. "Enjoy marital bliss while you can."

Viktor takes a step closer to her. The firelight glints on a knife in her hand that I swear wasn't there a second ago. "Now, now," she says softly, a hint of ice in her tone. "I didn't come here to fight, Romanov. I came here to warn you."

"Have you?" he says in a tone that makes my heart rate spike. I gulp.

"Your enemies are closer than you think, Viktor."

When he takes a step closer to her, she raises her hand in a gesture of peace. "I'm not here to fight, I promise." She laughs mirthlessly and bites her lower lip. She looks like she wants to devour my husband. "If I'd come here to harm either of you, I wouldn't have wasted time on small talk. I wanted you to know, Javier is planning an attack on The Cove. That quiet little brother of yours has caused too much trouble."

Ollie? His brother Ollie's the one in charge of international relations, but I can't imagine what he's done. Or Lev? Both are his younger brothers.

"My brother wants to use you to get to Lev," she reveals.

What?

"And why should I trust you, 'princesa loca'?"

Isabella's eyes shutter, and her voice turns to ice. "Because I want him dead as much as you do. He's a fool, a fool who's betrayed my family and our better interests one too many times."

Viktor studies her. "When?"

She shakes her head. "Now, now, where's the fun in this if I give you all the details? I don't want you to annihilate him immediately. It has to be a real, bonafide battle, you know."

She's crazy. This woman is insane. And yet... she came here to warn us, didn't she?

"I can tell you this. When he attacks, it will be swift and it will be violent. You'll want all of your brothers and associates near. I wouldn't let them travel all over the world like you have been. None of this gallivanting to Moscow or Barcelona."

She's been watching us.

What else does she know?

"Go. Tell your brothers you've been warned, but why don't you keep my visit a secret?" she says with a wink. She turns and sprints into the night.

"Wait!" Viktor shouts, running after her, but it's too late. She's already disappeared as suddenly as she came.

I feel oddly bereft.

"My God," I whisper, clutching his arm when he returns to me. "She was terrifying and yet... I don't know if I've ever seen anyone more beautiful in my life."

Viktor only shakes his head and pulls out his phone.

"We need to alert the others. We cannot fuck around when it comes to Javier Morales. She came here with a purpose, and I don't know if we can trust her, but there's no fucking way we can ignore her warning either."

I nod. "Absolutely."

Viktor leans in and kisses my cheek. "We've got this. Whatever this is, we'll weather it like we do every other challenge we've ever faced."

With my heart still pounding, I turn my head so our lips meet. The world fades away as I sigh into the kiss, and his warm, large hand rests at the small of my back. When we pull away, dawn breaks, casting a shimmer of gold over us.

We stand side by side, our fingers entwined. We've survived far more than this. We'll survive anything that comes our way because together... we are invincible.

THE END

CHAPTER ONE

Isabella

I grin into the chilly autumn night, nearly skipping with glee.

This disguise is so fucking awesome, literally no one would ever suspect who I really am.

This was no last-minute disguise. Hell, I've been practicing all day.

First, the fake mustache, because even the best disguise won't cover my Latina roots – Columbian men have beards and a five o'clock stubble by noon, so I used some makeup, just a touch of foundation to give me a slightly rougher complexion and a subtle contour to sharpen my jawline. A dab of an eyebrow pencil to give me the hint of stubble.

I refuse to cut my hair, so that was a tiny bit of a challenge.

It's slicked back and wound around my head, tucked under a black cap.

I had to wear a chest binder to flatten my chest which needed it thanks to my mama's generous genes, and that's a bitch, but I needed a masculine silhouette. The clothing was kind of fun — a dark hoodie that conceals my figure, baggy pants with multiple pockets to give me some bulk and a rugged appearance, paired with combat boots. I needed something masculine and practical for moving silently and blending in.

To mimic male body language, I adopted a slouched posture and broader stance, my walk more deliberate and heavy-footed. If they have a camera here I failed to see, they'll never suspect who I really am. Sadly, I have to mask the sexy hip sway.

And when I was ready to go, I took myself into The Cove — the prowling ground of our enemies – just to test it all out. I had a damn good time for myself. I spoke in a deeper voice when I needed to — ordered coffee, and asked for directions just to make sure I passed the test.

Not only did no one give me so much as a strange look, I caught a few girls making eyes at me.

"Hola, beautiful," I said in my guy voice to a slender blonde near Starbucks. She blushed but didn't respond, then whispered to her friend behind me, who I winked at. Heh.

Truth is, I wouldn't want to actually be a man for all the money in the world. I fucking love being a woman. But damn, it was fun to play.

And now, I'm ready. If they see me now, I'm still fucked, but at least they won't suspect who I really am. I'll get away – I always do – and *they'll* be none the wiser.

I intercepted communication between Aleksandr Romanov, one of the high-ranking officials in the Romanov Bratva, and his wife Harper. They have small children and long, sleepless nights, so I figured eventually they'd get sloppy, and I wasn't wrong.

I mean, anyone else might have totally missed the little tip-off, but when Aleksandr told his wife *got another late night* and she responded, *please be careful, it's so dark there and I don't trust you're safe,* I knew exactly where they were going.

Who's going? She asked.

My heart took a giant leap at his response: *All of us.*

It's rare that *all* of the Romanov men are in one place. Though some of their wives work for them, and I have it on good authority that Viktor's new wife Lydia actually set fire to her ex, the Romanovs are still in the Dark Ages. They'd deny it. Hell, their wives actually draw a salary, but I'm not impressed. Show me a Bratva group with a woman in actual fucking *power. Authority. Leadership.*

Now *that* would impress me.

The snap of a branch several yards to my left makes me freeze in my tracks. I stand as still as a hunted deer, listening. The Romanovs won't be here for several hours yet, but it's essential I'm not seen.

I wait, holding my breath. Listening. Is someone else here, or is it just an animal?

Another beat passes. Another.

Nothing.

I move on. I know exactly where to go: The abandoned warehouse, deeply hidden past a hiking trail in The Cove, is heavily secured with video surveillance. If the Romanovs see me on any security camera, they'll just see a random dude going for a hike off trail.

They might wonder how their security footage was destroyed but by then, I'll have everything I need.

The darkness and silence amplify every sound, making me hyper-aware of my surroundings. I only have about another mile to hike before I get to the entrance, but the night is young. I couldn't risk driving anywhere near here for fear of being seen.

"Who's there?" A deep male voice booms in the quiet woods. My heart stops for a split second.

Fuck.

I stand still and pull my hoodie over my head, sidestepping so I'm hidden behind a huge tree trunk. My heart beats faster. Did they actually send people here ahead of time? They never brought guards to the warehouse before.

Maybe they're getting wary.

My breathing's shallow as footsteps approach. Thankfully my vision is excellent even with the hoodie pulled tight. My hand tightens around my knife as I zoom in on my target. I don't need to *kill* any of their guards. Not yet, anyway. I just need to incapacitate and possibly maim.

He comes within ten yards but scans around and shakes his head. Is he alone? I take out the tiny pair of night vision goggles I brought and peek through them. Must be a new recruit. He looks young, and scared enough to shit his pants.

Ah, Romanovs, why did you make it this easy for me? I thought we would be a good match.

He turns his back to me and heads back to the warehouse. My green light.

The backside of the warehouse is camera-free with no entrances. But for me, it is perfect. I welcome a challenge.

I scale the side of the building, using a rusty drainpipe and ledges. My fingers grip tightly, my body tense with the possibility of being seen. I am in the zone when I am climbing, mentally placing my feet and hands into positions I cannot see.

A thrill races through me when I reach the topmost window, partially opened on the second floor, the hinges rusted. It's far away from the main patrol paths or any surveillance equipment. Since they use this place rarely, they haven't really secured it as well as their residences. I never would have dreamed to try to infiltrate one of their private homes.

I carefully pry the window open and slide inside just as the beam of a flashlight illuminates the leaf-covered ground below. My heart leaps into my throat. I crouch down, peering from the edge of the window as the useless guard walks past, leans against the wall and pulls out his phone.

When *I* get into a place of leadership in this family – and I fucking *will* – I'm going to fire that lazy son of a bitch. When my breathing slows and he's gone, it's go time.

The door to this vacant room is locked. Good. I thought this would be boring. I would be disappointed if I could not pick any locks today. With practiced ease, I do my magic and pick the lock in less than a minute.

Really, boys, a bit of a challenge would be nice.

I move quietly down the dim hallway, testing every footfall for creaky floorboards and ducking into shadows in case someone came in here unseen, until I find a shadowy loft area right above the main floor and quickly climb the ladder. It's a perfect vantage point to observe them without being seen.

I mean, I could've done something a bit safer, I guess. Planted a bug maybe. But Jesus, what is the fun in that? This is late night, the entire surrounding cast in shadows illuminated only by moonlight — it is eerie, tense, and dangerous. My favorite.

I settle into my hiding spot. I have got a few hours before they arrive, but my heart still hammers in my chest. I have waited *so long* for this. The entire trajectory of my life is at stake.

I lean back against the wall and imagine myself where I want to be. They say visualization is the key to leaning into a goal, for really making shit happen. If that is actually true, I have got it *made,* since I can already imagine what it feels like to give orders, to snap my fingers and watch grown men cow to me. I can already hear the respect in their voices and feel the surge of power coursing through my veins when they call me their Queen.

A flicker of sadness washes across me as I remember my father's cold, disapproving eyes. He'd kill me for what I'm about to do. Literally.

It's half the damn reason I am here.

To my father, women were a means to an end. A lower class of human, useless in his quest for domination, save their ability to provide offspring.

Even I was viewed as less than because of my status as *female*. My brother Javier, on the other hand, was much more highly valued.

I shake it off and focus on the task at hand.

I take mental notes and go over my plan again.

I went to Viktor and tipped him off. My brother would beat the living shit out of me before he murdered me with his own hands, but if he ever finds out, it will be too late for him. If my plan goes well, anyway.

That's one of several reasons he needs to go. I will see to that.

They are all coming — Mikhail, the eldest and one of the most dangerous. He took over when his father died and now rules the entirety of The Cove, the area between Coney Island and Manhattan. Next in command is Aleksandr, the computer geek, followed by Nikko, the group Assassin. He's got the eye of a sniper and a perfect shot, but I will not give him a target.

Viktor will be here, too. The largest one of all, heavily covered in tattoos and scars, Viktor is the group heavy, their loyal pit bull in human form. Ollie, the silent, quiet one who works in international relations, is home from Moscow, thanks to me. The youngest brother Lev will be here, too, but I do not worry about him. According to my intel, he is practically a kid. Javier has it out for Lev, but I'm not entirely sure why and I am not sure it matters. Javier hates everyone he sees as a personal threat.

I take out my goggles again and scan below. There is a table with detailed maps and documents below. Huh. Interesting. I would like to take a closer look at those, but do not dare risk moving out of my hiding spot.

The most challenging part of all this is that the Romanovs are so damn loyal. Any one of those brothers would lay down their lives for the others, including their wives, children, sister, and mother. It makes it nearly impossible to plot against a family so dedicated to each other. There is no weak link to exploit.

My family? Ha. Luckily for me, we're power-hungry animals, eager to kill for a meaty bone. It is only a matter of knowing whose hunger to stoke and stepping out of the way for the kill...*and* making sure you do not end up the one devoured.

I did not learn my skills for nothing, though.

I lean back in the loft, hidden in the shadows. The rain beats down harder on the tin roof, the relentless sound drowning out anything I would hear going on outside. It does not matter. They will show. I close my eyes, just for a little rest. I cannot risk falling asleep and someone finding out I am here, but it feels good to take a bit of a breather.

I wrap the oversized hoodie tighter around myself. It's fucking ice cold in here. The chill in the air and the drumming rain lull me. My focus wavers when a memory surfaces, unbidden.

I'm a child, only ten years old, standing in front of my father in his study. I'm swallowing back tears because of what I've seen and heard, another fight between my father and mother. He won. He always won, and even then I knew it was only because he was stronger and more powerful.

I made a vow then — that would *never* be me. I would never cow to a man.

"No crying," my father snapped, his black eyes merciless and unblinking. He scowled at me as he sat back in his chair, his arms folded across his chest. *"Las emociones son para los débiles, Isabella. Serán tu perdición si las dejas."*

Emotions are for the weak, Isabella. They will be your down-fall if you allow them.

I felt a chill at his words even as I made a solemn vow to rebel against him. One of the first steps toward adulthood is realizing that adults aren't always right. It wasn't true. Emotions are not for the weak.

Cowardice is for the weak.

Emotions are *human*.

My resolve hardens.

I am not my father and he has no power over me anymore.

I set my jaw and reaffirm why I am here: I will not let my father's legacy of hatred and cold detachment define me. I will use my skills to safeguard the people that I love and I will bring my brother to justice. I will protect the throne. I will stand strong to keep my family's name alive.

But first...the Romanovs.

CHAPTER TWO

Lev

"Who else is here tonight?" Ollie walks beside me, our steps almost silent on the damp forest floor. The cold autumn night is punctuated by a light rain, the drops spattering on Ollie's leather jacket as we approach the entrance to our abandoned warehouse. Nestled deep in the woods, far from any main highway, this location ensures the privacy and discretion we need. In the distance, the faint scent of smoke mingles with the damp moss, hinting at someone's campfire.

"Everyone," I reply, my voice low but firm. Ollie's brows shoot up silently, acknowledging the gravity of the situation. It's rare for all of us to gather like this. Viktor received a disturbing message recently, and when he relayed it to Mikhail, our pakhan, the alarm was sounded. We were all summoned back to The Cove.

A crackling sound to my left catches my attention. I swivel sharply, my eyes scanning the dimly lit surroundings. "Just an animal," Ollie mutters. To anyone else, that might not be reassuring, but I'd rather face a black bear or a poisonous snake than one of our enemies.

No one knows about this hideout, and we intend to keep it that way. Years ago, this warehouse was used ostensibly for repairing heavy machinery and industrial equipment, a plausible cover for its remote location and the noise it generated. Its real purpose was far more clandestine: a covert arms manufacturing and assembly plant. After my father's death, we acquired it through a friend of a friend, practically a gift.

As we approach the entrance, I spot Aleksandr's large black truck, nearly hidden in the shadows. That's how everyone else arrived. Aleks, our second-in-command and tech genius, and his wife share a home in The Cove. The young guard Aleks hired stands sentry by the main door. I nod to him, and he returns the gesture. If anything were amiss, we'd know by now.

Ollie steps aside, allowing me to access the security panel. I slide my thumb along the identification screen, casting one last glance over my shoulder as Ollie does the same. It's instinctual by now, ensuring we weren't followed. The screen flashes green, and the door unlocks. I push it open, bracing myself for what lies ahead.

"Stay sharp," I whisper to Ollie. "We don't know what's waiting for us inside."

Inside, the warehouse is dimly lit, shadows stretching across the concrete floor. The familiar scent of oil and metal hangs in the air, a reminder of its original purpose. We move quietly, every step calculated. This is our domain, but I never let my guard down.

Aleks is already here, hunched over a table covered with maps and documents. He looks up as we enter, his sharp eyes flickering with recognition and concern.

"Mikhail's waiting," he says, his voice a low rumble. "We need to move quickly."

I nod, my mind racing. The message Viktor received was cryptic but alarming. Something big is coming, and we need to be ready.

"Let's get to work," I say, taking my place at the table. My brothers gather around, each of us falling into our roles seamlessly. This is our family, our legacy. And I'll do whatever it takes to protect it.

"Someone paid Viktor a visit," Mikhail says. Under the dim overhead lighting, his golden brown hair nearly covers his eyes, his tanned skin showcasing ink that marks him as Bratva. I was scared of him as a kid and for good reason, but now that we're all grown, we're equals. We will defer to him as leader, though, for life.

"Right. I knew that."

Mikhail jerks his head toward Viktor, who tugs one of the folding chairs over and sits down. It sags under his weight. Beside him, our older brother Nikko, our personal family assassin, jerks his chin in greeting and folds his massive arms across his chest. Nikko was the one that taught me and Ollie how to shoot. He's an excellent teacher and an even better marksman. But in matters of strategy, he prefers to take a backseat and observe.

Viktor scowls. "Lydia and I had a visit from none other than Isabella Morales."

I nod. The Los Sangre Dorada Cartel, or LSD, is one of the most-feared cartels in all of the Americas. A visit from Isabella is not good news.

"And?"

"She said our enemies are closer than we think. Said we need to pull everyone in, close to home."

Ollie scowls. "And this is why you had me come home from Moscow?"

Mikhail nods. "We wanted to check the veracity of her statement before we made any assumptions or moves."

Ollie watches everyone thoughtfully but doesn't speak.

"Closer than we think," I repeat. "Does she mean a mole?"

"Possibly, yes, or she could mean her brother is planning an attack," Aleks says thoughtfully.

"Oh, she said that, too." Viktor scowls. "And she said when he does attack, it will be swift and merciless."

"Now *that* I believe," Mikhail says, leaning back in his chair. "Javier Morales knows exactly what he is doing. There's a reason we don't fuck around with any of them, even casually."

My mind whirs, putting pieces and details into place like a jigsaw puzzle. "Javier Morales is stationed in Columbia. Has he been sighted anywhere near here?"

Aleks, the tallest in the bunch, shakes his head. "No. As soon as Viktor alerted me, I zoned in on the surveillance we have in Columbia and found Morales still there."

I nod. Of course he doesn't have to be the one that attacked us. He could command an attack or call a hit anytime.

"But you saw Isabella in person?"

"In my fucking *home*," Viktor snaps.

Shit. I frown. "How did she get in?"

Ollie shakes his head. "It's what she's known for, brother. Word on the street is that the woman is made of vapor and smoke. One moment she's there and the next, she's gone. She can pick any lock, escape any shackle, escape any prison."

She'll be small, then, most likely. Lithe. Nimble.

Jesus, I'd fucking love to put her to the test. See what she's *really* capable of.

"Do we have any leads? And where's Kolya?"

Mikhail shifts, scowling, before he answers. "He's still in Moscow. His flight was canceled and I thought it best not to push answers on this right now with him."

Viktor tips his head to the side curiously. "What does that mean? What the hell?" The icy tone of his voice makes the rest of us go still. We're brothers, but no one talks shit in front of Mikhail without repercussions.

Mikhail holds Viktor's gaze as Viktor's hands clench into fists. Though all of us are loyal to Kolya, he took Viktor under his wing like the son he never had, even though he's only about twelve years older than him. Our father couldn't bully Viktor like the rest of us because of the sheer size of the guy, so he passed Viktor off to Kolya to train under the premise of Viktor being "too willful." We all knew the truth, though.

Kolya was a brother figure to Viktor, even more so than to the rest of us. Still is.

"It means that we keep as much as we can to ourselves," Mikhail snaps, his gaze on Viktor's challenging him to defy him.

Viktor gets to his feet. "Bullshit. It means you don't trust your fucking *mentor*."

Both men are on their feet now, their toes touching. Viktor's eyes are narrowed and Mikhail's hands are clenched into fists. There's no telling who would win in an actual fight — Viktor is stronger than the rest of us combined and would absolutely wipe the floor in a fistfight, but Mikhail's the *pakhan,* and if Viktor raises a hand to him, he'll lose that hand.

So yeah, this is *not* gonna happen.

I push myself between the two of them, and slap a hand on the chest of each of them. "We start fighting amongst ourselves and *everyone* bests us."

They both glare at me, but I'm not a kid anymore and they might be older, but I'm their equal.

I shake my head. "What the fuck are you going to accomplish with a pissing match? Mikhail kept this intel inner circle, so I'm assuming there's information he doesn't want to get out. It's not a slight to Kolya, and we're wasting precious time."

Only the leadership is here, none of our subsidiaries or captains.

"That's right." Mikhail says. "And anything we unearth of importance, we'll tell everyone immediately. So sit *down,* brother."

There's got to be another reason he chose this place and the inner circle, but I'll wait to find out. We all will.

Viktor's jaw clenches but he finally sits down. The chair bends and creaks this time.

"Refresh my memory," Aleks says, clearing his throat. "The primary method the LSD uses for earning their money?"

"Drugs," Ollie supplies. Our primary director of international relations, he knows the ins and outs of our rivals better than anyone. "They're pushing drugs hard. The LSD is spreading like a damn virus."

"They've moved from New York, haven't they?" I ask.

"Yeah," Aleks confirms, his fingers sliding across his tablet. "After those busts last year, they're trying to solidify their power. The Cove's a prime target."

They're known as a ruthless organization originating in Colombia, but with factions now spread throughout the Americas. They're mostly known for their extensive drug trafficking, particularly cocaine and heroin.

"Oh, right," I say. "They were the ones extradited for those high-profile drug busts last year, weren't they?"

"Yep. And word on the street is that they've expanded their influence into New York. Targeting The Cove because of our location and connections."

I nod. "Not to mention our affiliation with various groups." Due to several recent nuptials with my brothers, we've become allied with several other underground powerhouses, but still have no contacts south of the border.

"Exactly."

I stroke my chin and think this over. Aleks pulls out a tablet and his fingers fly over the keys.

"The cartel is led by Javier Morales Junior, son of the late Javier Morales. Javier is infamous for his ability to evade law enforcement while keeping a steel grip on his operations," Aleks mutters, shaking his head.

I nod, continuing to snap puzzle pieces into place. "They're not just known for drug trafficking, are they? And they have a mole in law enforcement here in The Cove."

Aleks nods. "Money laundering, arms smuggling, and human trafficking. Their presence here in America taints everything. We need them fucking exiled from The Cove."

Still, none of what we've learned here we couldn't discuss in our headquarters in The Cove. Interesting. There's more.

"But to really evict them, we have to know their next move. What's our in with them?"

Aleks nods. "We've had one of our new recruits in their ranks for the past three months. Isabella's warning came on the heels of his intel." I'd bet money on Dmitri. Dmitri Petrov joined our ranks after the death of our enemy several years ago, and after passing numerous tests to prove his allegiance to us. He'd rather die than betray us.

Ah. There we go. This is why we're here.

"Jesus," I mutter, shaking my head. "If they discover he's one of us—"

"Yeah, he's capital-F fucked," Aleks supplies. "He said it was a risk he was willing to take to prove his loyalty. Right now, he's managed to convince the sister of Carlos Ruiz that he loves her."

Ollie speaks up. "Carlos Ruiz is the cartel's chief enforcer, right hand man to Morales. Our buddy has used Carlos's sister to get intel we otherwise wouldn't have."

"Such as?"

"Such as locations of their safe house here in America, the schedules of their shipments, contacts of their supplier and even the name of one of the corrupt city officials on their payroll."

"Shit. He's playing a lethal game, but that's invaluable information." I nod.

"Yeah. We've already managed to intercept two major drug shipments because of information he's gleaned for us. We've let a few slide, even local ones, because we obviously don't want them knowing we're onto them."

"Fuck."

Aleks suddenly goes so still, I want to check to see if he's still breathing. It's like someone's just pressed the pause button on our conversation. He turns toward me and takes out his phone. I watch with interest.

My phone buzzes.

We have a visitor.

There's a reason he's texted me first, and not the group chat. Viktor would already be prowling, ready to smash skulls and Nikko's weapon would be drawn. He knows I'm slower to react and more methodical in my approach.

A chill skates down my spine and I immediately sit up straighter. Have they found us so soon? Have they tracked us here? We're not ready.

I keep my shit together.

Oh?

Biometric feedback in the loft. Someone small, maybe a woman.

Aleksandr takes safety so seriously, he has biometric readings on all of us at all times. Apparently he has the scanner on his ipad as well.

"Lev." My gaze snaps to Mikhail when he calls my name.

I nod.

"Put your damn phone down and pay attention." I blink at him slowly and look at my phone, then back up at him. Understanding dawns on him as Nikko and Viktor talk quietly to each other.

Aleks to group chat: No one move. Do not respond. Someone's watching from the loft. Let Lev handle it. He's the fastest and most lethal in tight situations. Lev?

My mind snaps into place, the strategy laid out in front of me. We have to move.

> Viktor, keep talking. Say some bullshit
> about Lydia and her family or the wedding
> or something. Mikhail, pretend you have to
> take a call. Nikko, go to a secure place
> where you can draw your weapon out of
> view of the loft and as soon as Ollie and I
> approach, cover me. Ollie, you and I will
> go. What do we have for weapons here?

Mikhail: got a gun and blade

Aleks: same

Nikko: carrying two fully loaded guns but
fucking arsenal in the car

Aleks: you brought your shit in my CAR?

Mikhail: drop it, stay focused

Ollie: smoke bomb in my jacket pocket,
could come in handy since it's a loft. Gun.

Viktor: my fucking fists

> At least one of you standby with Nikko,
> Ollie, get ready with the smoke bomb and
> for Christ's sake tell me later why you have
> that stupid piece of shit with you

Ollie: club last night. Let's go

Viktor starts talking about some nonsense about gardening and Lydia and fireworks or some such shit. Mikhail excuses himself to take out his phone and makes a fake call.

"I'm going to use the restroom," I tell them. "I'll be right back."

I walk in the direction of the loft to gauge the location. Is it near a window? How high is it? Is there a way for us to get the ladder away from the loft easily? I walk by it and quickly note everything — tucked away from any windows, it's at least ten feet off the floor and the ladder looks nailed in place. In this case, that is not good.

I walk into the bathroom and pretend to use it, quickly coming back into the room where my brothers are located. None of them even look at me but my phone quickly buzzes with a text.

> Mikhail: Plan?

I have to admit I fucking love that he's actually deferring to me with this. My father is turning over in his grave. *Imagine that, you asshole, the one you hated most actually knows his shit.*

> We have two options given that it's a loft with only one way up. Either one of us goes up and forcibly drags him down, or we demand he comes down of his own accord. There's no way for us to get there unannounced and there's no other way to get to him.

> Viktor: Bring him down. Drag him down here and let me show him how we deal with a spy.

I shake my head and reply.

> My preference would be to demand he
> come down on his own. Anyone who went
> up after him would be at a disadvantage.
> There's no easy way to dislodge the ladder.
> A third option is to forcibly make him come
> down with the smoke bomb. Then, we'll
> deal with him.

Nikko: Ready.

Mikhail: Let's go

Aleks: Go time

Ollie: I'll cover you

I lift my head and stare at the darkness above the loft ladder. I feel kind of dumb, because it looks like I'm glaring into blank space, but I trust Aleks. If he says someone's there, then someone's there.

I nod to my brothers and face the loft.

Pre-Order your copy of 'Shackled: A Dark Bratva Enemies to Lovers Romance' by scanning the QR code below (Available August 16, 2024):

Fueled by dark chocolate and even darker coffee, USA Today bestselling author Jane Henry writes what she loves to read – character-driven, unputdownable romance featuring dominant alpha males and the powerful heroines who bring them to their knees. She's believed in the power of love and romance since Belle won over the beast, and finally decided to write love stories of her own.

Scan the QR Code below to receive Jane's Newsletter & be notified of upcoming new releases & special offers!

Be sure to visit me at www.janehenryromance.com, too!